Welcome to Ero-TEA-Ca: We're Open!

Alyson Root

J&M Books

For permission requests, write to a.rootauthor@alysonroot.com

Published by J&M Books

Lytchett House, 13 Freeland Park, Wareham Road, Poole, Dorset, BH16 6FA

Print ISBN: 978-1-917785-07-5

Ebook ISBN: 978-1-917785-25-9

Developmental Edit & Cover design by:

Tara Sullivan, The Write Gal Co.

www.thewritegal.com

Line & Copy Edit by:

Linda Slate

Proofed by:

Crystal lee-Wren, COLProof

&

Morgan Bonito

Welcome to Ero-TEA-Ca is written in British English.

1

Harriet

"Crumpets! But not just any old crumpets—boob crumpets."

Harriet looked up from her long list of things she needed to get done. "We've got cherry Bakewells and muffins. They cover the breast quota," she replied, "but I like your thinking."

"Okay," Nabi, Harriet's best friend, murmured. "Titty muffins and Bakewells. Got it. No boob crumpets."

"We will still serve them, though. Can't have a breakfast menu without crumpets."

"No, indeed, we cannot." Nabi smiled. "Are we missing anything else from the food side of things?"

"Nope. All good. In fact, we have everything. We just need to move it all into the shop."

Nabi did a little squeal and a happy dance. "I can't believe we're almost ready to set up."

Harriet beamed a smile right back. "I know, right? God, it only feels like yesterday we came up with the concept."

"Who says you can't come up with a winning idea when smashed on cheap wine?" Nabi scoffed playfully, her long black hair swishing as she jiggled excitedly.

"My mother," Harriet replied, grinning.

"Mrs K still not onboard, huh?" Nabi asked, already knowing the answer.

To say Mr and Mrs Kirkwell were less than impressed with their youngest daughter's latest venture would be an understatement. Patsy and Ronald Kirkwell were two of the most strait-laced humans on the face of the planet. They subscribed to *Reader's Digest* and *Gardener's World,* enjoyed annual trips to Skegness, and believed watching snooker on mute was the only way to enjoy the weekend. How they'd produced three children was baffling. Harriet often thought her mum must have gotten pregnant via immaculate conception, because the possibility of her parents getting raunchy was, quite frankly, laughable.

Not to mention, they'd spawned three kids who were the *complete* opposite of their parents. Diane, the eldest, was a sex therapist to the stars. Kevin made erotic art, and Harriet...well, Harriet was about to open the first erotic tea shop, not just in Oxford, but the whole county of Oxfordshire.

Ero-Tea-Ca was the brainchild of Harriet, Nabi, and Kevin. Sure, it had come about after one too many merlots, but that didn't change the fact it was going to be a roaring success. Diane had even taken time out of her very busy schedule to help her siblings curate a sex-positive environment that hoped to cater to as many people as possible.

Plus, two of the three kids were on the rainbow spectrum. To be fair to Patsy and Ronald, they'd taken the news their son liked to sleep with men, and their youngest daughter was a card-carrying lesbian, pretty smoothly. Well, if you discounted the week where Patsy cried because she wouldn't get the brood of grandkids she wanted, or the fact Ronald had a mild panic attack about having to entertain men who acted like women and women who acted like men. That antiquated stereotype was the collective belief between the two parents: all lesbians were butch, and all gay men were effeminate.

Thankfully, Diane helped stage an intervention and educated them over the course of a long weekend. Harriet and Kevin kept their expectations low, but were both pleasantly surprised when they took girlfriends and boyfriends to meet their parents. Yes, it was awkward, but Mr and Mrs Kirkwell did their British manners proud.

"Ladies, I come bearing gifts," Kevin announced as he barged through the door, holding a large brown box.

Leaning back in her seat to look around Kevin and at Nabi, Harriet smiled, then chuckled. "Um, to answer your question quickly, Nabi, Mother is not suddenly enthusiastic about supporting the shop."

"Oh, Mum is going to spit feathers when she sees what I made." Kevin laughed, placing the box on Harriet's kitchen table. His face was flushed with excitement. Harriet wondered if she would finally see the big surprise he'd promised a few weeks ago.

Intrigued, Nabi scuttled over to peer inside. "That's a lot of packing peanuts," she commented—packing peanuts that would end up all over the kitchen floor if someone didn't stop Nabi from flicking them in amusement at Kevin.

"Yes, and you will see why in just a second." Kevin grinned, batting away another Styrofoam missile. He carefully plunged his hand inside the box, and after a few seconds of rummaging, gently withdrew his arm. Cradled in his hand was the most beautiful glass dildo Harriet had ever seen. It was a transparent model with red streaks running through it.

"Oh, Kev, it's gorgeous!" Harriet gushed. She'd floated the idea a few months back of putting handcrafted dildos or vibrators in gift boxes, but became disheartened when she'd asked for a few quotes through local artists.

"I know," he breathed. "I have forty ready and waiting at the studio. I didn't want to tell you about them until I knew I could get them done. Glassblowing isn't my usual medium, but I asked Kiki to help, and, well, you can see how fantastic they came out."

"Look at it," Nabi cooed, her eyes big and bright. "You've outdone yourself this time, Kevin."

"So that's it, then," Harriet began, her heart full of joy. "The final product for the gift sets. We have the teapots, cups and saucers, tea, and dildos."

"I'll pick up the gift boxes tomorrow from Raine. She's done a wicked job on the artwork," Nabi said as she collected another dildo from the box.

"And…guess who got you an interview with *Out* magazine?" Kevin grinned.

Harriet jumped into his arms. "How the hell did you swing that?" she all but screamed, squeezing him tightly. Getting their name and the tea shop featured in *Out* magazine was going to help boost the business magnificently. *Out* was Britain's biggest LGBTQ+ print and digital magazine. Harriet had been an avid reader of the magazine for the past fourteen years, picking up her first copy at the tender age of sixteen, when all she could think about were girls and how much she liked looking at their boobs.

"I called in a favour. Remember Pinky? Well, they owed me one after…never mind, let's just say they were more than happy to help us out. Anyway, Boadicea…you know her, right?"

"I've never met a Boadicea in my life, Kev." Harriet laughed.

"Really? I thought you met at Gogo's Pride party last year?"

"Boadicea? Really?" Nabi asked. "Who the hell calls their kid Boadicea?"

"Her parents, obviously," Kevin deadpanned. "So, Boadicea Harrington-Smythe—"

"Now you're just fucking with us," Nabi laughed. "No way is that her actual name!"

"Jesus wept. Would you stop interrupting?" Kevin laughed. "And yes, it is her full name. She comes from old money, but she's no trust fund baby. I mean, I bet she has a trust fund that could bankroll a small country, but the point is, Boadicea has worked hard to make a name for herself. She's the reporter everyone wants to write about them, and we happen to have that chance. Not only are we going to be featured in the magazine, but they're sending Boadicea to do the article. This is going to be huge for the shop!"

Harriet finally let go of Kevin and sat down. Her dream was finally coming to fruition, and she suddenly felt lightheaded. The dreamer of the three, Harriet, had struggled for years to find something she wanted to do. Diane and Kevin found their passions early in life, but Harriet never quite pinpointed what made her happy.

That was until one fateful night when Harriet's best friend and brother came over after she was dumped by stupid Georgina. They mainlined merlot and started talking about the future. It was Nabi who said Harriet should do something with tea, because the woman knew Harriet was obsessed. Her pantry was like a small tea shop in itself. Then Kevin suggested she should open a sex shop, because Harriet's toy collection was just as impressive as her tea selection. Harriet then merged the two ideas together, and voila! The Ero-Tea-Ca tea shop was born.

The morning after the brilliant idea, Harriet dived in headfirst and hadn't stopped working until the tea shop was no longer just an idea, but a reality. She'd had support from both her brother and sister, plus Nabi and several other friends. It was just her parents that couldn't get behind it.

"When is Boadicea coming to do the interview?" Harriet asked, her face feeling a little numb.

"Opening day," Kevin replied. "Hey, Harriet, take a breath, okay?"

"Is it that obvious I'm panicking?" She laughed.

"Yes," Nabi answered, still taking out dildos. "But that's cool. You can get nervous with us. We have your back, my little chickadee."

"We do," Kevin reiterated, squeezing Harriet's hand. "And it's totally normal to freak out a bit. God, can't you remember the state I was in when I did my first gallery show?"

"Yeah, he was a thousand times worse than you," Nabi commented. "And he had bright pink hair, which was a travesty."

They all laughed. Kevin *had* looked ridiculous with pink hair.

"I just want it to work, you know? I finally feel like I'm doing something I love, and I don't want it to fail," Harriet said, returning Kevin's hand squeeze.

"Ugh, you've let Mum and Dad get under your skin. Listen, Harriet, you've done the market research and spoken to God knows how many people in the industry. Ero-Tea-Ca will work because it's unique. The British love their tea! Plus, unlike our alien parents, they also love sex. The world is changing, and people are open to sex positivity like never before. Your tea shop is offering a space where the public can indulge in fine teas from around the world, catered to the body's every need...plus, treat their naughty side. And yet, you've managed to keep the elegance of a traditional English tea shop."

"Yeah, I mean, the space you found to house us is legit perfect," Nabi said.

Kevin nodded in agreement. "Have some faith in yourself, Harriet. This is going to be amazing!"

"It is not going to be amazing, Harriet. It is going to be humiliating," Ronald Kirkwell scoffed. "Our friends and family will pass by the shop daily and know it's you who has brought debauchery to Oxford."

"Dad, come on." Kevin laughed. "That's a tad dramatic, dontcha think?"

"I do not," Ronald continued. "Where has all the decency gone?"

"It stayed where it belonged—in the 1800s," Kevin supplied.

"Kevin," Patsy huffed, "don't speak to your father like that."

Kevin rolled his eyes.

"Look, I only wanted to see if you were coming to the grand opening. I don't need another lecture as to how much of a disappointment I am." Harriet sighed.

"We're all disappointments." Kevin nodded.

Harriet wished she were as easygoing as her brother. Kevin didn't give two shits what their parents thought.

He never had, whereas Harriet always strived to gain their support.

"No, Harriet, we will not be in attendance," Ronald stated. A weight of sadness sat heavily on Harriet's chest.

"You know she's going to be massive, right?" Kevin blurted. "Harriet is going to have a chain of tea shops around the country by the time she's finished. She's going to be the biggest success out of us all."

Patsy and Ronald both huffed at the statement. Harriet felt her eyes fill with tears. Not because her parents were prudes or had such little faith in their kids, but because Kevin had such unwavering belief in her.

"You really think so?" she choked.

"I know so, sis. And I will be with you every step of the way. So will Diane."

"We're not saying we aren't happy you are finally doing something with your life," Patsy began, "but couldn't it be less vulgar?"

"There is nothing vulgar about Ero-Tea-Ca," Harriet said, feeling her temper fray. "The shop is full of art, not porn. You would know if you took the time to look at what we've created. And as for your friends...when they walk past, all they will see is a beautifully classy English tea shop."

"That sells *sex toys*," her mother whisper-hissed. Harriet wanted to burst out laughing. Patsy and Ronald were the type of people that barely said the words *lesbian* or *gay* above a mumble. Uttering the phrase *sex toys* must have taken a herculean effort to croak out.

"They are handcrafted toys. Made by Kevin and other artists. Same for the teapots and cups—all locally made to the highest standard. The artwork is phenomenal," Harriet said with pride.

"Face it, guys," Kevin butted in. "People like sex."

"And tea," Harriet added.

"This *is* going to be amazing," Kevin declared.

"It is," Harriet agreed, using Kevin's confidence to boost her own. "Now, we need to go. The shop opens next weekend and we've got to start moving everything in. I'll leave your names on the guest list, just in case."

With renewed energy, Harriet left her parents sitting in their armchairs with the TV muted. If they couldn't see how great this venture was, then fine. She'd just prove them wrong.

"One week, Kev. That's all the time we have to get Ero-Tea-Ca ready for the grand opening."

Kevin trailed behind Harriet as they left their parents' house. "Plenty of time. Gogo is popping over tomorrow to help move the merchandise in. The van will arrive at the shop at 8:00 a.m. Diane said she'd come over if she could rearrange one of her clients. I'm pretty sure Nabi has been sleeping on the stockroom floor in anticipation, so I wouldn't worry about manpower."

"She hasn't, has she?" Harriet wouldn't put it past Nabi. Her best friend was quirky like that.

"I'm not certain, but she *was* mumbling about 'becoming one with the building so their energies match,'" Kevin said, straight-faced.

Hopping on her Vespa, Harriet waited for Kevin to jump on the back. "Then she has definitely been sleeping in the shop. It'll smell like incense when we get there tomorrow, mark my words."

Nabi was a strong believer in energy. Harriet had lost count of the number of crystals Nabi had gifted her over the years. All her friends received rocks of some sort for birthdays and Christmases. Nabi learned everything from her grandma, who was basically known around town as a Chinese shaman. Mrs Choi had a crystal or herb for everything. She was so well known, even the local doctor pawned off his patients to her when he was too busy to see them.

"Do you want to head over to the shop and find out?" Kevin called over the noise of the engine.

Shaking her head, Harriet clipped her helmet in place. "No, let's leave her to do her thing. I want to order a pizza and try to relax tonight. Because, Kev, come tomorrow, it will be a while before we have a lot of downtime."

"Agreed. Okay, sis, hit it!" That was Harriet's cue to hammer the throttle. Which would be impressive on a Harley Davidson or something, not so much on a single-cylinder Vespa. They didn't exactly look like Hells Angels. To be honest, the bike sounded like a hairdryer on wheels.

At least they were able to zip through traffic with relative ease, landing them at Harriet's flat fifteen minutes later, cheese and pepperoni pizza strapped to the bike's parcel shelf.

They fought their way through piled boxes of tea to get into the kitchen. Having her place back was just another advantage of the shop opening soon. Weeks upon weeks of climbing over shop inventory was tiring, but as Harriet settled at the kitchen table and looked around at all their hard work, she knew any struggles and sacrifices would be worth it.

2

Cassandra

"Unacceptable," Cassandra hissed to herself as she peered through the blinds. "I won't stand for it," she growled as she watched the moving van's rear door open. "They'll ruin us all."

"Now you're just being dramatic," Kendal scoffed from behind. "You're just sour because Old Man Beedle didn't sell you the shop."

Kendal was wrong...entirely wrong. Cassandra was neither sour nor harbouring ill feeling towards the old man. Her anger was justified.

"It's a porn tea shop, Kendal. This has nothing to do with the building. Our street is full of respectable businesses and they're going to ruin it!"

Another scoff. "Give it up, Cass. I know you better than that."

Dammit. Kendal did know her better than anyone. After all, they'd been married for ten years, divorced for seven, but were still best friends.

"You can't tell me you think this is a good thing, can you?" Cass asked, jabbing her finger towards the van. There were several people milling around, beginning to unload boxes.

"I think it's awesome."

"You would," Cass mumbled.

She felt Kendal's eye roll. "You don't have to like it or agree, Cass. It's done. The shop will open, and you'll have new neighbours. What are you gonna do? Just be a grump for the rest of your life?"

"Yes!" Cass declared. "I have everything to be grumpy about. I'll lose customers. Mark my words. They'll either bugger off to the porn tea store or stop coming around because they feel uncomfortable. I'm tellin' ya, Ken, this isn't going to end well."

Kendal stepped up to Cassandra's side and peeped through the tiny slit of the blind. "Have you even met them yet?"

"Nope. And I have no intention of doing so, for as long as humanly possible."

Cassandra and Kendal couldn't have been more different—in opinion or appearance. That they'd once been married—and were still best friends—amazed most people. Cass was tall, pale, and freckled, with long, straight jet-black hair and a no-nonsense edge to everything she did. Kendal was shorter and curvier, with rich brown skin and deep-set eyes. She alternated between a natural crown of picked-out curls or waist-length braids, but always carried a kind of unshakeable calm that made her feel like the safest person in any room.

Kendal sighed and shook her head. "Cass, just give them a chance. If you really lose customers, you can take it up with the Shop Owners' Guild at the end of the quarter. But being outright arse-y won't win you any favours. You're already on thin ice with Mandeep."

"He left litter all over the place."

"He placed leaflets on his *own* tables. Nowhere near the café, Cass. Stop antagonising everyone. You can't force people to work the way you want them to, sweetie."

Cass furrowed her eyebrows. "I just want the high street to succeed. We need to hold ourselves to a higher standard."

"And I'm sure the other shop owners agree, but it's not for you to police."

Cass waved her hand, dismissing the conversation. "We're not here to talk about that. We were talking about *them*," she shot, pointing to a very upbeat Asian woman and her now absent cohort skipping around the truck.

"Look, if you can't play nice, just stay out of the way. Leave them to their shop and you concentrate on yours, okay?"

Silence.

"Cassandra. Okay?"

Dropping the blind, Cass huffed one last time before turning to face Kendal. "Fine. Now, can we get this place ready for opening?"

Kendal chuckled. "You say it like I'm the one who's stood here wasting time."

Cassandra's mood was in the toilet, and her ex-wife's comments weren't helping. Couldn't Cass indulge her own grouchiness for once? After all, she now had to work next door to a raunchy tea shop, for crying out loud.

"I wasn't wasting time," she mumbled to herself as she set about turning chairs over. The floor was dry after an early morning wash. Cass liked the café to be sparkling clean every morning, even if it meant getting up at the butt crack of dawn. Her reputation was worth it.

The Shop Owners' Guild might find her ornery, but her customers didn't—or at least they didn't complain about her naturally spicy character. Probably because ninety percent of people who came to The Oxford Beanery were just as irritable as Cass before their first cup of coffee and didn't pay her any attention, choosing instead to focus on mainlining caffeine to face the day.

With one last sweeping look, Cass nodded her satisfaction at the café's readiness and went to the door. Opening the blinds was the last job on her list before flipping the *Closed* sign to *Open*.

Of course, her eyes went straight to the oversized van still parked outside, its cargo door jutting over Cass's property. She gritted her teeth and took a ragged breath. If they hadn't shifted the thing by the time the daily rush hit in an hour, Cass wouldn't have a choice but to confront the new owner, would she?

Scowling one last time for good measure, Cass spun around and marched to the till with purpose. Kendal already had the coffee machine up and running and was making them both a cup of Peruvian Gold. It had a kick no other coffee could match, with just the right blend of acidity and smoothness as it sat on the tongue. Delicious.

"Here, neck this before the morning crowd arrives," Kendal called. She was already throwing back her own espresso-sized cup.

Inhaling the rich aroma, Cass let the black gold engulf all her senses. This was what she lived for. Coffee was everything. Her mind flitted to the tea shop again, causing her to scoff. Coffee outshone tea by miles. Maybe Cass wouldn't have to put up with the new neighbours for long. They'd probably crash and burn within the first six months. Most new businesses did, and for the life of her, Cass just couldn't see an erotic tea shop lasting long. This was Oxford, for goodness' sake.

Feeling satisfied with her predictably correct assumption of the tea shop's inevitable demise, Cass welcomed the first customers. They were bleary-eyed and mute—just how she liked them. It stayed quiet until Gordon marched in. He was the resident busybody and had taken over the mantle of Chief Gossip when his wife, Mary, passed away three years ago.

"It's happening then," he stated the second he reached the front of the queue. "We're really getting a sex tea shop?"

Cass grunted a response. Kendal positioned his usual order in front of him. Gordon was as predictable as he was loose-lipped. He never strayed from a flat white, no matter how many times Cass and Kendal tried to get him to deviate.

"It's a tea shop," Kendal replied.

"With sex stuff," Gordon shot back. "I mean, who comes up with something like that?"

Exactly what Cass would like to know! Probably some new-age hippy with Mum and Dad's money backing it.

"It's a new concept, sure," Kendal added. "I think it's ingenious. I mean, everyone loves tea. And we could do with a few more open minds around here. We take being British to a new level sometimes. Time to take the sticks out our bums, if you ask me."

Gordon's bushy eyebrows rose so much, Cass could almost see his entire eye. "You think it's a good idea?"

Kendal nodded. "Yes, and I'm looking forward to attending the grand opening."

Cass almost cricked her neck with the speed she looked at her ex. "You're going?" Cass had received an invitation through the post two weeks ago and had promptly put it in the recycling bin. "When were you invited?"

"I wasn't, personally. But as co-owner of the café, I was. I found the invitation in the bin, Cass."

"It should've stayed in the bin. You can't go on behalf of The Oxford Beanery, Kendal. That sends the message we're okay with them being here."

Kendal shook her head. "I *am* okay with them being here. And I'm going."

Cass was gobsmacked. "I forbid it," she declared, far too loudly.

Kendal's eyebrows shot up. "Oh, do you now? And how exactly are you going to stop me, *Cassandra*?"

Cass fidgeted with her apron string. She couldn't forbid Kendal and they both knew it. "Okay, I can't forbid you. But I strongly urge you to change your mind. I don't want the café linked with that place," she shot, jabbing her finger towards the west wall. A pang of disappointment hit her square in the chest. Cass had planned to breach that wall and create an archway into her very own library. *Stupid Old Man Beedle.*

A hand gripped her shoulder, tugging Cass from a downward spiral. "Beedle never promised to sell you the shop, Cass."

"He said I'd have first refusal," Cass growled, unsurprised Kendal had read her thoughts so well.

"You were travelling, sweetie. He did try and get hold of you. You know that."

"I was in the middle of a rainforest, Kendal. The phone signal wasn't exactly great. He knew I planned to be back a week later. You're telling me he couldn't have waited seven more days? I had plans for that shop—big plans—and he knew it. Beedle wrecked my dreams!"

"You should sue him for emotional distress," Gordon interjected.

"He's eighty-three years old," Kendal scoffed. "And it was his right to sell the shop to whomever he wanted to."

Cass slapped her hand on the counter. "It doesn't matter. Gordon's right. I should sue him."

"Cassandra Beaufort. If you even think about contacting a lawyer about this, I will sell my shares of the café to your mother!"

Cass recoiled in horror. "That's low, Ken."

Kendal narrowed her eyes. "I'm deadly serious."

They stared each other down for a few moments before Cass backed down. Nothing was worth her mother getting involved in the business. "Fine, I'll leave Beedle alone."

"And you," Kendal interrupted, pointing at Gordon, "stop meddling. Drink your coffee and eat some cake. Nothing more." Gordon looked suitably chastised. He picked up his coffee and shuffled off to find a seat.

"Please don't go to the opening," Cass began.

"I'm going. I'll leave out the fact I'm part owner of this place if it helps, but I'm looking forward to meeting some new people. The high street is full of old fuddy-duddies. It's about time some life got injected into the place."

"Are you calling me an old fuddy-duddy?"

"If the shoes fits, Cass."

Well, wasn't that just peachy? Sure, Cass was a bit of a grouch, and she liked things to be a certain way and hated change, but a fuddy-duddy? Rude. Just rude.

"I'm going to do a stock take," she huffed, leaving a smirking Kendal at the till. Matt would be in soon to help her with customers, so Cass didn't feel too bad. And Kendal deserved some payback after that comment, anyway.

The stockroom remained as organised as ever and Cass regretted exiling herself to it. After all, they'd completed the stock take just last week, and Cass knew she didn't need to recount anything for a few more days. Kendal would call her any second for help. Any second...

Cass slumped in the chair used to reach the higher shelves. Kendal had not called for help, and after a peek through the door, Cass saw her business partner was doing absolutely fine by herself. There wasn't a long queue and everyone seemed affable. Huh. The customers never smiled at Cass like that.

Grumbling to herself, Cass's nose twitched. The smell was back! Instead of the gorgeous aroma of coffee, Cass's olfactory centre was being assaulted by some sort of plant. Not perfume...something earthy, and wholeheartedly unwelcome.

Scrambling to her feet, Cass sniffed the air. Where was it coming from? She shifted a few boxes, sniffing as she went. On her hands and knees, she crawled across the floor with her nose millimetres away from her pristine laminate. The smell was weaker down there.

Back to a vertical position, Cass flattened herself against the stock shelving. Coffee. That's all she could smell. Pushing away, she brought hands to hips, scanning the room. One step to the left and the smell was a fraction stronger. Another step and Cass knew she was getting warmer.

Cass grabbed the chair she'd been slumped in minutes before, leaned it against the shelves, and hauled herself up.

The earthy stench got infinitely worse as she rose to her tiptoes. Carefully lifting a box of her favourite coffee out of the way, Cass caught sight of an air vent in the top corner of the wall shared with…no, she couldn't even say the name. Who called their business Ero-Tea-Ca, for goodness' sake?

Craning her face closer, Cass took a giant whiff. The smell was coming from next door! Cass gasped, "Oh my God, they're smoking marijuana!" She was right! They *were* new-age hippies, hellbent on destroying the neighbourhood. First sex, and now drugs.

Jumping down, Cass tore out of the stockroom, intent on having it out with the new owner, or whoever was there when she arrived. Her frustration and anger were already close to spilling over, and the way Cass saw it, if a new employee got the brunt of her ire, then so be it. More fool them for choosing to work in a porn tea shop where drugs were liberally used in broad daylight.

Cass didn't give Kendal the chance to say anything. She was busy with a customer anyway. And Cass didn't need her ex-wife's rationality poking its nose in. A new wave of fury washed over her as she exited The Oxford Beanery. The blasted moving van was still there, and it didn't look like it was going to move anytime soon. There were piles of boxes sitting on the curb and inside the vehicle.

Bypassing the clear health and safety violation, Cass marched next door. The windows were frosted, making it impossible for Cass to see inside. Just as she was about to barge her way in and give them all a piece of her mind, the young Asian woman came dancing out. Literally, dancing. Her hair was up in two buns on top of her head, and she was wearing neon pink eye makeup.

Cass glared. "A new-age hippy! I knew it," she mumbled.

"Oh, hey," the woman said after she'd twirled one more time. "I'm Nabi."

"I couldn't care less," Cass seethed. "That van is blocking access to my café. The boxes are causing a safety hazard, and whatever illegal crap you're smoking in there is leaking through to my stockroom."

The Chinese woman—no, Nabi—pulled her EarPods out and stuffed them in her dress pocket. "I'm totally sorry about the van. The people who were here earlier had to leave, but reinforcements are on the way. I slept in the back room—"

"You're not allowed to live in your shop!" Cass bellowed. "Christ, how many laws do you plan on breaking?"

Nabi laughed. "Oh, no worries. I don't live here. I was cleansing the space and connecting with its energy."

"Cleansing the space," Cass deadpanned.

"Totally. Energy is so important. Don't you think? Anyway, I'm not the owner, but I will be working here."

Cass could feel her jaw muscles locking. "I don't care," she hissed. "Just get that bloody van moved before I call the council and lodge a complaint."

Unsatisfied and still raging, Cass stomped back to The Oxford Beanery. The council was about to get a strongly worded email.

3

Harriet

Harriet's breakfast choice of half an apple was a mistake, one she only realised she'd made halfway to the tea shop. Her tummy was cramping and if she didn't get something substantial in her body soon, she'd likely fall over within twenty minutes of shifting boxes.

Kevin was the one at fault. He'd forgotten to set the alarm. And—due to the fact Harriet hadn't fallen asleep until 4 a.m. because she was riddled with nerves and falling down the rabbit hole of worst-case scenarios regarding the shop opening—she'd slept through. That was, until her brother scared the living shit out of her by shaking her and dramatically declaring, "Harriet, the world is ending! Run for your life!"

He thought his tried-and-tested routine was hilarious. Harriet hadn't liked it when she was a kid, and she certainly didn't appreciate it now. Who the hell wanted to be ripped out of sleep like that? She'd get him back somehow, but revenge would have to wait.

They were two minutes from the shop, and Harriet's tummy and nerves were not helping. This was it. After today, the tea shop would be stocked and ready to launch. There would be a soft opening next week and then the grand opening ceremony. Nabi had convinced her to buy one of those ribbons and a giant set of scissors to make it official. Was it a bit OTT? Probably, but like her friend explained, it wasn't everyday one made their dreams come true. And this shop was Harriet's dream.

Spotting the moving van parked up and with multiple boxes sitting beside it, Harriet cringed. They should have been here hours earlier to get the stock inside. God knows the inconvenience they were causing right now. Probably some health and safety issues too. It was still earlyish, though, so maybe they'd get away with it if they shifted the boxes double time.

Harriet pulled the moped to a stop a few metres away from the truck. She was just removing her helmet when a blur of dark hair and muttering anger whipped past the bike and stormed into the coffee shop next door.

Whoa, someone really needs their java!

Nabi came floating over with a serene smile on her face. "Hey, guys."

"I'm so sorry we're late, Nab. *Someone* forgot to set the alarm."

Nabi waved off Harriet's apology with an actual wave of her hands. "It was meant to be. I had more time to connect with the building. We're good now. Totally in sync with the energy. Just don't move the crystals."

"Never," Kevin commented from the back of the bike. "We know better than that, Nab. So, shall we get this bitch moved in?"

"Yes," Nabi sang. Harriet tried to ignore the raging hunger and light-headedness. They had work to do. *She* had work to do. Everything rested on her shoulders. If Ero-Tea-Ca failed, her parents would never stop gloating, and Harriet didn't know if she could handle a failure. Not again. Everything up to this point she'd tried, had failed. She couldn't let Ero-Tea-Ca join the club.

"Game plan," Kevin called, dragging Nabi and Harriet into a huddle. "Nabs and I will start shifting boxes. Harriet will go to the coffee shop, eat something, and then return."

"Hey—"

"Sweetie, your stomach sounds like an extra from *The Walking Dead*. You're no good famished. We've got a lot to do, so go eat," he said in all seriousness. Her stomach made the point for him by rumbling obnoxiously loud again.

"Why didn't you have breakfast?" Nabi asked, popping a neon green lollipop in her mouth. God knows from where she'd produced it. Harriet stopped asking how and why Nabi did things years ago.

"We were late and I thought an apple would be fine, but then I dropped half of it and didn't want to waste any more time."

"But you're like, *the* worst person ever when you get hungry." Harriet wanted to protest, but it was true. She brought a whole other meaning to the word *hangry*. "I'd say you're ten minutes from unleashing the beast. Kevin's right. You need to eat first."

Unleashing the beast was a bit much. Sort of. Rolling her eyes, Harriet agreed to nip next door. But only for a pastry and take-away cup of coffee. Organising the shop had to take priority. Ero-Tea-Ca had to be her life from now on. Nothing could get in the way.

With the lamest "Break" chant she'd ever heard, Harriet spun on her heels and headed for The Oxford Beanery. An additional set of nerves rattled in her chest. The owners were her new neighbours, after all, and she wanted to make a good impression.

Pushing through the door, Harriet took a second to scan the shop. It was gorgeous. The café was industrial modern, yet cosy. The smell of coffee saturated the air and made Harriet's mouth water. Yes, she preferred tea. Obviously. But who the hell didn't like a good cup of coffee, too?

Plush seats were positioned to her left, tables and chairs to the right. Behind the counter sat the biggest coffee machine Harriet had ever seen. It had more dials and knobs than a spaceship. All she had to contend with was a kettle and teapot, and thank God for that.

A lovely-looking woman smiled at her from behind the counter. "Hi, welcome to The Oxford Beanery. What can I get you?"

This boded well. If she happened to be the owner, Harriet was in luck.

"Can I take a black coffee and…any type of pastry to go, please?"

Harriet startled when a door to the left crashed open, and a very irate woman pushed through it. "There, let's see the council ignore that!"

The server rolled her eyes. "Cass, we have customers," she murmured.

The angry woman's jaw set. "I can see that, Kendal."

Harriet stood frozen in place. Both women looked fierce and very intimidating. They glared at each other for a few seconds before the angry one, or Cass, as Harriet now knew, huffed and walked off. Kendal completed Harriet's order with a smile, but it was strained. Maybe now wasn't the best time to do introductions.

Collecting her coffee and food, Harriet retreated to the safety of her own shop. Nabi was singing to the music piping out of the shop speaker and Kevin was dancing as he shifted boxes. Finally, Harriet smiled. Okay, so the day had started out a little stressful, but everything was fine now. The pastry was excellent, and the coffee was orgasmic. Time to get moved in.

Wow, glass dildos and teapots were heavy. Harriet had sweated through her T-shirt hours ago and she desperately needed to change, but they still had a lot to do. A hot shower and clean clothes would have to wait a little longer.

Kevin had gone to return the removal van and Nabi was in the stockroom, chanting. Harriet didn't ask. Instead, she stood in the middle of her shop and marvelled at the work. When she'd taken over ownership, the shop resembled a workshop. Mr Beedle explained it had been a local hardware store for decades.

With hard-earned money and some investment from her siblings, Harriet put everything into buying the shop and getting it refitted. The end result was beyond her expectations. The fitters had turned the space into a gorgeous vintage English tea shop. It was a beautiful blend of old and new. The furniture, till, display cases, and shelves were all vintage. Harriet wanted her customers to have an *experience* when they walked into her shop. Of course, she had all the latest technology too, but the idea was for customers to lose themselves for a while…forget about the outside world and all its judgements. Inside Ero-Tea-Ca, people were free to enjoy fine tea from across the world and explore their desires.

It might be a weird concept for some, Harriet understood that, but in her gut, she knew it would work, especially for women. Yes, British people might have a reputation for their prudish natures, but times were changing. Friends were more open about their sex lives. Sex was becoming less taboo, and Harriet wanted to foster a safe space for people to have those conversations. Plus, tea—the number one staple in all British households.

A winning combination.

"I can't fit any more boxes in the stockroom. We need to start unloading and filling the shelves," Nabi called.

Shaking out her aching arms, Harriet began opening box after box. She'd amassed an impressive collection of tea over the past few months. She had blends for nearly every need: heart health, anti-anxiety, sleep, anti-inflammatory, detox, and, of course, libido.

Pulling out her phone, Harriet scrolled to her floor plan. She was a natural organiser and had plotted the layout of the shop months ago. Everything had its place. And now it was time to put the floor plan into action. Nabi gave it a once over before grabbing a box of Kevin's glass dildos. They would be displayed behind the serving area. Harriet couldn't afford for them to be smashed by over-excited clients. If a customer was interested, she or Nabi would take the time to show the customer personally—the product, not how to use it. Huh, maybe she needed to make a sign.

The last thing Harriet wanted was any misunderstanding. She knew the other shop owners might not be thrilled to have Ero-Tea-Ca open up so close to their businesses, so she needed to ensure they understood she sold tea and toys, not sex. This wasn't a brothel or porn shop. It was so much more. However, Harriet was sex work positive, so she'd happily go to bat against anyone who wanted to open their bigoted mouths.

"Harriet, you're gritting your teeth. Are you hungry again?" Nabi asked with concern, her lollipop hovering in front of her mouth. How many was that now? Four? No wonder Nabi seemed to have endless energy. She was high as a kite on sugar.

Shaking her head, Harriet let out a breath. "No, sorry. I got in my head for a second there. It's nothing. I'm fine."

"No, that was definitely something. You're not worried about opening the shop still?"

Placing a box of Maca tea on the floor, Harriet sat at the closest table. "I was thinking about the other shops around us, actually."

"'Kay. What about them?"

"Just that some aren't happy, are they?"

Nabi shrugged. "Sure. But so what? If they don't like it, they don't visit. Simple. You've already put frosted glass in to stop kids from being able to look in and see adult stuff. You've got a warning on the door and you've been super clear in all the ads that this is an adult space. The council signed off, Harriet. Fuck what anyone else thinks."

"Maybe I should have invited the owners for a cuppa? Let them take a look around?" Yeah, she should have done that.

"You can still do that if you want. But you need to be prepared that not all of them will change their minds."

Harriet narrowed her eyes. There was something Nabi wasn't saying. "Nabs...did something happen?"

"Oh, nothing super bad. The owner of the café got a little huffy, but nothing major."

The owner of the café? "What did they look like?"

Nabi sucked on her lollipop, deep in concentration. "Dark hair in a ponytail. Kind of intense. Some serious blocked energy. Her chakras are all out of whack."

Harriet closed her eyes. She knew who Nabi was talking about: Cass, the angry woman. Shit, the tea shop hadn't even opened and Harriet already had an irate neighbour. "What was she upset about?"

"The van. Something about safety and blocking access. Oh, and smoking weed in the shop."

Harriet's eyes bugged open. "What? Who the fuck was smoking weed in here?"

Nabi chuckled. "No one. I'd done a sage sweep and lit a few other incense sticks. No drugs, I swear. It seemed the smell made its way through the air vent and into her stockroom. She was pissed."

Harriet's shoulders sank. "Great."

Flinging an arm around Harriet's shoulders, Nabi pulled her close. "Don't worry. Take her a box of tea and a dildo as an apology for the inconvenience."

"I'll take the tea, not the toy. Boundaries, Nabs. Do we know if she's the sole owner of the café?"

"No clue. Why?"

"Just that when I went in for coffee, there was a really nice woman working that I hoped would be the owner."

"Maybe she is, maybe she isn't. Don't let the negative in, sweetie. You're in a great place. You've successfully kept Patsy and Ronald's negativity at bay, you can do the same for some rando café owner. This is your moment to shine, Harriet. And the people of Oxford deserve to have a sexy tea shop."

"Well, when you put it like that..." Harriet laughed.

The door opened and in strolled Kevin, followed by Gogo. Gogo was a six-foot-five giant. They always styled their hair in intricate braids. Their clothes were always unpredictable, and Harriet absolutely adored them.

"The queens have arrived," Gogo announced. "Set me to work, my beautiful Harriet. Let me bask in all your sexual glory."

"Hey, G. Thank you for coming." Harriet was swept into a hug that felt like home. Gogo was the master of hugs. They always seemed to know exactly what people needed.

"I wouldn't be anywhere else. Now, what needs doing?"

Showing Kevin, Nabi, and Gogo her schematic, Harriet left them to unpack. Unfortunately, her mind was on this Cass woman. She'd never been very good at letting things go. Not when those things included someone being mad at her. How the hell was she going to get Cass on board?

Her gut feeling was Cass wouldn't be a big fan of the shop. She thought back to the simmering ball of ire she'd witnessed barge into the café. Crap. Cass had said something about the council. Had she reported Harriet already? Jesus Christ, what a disaster.

Damage control. Harriet needed to calm the waters. She didn't need a complaint against her before she'd even opened her doors. Should she take some tea as an olive branch? What else could she do? Anxiety spread through her limbs. She hated confrontation. That being said, she wouldn't let anyone bully her. The van was gone now and all the boxes were removed. There were no more safety issues. She'd need to explain about Nabi's herb-burning sessions. Hopefully, that would be enough to stop Cass from complaining to the council again.

Somehow, Harriet didn't think so. Cass was going to be a pain in the arse. She could feel it.

Crap.

4

Cassandra

Three and a half hours. Surely that was enough time for the local council to have read Cass's email and responded. Obviously not. How irritating. Clearly, Cass's concerns were worth a quick response. They couldn't ignore drug use, right? As if she believed Nabi The Hippy and all that nonsense about connecting with the shop's energy. Puuuleeasse! She was on wacky baccy, for sure.

"Cass, if you're just going to stand there scowling, can you bugger off to the back?"

"I'm not scowling. I'm waiting."

"I can't believe you sent an email."

"I can't believe I waited so long. Drugs, Ken. Drugs. I knew the shop was a bad idea. Can you imagine the clientele they'll attract? Not on my watch."

"Please stop. Seriously, Cass. If there really is a drug issue, the council will sort it out. I don't want you getting involved. Whether you like it or not, the tea shop is here for the foreseeable future. We need to be civil."

"Kendal, I'm always civil." Cass didn't appreciate the snort or the slap on the back.

Brushing off Kendal, Cass did a sweep of the café, clearing tables and chatting with the regulars. The dinner rush was over, and the late afternoon lull was in full force. They had an hour or so until the workaholics came in to refuel their fried brains.

Time for a cup of coffee.

Cass had just poured herself a shot when the doorbell rang. Setting her espresso to one side, she turned, ready to take the order. Huh, it was the woman from earlier. Cass remembered her because she was momentarily distracted from her high horse. The woman was clearly younger by several years—maybe ten. Her hair was sunshine, as was her smile. Wow, it had been a few years since anyone had caught Cass's attention for even a second.

Why was she back? Was she a coffee nut like Cass? Or had there been a problem with her coffee? Cass scoffed. No way. The Oxford Beanery only served Grade A coffee. Could the pastry have been soggy?

"Hi," the woman said, causing Cass to jump.

Clearing her throat, Cass put on her best smile that she hoped didn't come across as a grimace. "Welcome to The Oxford Beanery. What can I get you?"

She watched the woman shuffle from foot to foot. "Oh. Um...nothing actually. I was hoping I could speak to you. You're the owner, right?"

"Yes, I own the café. What can I help you with?"

"My name is Harriet Kirkwell."

"Cassandra Beaufort."

"Right. So, this is awkward. I'm the owner of Ero-Tea-Ca. I'm your new neighbour."

Well, shit.

"What can I do for you?" Cass repeated in a monotone voice.

Harriet placed a box on the counter. "I brought you some tea as a way of apology. I understand my tardiness this morning meant the moving van was in the way of your shop and also caused some potential safety issues. I truly am sorry. I was supposed to get here super early and get all the boxes in the shop before you opened. I also want to apologise for the smell that wafted through to your stockroom. Nabi, my best friend and employee, was burning sage and several other herbs."

So, Harriet was sticking with the same story as Nabi. No doubt she wanted to stop any investigation from happening. "Likely story," Cass mumbled. "I don't need tea, Ms Kirkwell. As you can see, I only serve coffee."

"I know that." Harriet chuckled. "The box is for you. It aids sleep."

"I sleep just fine, thank you. Even better when the council launches an investigation into drug use in your shop. That and the fact I'm positive your employee is living in your back room."

Harriet looked panicked. Good. "I promise, no drugs are being consumed on my property. Nabi doesn't live in the back either. She has a lovely house."

Crossing her arms, Cass huffed. "That's for the council to decide."

"You already contacted them?" Harriet asked in a high voice.

"Oh, hey, you're back. Enjoy the coffee that much, huh?" Kendal called as she pushed through the door from the office. Cass watched Harriet shift her pale face to

Kendal. She tried to put on a smile, but it didn't really work. Cass faltered. Was she being too harsh? Then she remembered this woman was opening a sex shop next door, and that concern flitted away pretty damn fast.

"Hello," Harriet stammered. "I just came to introduce myself to Cassandra. I'm opening the tea shop next door."

Of course, Kendal had the complete opposite reaction to Cass. Sometimes Cass swore her ex-wife did it on purpose just to wind her up. Instead of the scorn Harriet deserved for opening an inappropriate shop in their respectable street, Kendal's eyes lit up.

"Oh my God, hi. Why didn't you say something earlier? I'm Kendal, co-owner of The Beanery. I'm so happy to meet you and I can't wait to visit your shop. What a unique idea. I'd love to talk more. Maybe you could come over for coffee when we close?"

"Kendal," Cass growled.

Harriet looked suitably uncomfortable. Hopefully, she'd just leave. "I don't think that's a good idea, but thank you," Harriet replied, her eyes flitting between Cass and Kendal.

Kendal squinted her eyes at Cass. "Well, if you change your mind, just pop by."

"Have a lovely rest of your day. Um, bye." And then the ray of sunshine left…a little dimmer than when she arrived. A thread of something tugged on Cass's heart. She wasn't a bitch—really, she wasn't—but there was a time and place for things, and that shop, on this street, was neither.

"I'm going to fill in the rota," Cass said before she inevitably got an earful from Kendal.

Her peace and quiet lasted three minutes. Kendal shattered it by banging open the door and launching the box of tea Harriet left on the counter. "You are an arse, Cassandra Beaufort."

"Ow, Christ, Ken, you hit me in the eye!"

"Good! What in the ever-loving fuck was that?"

"Do you have to swear?"

"Yes, you lunatic. That poor woman came in here offering an olive branch and you were awful. No way this is just about her shop. What the hell has gotten into you?"

"It *is* about the shop. It's about decency and keeping some decorum in the world. She could open up her porn shop anywhere! Why here?"

Kendal shrieked in frustration. It reminded Cass of one of their countless arguments over the years. "It doesn't matter, Cass. It's none of your business. You certainly don't have the right to bully the woman."

"Who the hell is bullying? I simply did my civic duty and reported unlawful behaviour."

"Unlawful my arse. You couldn't wait to report them, because for some reason that is beyond my understanding, you've become overly upset over another business that, in reality, is very unlikely to affect you, me, and the café negatively. In fact, I'd be so bold as to say they will attract new people to the area."

"The wrong kind of people," Cass shot.

"Oh, wow," Kendal scoffed. "This is a new level of shit, Cass. Since when did you become such a snob?"

"Why is it so wrong to want to uphold a certain level of propriety?"

"Are you hearing yourself? I can't listen to this anymore." Kendal stormed back out, slamming the office door. Heat rushed up Cass's neck. She hated arguing with Kendal. It reminded her of their worst times, which then reminded her of how *she* had failed. The only thing Cass succeeded at was the café. She couldn't let anyone taint that.

"Mr Whiskers, it's not dinner time yet. Young man, I will not allow you to manipulate me." She was definitely going to be manipulated, and Mr Whiskers would get two dinners. At least he would be happy to be around her. Kendal had cancelled their usual Friday night dinner because she was still angry.

Cass let her hair down and ran her fingers through it. She was getting a stress headache. It wasn't the ponytail; she knew that. It was the entire day and the lingering doubts she'd gone a step too far. Was Kendal right?

A *bing* drew her attention away from her darkening thoughts. Cass sucked in a breath when she saw it was from Roger at the council. Nibbling her lip, she opened it. After reading the email three times, Cass was both pissed and relieved.

The council couldn't do anything without a police report. The police! Cass felt a cold sweat start at the base of her spine. Reporting Nabi and her possible weed-huffing ways was one thing. Involving the police, quite another, especially if Cass was wrong.

The next part of the email explained in detail how the council was fully aware of Harriet's business plan, and they didn't intend to reverse their decision allowing Ero-Tea-Ca to open. Well, that was that then, unless Cass decided to take her complaint to the police, which she didn't think Kendal would ever forgive her for if she did.

"So, Mr Whiskers, it looks like the naughty tea shop is opening. I still don't like it, but what else can I do?" Mr Whiskers, unsurprisingly, didn't answer. In fact, he turned his back and sauntered off to his scratch post. Cass wouldn't get any more attention from him until she held up her end of the deal of putting food in his bowl.

Sticking a frozen pizza in the oven, Cass paced through every room on the ground floor. She was irritable and didn't know what to do with herself. She needed to talk to Kendal and make amends.

She'd done a lot of work on herself since their divorce, mainly on communicating, which had been a big reason they'd ended up splitting. Kendal was Cass's rock. Her ex-wife might be angry at her and not understand her point of view, but they were best friends and owned a business together. They couldn't go days without talking. At least

Cass couldn't. She needed to clear the air, otherwise she wouldn't be sleeping.

"Kendal, please don't put the phone down," Cass shot as soon as the line connected.

"I need some space, Cass. Today was a lot. You were a lot, and I don't say that lightly."

"I know. But please talk to me."

"What's there to say?"

"I got an answer from the council."

"Jesus, Cass, you're still on that?"

"No. They said I'd have to report my suspicions to the police."

"Cass, I swear—"

"I'm not going to do that, Ken. I promise."

"I should hope not. You owe Harriet an apology. You've made her first day on the street awful. I can't get the look of panic she had all over her face out of my mind, Cass. We don't do that to people. We both know better. Or I thought we did."

Great. Big swirls of guilt swam in Cass's stomach. She could see Harriet's ashen face, clear as day. "I...I really thought there were drugs, Ken."

"You were looking for something, Cass. You need to work through whatever's going on with you, but leave Harriet and her business out of it, okay?"

"Fine. I still don't think an erotic tea shop is right for the street, but I promise I won't actively try and harm her business. Time will tell, I guess."

"Did you put a pizza in the oven?"

"Maybe."

Cass heard shuffling and a few expletives. "I'm coming over, okay?"

"Okay," Cass replied with a smile. Her world was righting itself, thank God.

"We can discuss how you're going to grovel to Harriet. See you soon."

Cass laid her head against the closest kitchen cabinet and banged it repeatedly on the wood. As much work as she'd done on communication, Cass still sucked at admitting when she was wrong—even though she wasn't completely convinced she *was* wrong...not entirely. Either way, she had to apologise to Harriet.

"But I'm not apologising for my opinion. The shop is still incompatible with the street," she uttered to the room.

Twenty minutes and one boiling-hot pizza later, Cass sat silently as Kendal eyed her. "So?"

"So?"

"Cass, don't act dense. How are you going to apologise?"

Cass ruffled her hair. "Um, how about a note?"

Kendal dropped her piece of pizza, picked up a napkin, and wiped her mouth. "Try again. You reported her to the council. Do better."

"Right. I...I could give her a bag of our best beans. You know, in reciprocation to her for giving me tea."

"That would be nice. Also, maybe apologise to Nabi. She might not be the owner, but you accused her of using drugs and living in the shop."

"Yeah, that's fair." Cass poked at her last bit of food. Tomorrow was going to be painful.

"Cass, what's this really about?"

"I've told you."

"Yeah, and I don't buy it."

Curse her overactive tear ducts. Cass could feel her eyes welling up. "Dammit," she grumbled, swiping her face as fast as she could.

"Tears? Come on, Cass, it's me. Talk to me."

"The café can't fail, Ken," Cassie burst. "Opening up such a controversial shop next door to us could tarnish the café. It's the only thing I've done right, and I can't lose it!"

"Whoa, whoa, whoa. Where's this coming from? What have you failed at?"

Cass glared at her ex in astonishment. "What do you think?"

"Cassandra, you can't mean us?"

Cass shrugged. "I mean, it's true, right? I couldn't change to give you a life you wanted, and we divorced."

"Sweetie, we wanted something different. And neither of us should've had to compromise on something so big. We talked through this in therapy."

"Maybe I'm just hormonal." Cass chuckled.

"Well, you're old enough to be pre-menopausal," Kendal sassed.

"I'm forty-one!"

"Your mum was young when she started."

"I hate you know that about her."

Kendal laughed. "She sure shared a lot of detail."

Cass screwed up her nose. "God, didn't she just."

Kendal smiled softly. "Cassandra. Whatever you're going through, you have me, okay? You're my person, even if we aren't married. And because I'm your person, I get to tell you to chill the hell out about the café. We have a great business, and nothing will screw it up. Well, maybe if you piss off all the owners and they kill you and bury you under the outside terrace…"

Cass grinned. "Thanks, Ken. I needed this."

"Anytime. But please promise to just stay out of Harriet's way. You don't have to agree with Ero-Tea-Ca, but you can't undermine her business. It's her life, like The Beanery is ours."

Cass patted Kendal's hand. "I promise. I'll make things right in the morning and then I'll mind my own business."

5

Harriet

It was a brand new day and the sun was shining. Saturday was looking to be much better than yesterday, which Harriet was immensely grateful for. It hadn't been the best introduction to the street, and no doubt she'd have to deal with Cass again, but that was fine. Harriet could handle it.

No way was she going to let one person bring her down. There was too much at stake, and Harriet wanted to bask in the excitement of her new journey. The scary shit would happen next week when they had the soft opening and party. So, these next few days were Harriet's chance to perfect the shop and just...be.

She'd waited long enough to reach her goal. This weekend would be her time to enjoy that, no matter who had a problem. It irritated Harriet that her mind kept latching on to yesterday and the way Cass reacted. Surely the idea of an erotic tea shop couldn't be *that* distressing?

Well, she'd just have to prove the moody busybody wrong! Harriet would attract new clientele to the street, boosting not just hers, but all the other shops' sales. Then Cass would have to admit she was wrong, wouldn't she?

Hm...unless the issue went deeper than that? Could Cass be a homophobe or something? She'd met Nabi, who looked all kinds of queer. Harriet didn't exactly look straight, or so her brother and sister had told her multiple times.

Why hadn't she thought of that? It made sense, right? None of the other shop owners were kicking up such a fuss. But then Harriet thought of Kendal, and that didn't seem right. Kendal definitely didn't give off bigot vibes, and she doubted Kendal would hang out with someone who did. But how could Harriet be sure just from first impressions?

Maybe this was a *wait-and-see* situation. Harriet would get on with her life and business and see if Cass caused any more issues. If the woman *was* a homophobe, she was going to freak when she saw the modern Pride flag decals Harriet planned to stick on the windows, let alone if she ever entered Ero-Tea-Ca and saw all the artwork.

Whatever. Cass didn't deserve all the mental attention Harriet was giving her. There was plenty to do, even though it was Saturday, which normally meant cleaning the flat, then meeting up with the siblings for lunch, followed by a movie and a pizza. Harriet would be alone in the shop, cleaning, organising, and settling into her new role as a business owner.

Nabi had wanted to help, but Harriet made her stay home and sleep. Nabi may not have been living in the shop, but no doubt she's spent the odd night or two camped on the stockroom floor, blessing the space and connecting with the shop's energy. All that meant Nabi was running on way too little sleep and far too much sugar. Harriet needed to find where her best friend stashed all those lollipops and destroy them. Would a fruit smoothie really be so terrible?

The tea shop was looking good. They'd got a lot done yesterday. A few more shelves needed to be stocked, and Harriet wanted to familiarise herself with the till and the card machine. Arranging the gift boxes would require a little time. Harriet knew herself enough to understand it would be a slow process. She'd arrange them, then rearrange things several times before she was satisfied.

Pouring out her perfectly steeped Ashwagandha, Harriet picked up her personalised teacup and slowly paced the room, taking everything in. It was fun to watch the outside world pass by without them knowing she was watching. The frosted windows were a great idea. Who knew one-way frosted glass existed? Not Harriet, until Nabi mentioned it as a way to get around any privacy issues.

One particular person made Harriet stop and stare. Cass, to be precise, who'd arrived outside the shop door. Thank God the roller blind was down. Harriet watched her screw up her very pretty face as she stared at the *Closed* sign. As harsh as Cass had been, Harriet still noticed her beauty, which was somehow intensified by her brooding character.

What's she doing here?

Instead of rushing to find out, Harriet sat down and watched. Cass had one hand balled into a fist and the other gripping a bag of coffee beans so hard she was about to cause a mess all over the pavement.

Cass seemed to be muttering to herself. What on earth was she doing? It took everything in Harriet's power not to flip up the shade and ask. No, she'd wait. And keep waiting.

Wow, Cass was taking a long time to decide whatever the hell she was trying to decide. At one point, it looked like the woman was going to throw the coffee beans at the door and run.

Harriet had finished her tea by the time Cass straightened herself up and tentatively knocked on the door. Placing her cup down gently, Harriet took her time walking over and unlatching the door.

Like yesterday, Cass had her hair in a low ponytail. She wore plain black trousers and a short-sleeved shirt with The Oxford Beanery embroidered over the left pocket. Her little apron was cute, and she gave off a strong coffee smell. It was nice.

"Can I help?" Harriet asked in her most pleasant and non-sarcastic voice. Cassandra Beaufort wouldn't make her sink to a level of pettiness. Harriet was better than that.

"He-hello. Um, good morning. Sorry to disturb."

"No worries. What can I do for you?"

Cass thrust the bag of beans in Harriet's hands. "Here. As a welcome gift."

This was so weird. "Right, thanks. Anything else?"

This time it was Cass who shifted nervously from foot to foot. "Yes. Well, I'd like to apologise...if I may."

"I can't stop you." Harriet chuckled. "Would you like to come in?"

Cass's eyes went wide. "Oh, no. No, thank you. Out here's fine." Wow, so even the thought of entering the shop was too much.

"As you like." Harriet leaned against the door frame and waited. Cass cleared her throat several times. Did she need a glass of water? God, it was becoming painful. "Listen, I don't mean to be rude, but I have a lot of things to do today, so..."

"Right, of course. Okay, so I wanted to say sorry for accusing your employee of using drugs and living in the shop. I won't say sorry for complaining about the van or boxes, though. They *did* cause safety issues and blocked access to the café."

"And sending an email of complaint to the council? What about that?"

"I may have been a tad premature. In any case, the council won't be taking anything further without a police report."

That made Harriet stand up straight. "You're calling the *police*?"

"No!" Cass rushed to voice. "No, I'm not. I wouldn't. Not unless I was one hundred percent sure you were doing something illegal."

"Which you're still not convinced is the case, right?"

"I didn't say that," Cass argued.

"No, your face did. I really don't know what I've done to earn this, Cassandra." Should she be using informal names? Maybe sticking to Ms Beaufort would be better.

"Harriet, I swear, I will not be calling the police. What I think of you and your shop doesn't matter, does it?"

"Wow. Yeah, sure. Can I ask you something?"

"Um, sure."

"Are you homophobic? Is this what your campaign of terror is about? You don't like a bunch of queers moving in next door? Afraid we'll corrupt your precious street?"

Cass bit her lip and flared her nose. "Yes, I'm a massive homophobe. Just ask my ex-wife—the one I run the café with. You know, the stunning Black woman with legs for days? She'll tell you how much I hate queer people."

"Fine, you're not bigoted. But you *do* have a problem with Ero-Tea-Ca, right?"

"I didn't come here to discuss this. Do you accept my apology, or not?"

Harriet wasn't going to get any further, so she figured it was better to cut her losses. "Yeah, I accept. I'd like you to promise you're not going to run off to the council every five minutes with bogus complaints, though. It's already stressful enough opening a brand-new business. I don't want to have the threat of inspections hanging over me all the damn time."

"I plan to stay out of the way. That you can be sure of."

Huh, Harriet didn't like the sound of that. "Fine. But I was hoping you and Kendal would join the other shop owners on Monday evening for a small gathering I'm having. It's a soft opening with friends and family. I think it will go a long way towards squashing any fears you may have about the business I plan to run."

Cass was back to looking uncomfortable. "Thanks. I'll pass the invite over to Kendal. She'll more than likely attend. Have a good day."

Harriet watched Cass until she disappeared into the café. Softly closing her own door and relocking it, she squashed the bag of beans between her fingers. It was like a fragrant stress ball. Was that it, then? Cass had apologised. Kind of. And she planned to stay away. That was a good thing. Or was it? Why was Harriet so hung up on what Cass thought?

Maybe the idea of another person shitting on her dreams was the reason Harriet couldn't let it go. It was bad enough she had to fight with her parents over it. Now she was dealing with her next-door neighbour, too. Harriet was sure Kendal would love the shop and everything in it. Call it a gut feeling, or whatever. That made Cass's reaction even more infuriating. Kendal and Cass had been married. Maybe they divorced because of how glaringly different they were.

If Cass was a big ol' lez, why didn't she like the idea of an erotic tea shop? Lesbians were all about sex positivity...well, the ones Harriet knew. Cassandra Beaufort was a conundrum, a grumpy mystery Harriet had to figure out. If anyone was going to cause Ero-Tea-Ca problems in the future, it was sure as shit going to be Cass. So, if Harriet worked on her and got Cass to see the light, i.e., how awesome the tea shop was, Harriet would be securing her future in the shop owner's community.

A new goal then. Step one: finish stocking shelves. Step two: make sure Cass attended the soft opening. Step three: no clue. Having the first two steps figured out was good enough for now.

So how did she make sure Cass attended? Kendal, obviously. Harriet was an astute woman. She knew damn well Cass hadn't come over to apologise out of a sense of guilt. Oh, no. Harriet would hazard a guess she'd got an earful from Kendal last night.

If Kendal was the way in, Harriet had to make contact without Cass knowing. The last thing she wanted was to aggravate Cass further. Maybe taking Kendal up on the coffee she offered was the best way. Surely Cass had to take a day off now and then?

As if the universe itself embossed Harriet's plans with its seal of approval, she watched Cass leave the café with a satchel slung over her shoulder. Face-planting the window so she could see the second Cass was out of sight, Harriet realised just how ridiculous she was being. Did she really need the woman's approval that badly?

Yes. Yes, she did.

Step one of stocking the shelves was going to take a back seat until later. This was her chance. Grabbing her own satchel, Harriet locked up the shop and practically skipped next door.

Kendal greeted her with a wide and genuine smile. Maybe even a bit of relief was mixed in there, too. "Harriet! Come in. What can I get you? On the house. Pick anything you want."

"You don't have to do that. I can pay."

"Nonsense. Black coffee and a pastry?"

Harriet liked Kendal had remembered her order. Not that it was a particularly complicated one. "Thanks. I'm going to sit in if that's cool."

"Only if you let me join you?"

Bingo! "I'd love that."

"Find a table and I'll be right over."

Choosing one of the comfy seats, Harriet dropped her satchel to the floor and made herself at home. The atmosphere felt chill. The customers seemed happy. Some were reading. Others were typing on laptops. It was nice. Hopefully, Ero-Tea-Ca could adopt the same vibe, although the one big difference was Ero-Tea-Ca had actual vibes to offer—batteries included.

"Here you go. Fresh from the oven," Kendal said in her melodic voice. She also had a pastry and a large cup of dark coffee. Cass was right. The woman had legs for days.

It still stumped her how Kendal and Cass had ever been married. Was that super judgemental of her? Probably. Hell, Harriet was only human. And it wasn't like Cass came over as warm and cuddly. Not like Kendal did.

"These pastries are to die for," Harriet mumbled through her first bite.

"Right! I have to regulate myself to one a week otherwise I'd need cholesterol pills, and I'm still too young for that."

How old was she? And Cass, too? Maybe late thirties? "You look great. You can't be anywhere near the age of cholesterol pills." Harriet chuckled.

"Forty-nine. I'm getting there."

Harriet almost choked on her croissant. "You look amazing!"

Kendal laughed. "I have great genes. You should see my mother."

"Is Cass the same age?" *Subtle, Harriet. Real subtle.*

Kendal's eyes twinkled as she gave a sly grin. "Cass is forty-one but has the character of an eighty-year-old grouch."

Harriet snickered. "Yeah. You seem quite different."

"Oh, we are. But it works. I take it she came and apologised? I can only back that up with my own. I'm so sorry, Harriet. I really don't know what's got into her. She's always been a bit over the top where the café is concerned. The other shop owners will attest to that. But for whatever reason, she's got a real bee in her bonnet about Ero-Tea-Ca opening."

Harriet shrugged. "I knew some people would have an issue. That being said, I want to invite you to a soft opening on Monday evening. Friends and family will be there, plus, I hope several other shop owners. I want you all to see the tea shop is nothing but that: a place to drink tea, and eat cakes and sandwiches...just surrounded by erotic art. It's not porn."

Kendal laid a hand on Harriet's arm. "You don't have to convince me. I'm really excited. As much as I love coffee, I love tea too. And I think it's about time we felt comfortable enough to not only talk about, but be surrounded by, the beauty of the human form and all the pleasure we can get from it."

"Wow, thanks. That's exactly what I want—to show people there's nothing wrong with our bodies. That talking about sex shouldn't be taboo."

"I'll be there, then. What time?"

"Around seven. Um...do you think Cass will come?"

Kendal winced. "I wouldn't count on it."

Harriet sighed. "Okay. Complete transparency. Cass let it slip you are her ex-wife after I asked her if she was a homophobe." Kendal snorted. "I figured her apology was your brainchild and hoped you'd help me get her to come to the opening on Monday night."

Canting her head to the side, Kendal smiled. "Can I ask you why? I mean, she's been nothing but a shit to you."

Swallowing a large gulp of coffee, Harriet nodded in recognition of the fact that Cass had definitely been a shit to her. "Honestly, I just don't want another person to fight with over the shop. My parents are less than pleased with my idea and have fought me all the way. Thank God my siblings backed me up, otherwise I think I would have caved by now."

"I'm sorry, Harriet. That must've been hard."

"It wasn't fun," she laughed, "but Ero-Tea-Ca is important. I know it is. And it's worth the discord between me and my parents. Hopefully one day they'll come around. I'd just like Cass to come around sooner. We're going to be neighbours for—fingers crossed—a long time. I want us all to feel comfortable."

6

Cassandra

"**I**t's been a while since you've called for an emergency session, Cassandra."

Cass crossed one leg over the other. "I know, and I'm sorry."

"What are you apologising for, exactly?"

Ugh, Cass hated this, but she'd sworn to herself to keep growing and evolving after she and Kendal divorced. The only way that was possible was by talking to a professional.

Dr Herman was a pleasant woman. It took Cass a while to open up to her, but over the past three years they'd made some significant progress. The only thing Cass still struggled with was the initial delving into her feelings as soon as she sat down. It felt foreign and uncomfortable.

"Fine, I'm not sorry. I needed to talk to you because I'm struggling lately."

Dr Herman mirrored Cass's position. The only difference was the good doctor had a notebook and pen. "Elaborate."

"A new shop is opening next door."

"In the space you wanted to buy?"

"Yes," Cass grumbled. It was still a sore point. "The owner is opening a tea shop."

"That sounds nice."

"An erotic tea shop that sells...toys and things."

"And you're unhappy about that?"

Cass's face flushed. "Well, yes. Of course I'm unhappy. It's...it's crude and...and..."

"Cassandra, take a breath."

Cass fell into a breathing exercise Dr Herman had shown her early on in their sessions. "I'm okay."

"Carry on when you feel ready."

Where did she start? Ever since she found out Harriet's shop would open, Cass felt off and out of control, and she couldn't put a finger on why. All she knew was her behaviour had escalated. She'd really fudged up yesterday. If she'd truly thought something illegal was going on, she'd have gone straight to the police, not the council. Her intentions had only been to cause Harriet trouble.

"If an establishment like that opens, it'll change the dynamic of the street. Who knows what kind of people we'll attract. I've worked too hard to develop a stellar reputation to have it marred by...by people like Harriet Kirkwell."

"Harriet Kirkwell is the new proprietor?"

"Yes. She's young and bubbly, and clearly a liberal hippy."

Did Dr Herman just smirk?

"Okay, Cassandra. Let's break this down."

"Sure. But this time can you just tell me what my problem is, so I don't have to spend all day trying to figure it out through your cleverly worded questions?"

That *did* earn Cass a small smile.

"You know that's not how this works."

Cass huffed, "It was worth a try."

"From the little you've said, I've picked up two threads. Let's follow them individually and see where we end up."

Cass nodded. It already felt good knowing Dr Herman had a clue where to start. The pre-menopause idea was still on the table, though. "Ready to go down the rabbit hole, Doc."

"Let's start with your worries about the reputation of the café."

Scratching the back of her neck, Cass tried to pull her thoughts into something understandable. "Well, surely people who go to erotic tea shops…"

"Are people who like to drink tea and talk about sex?"

"Yes. A tea shop is one thing. I think that would actually be a nice addition to the street. But why the need for all the X-rated stuff? What kinds of people like that sort of thing? And why do they need to push it in others' faces?"

Dr Herman cocked her head. "But how does that affect the café's reputation? You won't be involved with the tea shop. It's a completely separate business, in no way associated with you or Kendal."

"The overall reputation of the street matters."

"The overall reputation isn't what's upsetting you. It's the idea the café could be affected. You're feeling out of control and imagining the worst-case scenario."

"Wouldn't you?" Cass shot. "The café is the one good thing I've done. The one good thing that works as it should."

"Okay, let's pause there for a second. You're referring to your marriage and subsequent divorce. No need to beat around the bush on that one."

Cass appreciated it. "I just don't want to fail at something else."

Dr Herman paused for a second. "Cassandra, you know that's not what happened. Tell me why you and Kendal divorced. The facts only."

The loose thread on the arm of the couch became very interesting. After pulling it several times and causing a small hole that made Cass's heart rate increase by several beats per second, she finally looked at Dr Herman, who sat as patient as ever. "Kendal didn't want children, and I did. Do."

"And..."

Cass rolled her eyes. "And something like that isn't a compromise."

"No, it's not. You and Kendal spent months discussing it."

"I know. But maybe I could live without kids."

Dr Herman placed her pad and pen down. "Are you still in love with Kendal?"

"I'll always love her."

"But?"

"She's my best friend."

"But do you still love her romantically?"

Cass dropped her head. "No. And I think she's seeing someone."

"Ah. And when did you discover that?" Cass became overly interested in the plant to her right. *Was it an Aloe?*

"Cassandra..."

"A few months ago. A couple of days after I found out Mr Beedle had sold the shop to someone else." Cass didn't need to see the doctor's reaction. "I know, I know."

"You know *what*, Cassandra?"

"That I'm reacting to a change of circumstance and not dealing with it very well."

"Elaborate."

Oh, for crying out loud. She may be forty-one, but right now Cass just wanted to stamp her feet and throw a hissy fit. "Even though Kendal and I are divorced, we have a routine. Our lives are still inextricably linked, and if she's seeing someone, that will inevitably change our dynamic, and that scares me. What if this woman is the love of her life and Kendal decides she wants out of the business to go travel the world, or live in Aberdeen?" Why Aberdeen had come to mind, Cass didn't know. Either way, it was nowhere near Oxford.

"Has Kendal mentioned any of that to you?"

"No. She's said nothing, which makes it worse."

"How?"

"Because it means she's worried how I'll react, right?"

Dr Herman shrugged. "Or, it has nothing to do with you, and Kendal wants some time to figure out where the relationship is going. She has that right."

"Of course she does. But it will affect me...the café."

"Time to take a step back from you, Cassandra. Try to look at this solely from Kendal's point of view."

This was one of Cass's issues, still. When her anxiety reared its ugly head, she found it hard to look past her own nose. But that was what the doctor was for. Now, with a few questions and well-timed words, Cass could put herself and her ego to one side and see the situation from another perspective.

"You're right. I know Ken. She loves the café as much as me. She'll tell me about this person when she's ready. I hope."

"She will."

Dr Herman had counselled them both at the end of their relationship. Sometimes Cass wondered if the doctor was the reason they could move past the hurt and forge a new relationship based on mutual respect, love, and friendship.

"But understanding that, doesn't change me not wanting an erotic tea shop opening right next door."

"True," the doctor began. "That's the second thread we need to follow. One that you're not going to like."

Cass didn't especially like any of it. "Okay. What's your theory?"

"It comes back to a subject we're yet to fully dissect: your mother."

Fuck.

Only a bag of Maltesers and a tub of Ben & Jerry's could lift Cass from her horrendous mood. The doctor had really pushed her, far beyond her comfort level, but Cass knew she needed it. Talking about her mum in detail was long overdue, and Cass had avoided it to the best of her ability. But if she really wanted to grow, she had to face the tough stuff.

Opening up about her childhood was hard and there were very few people who knew about Cass's struggles when it came to her mum. Lolita Beaufort was a tornado of a person. She was full of life and love, which, for most people, sounded great. Not for Cass.

Cassandra had always been a reserved person. She needed time to adjust to situations and people. Simple things that were water off a duck's back for most gave Cass anxiety. Eventually, she'd process and acclimatise, but more often than not, people, including her mum, thought she was being ridiculous or overly sensitive.

That wasn't the worst of it, though. Lolita was a sexually vivacious woman. She was a single mum, but that didn't stop her from having men over. Cass once referred to their front door as a conveyor belt for horny blokes. If it hadn't been for the fact that kids called Lolita all manner of nasty things and treated Cass like a leper, maybe Cass wouldn't have found her mum's love life so traumatising.

Now, as an adult, Cass could understand the kids at school were just being arseholes. If it weren't jabs about her mum, they'd have found something else to pick on Cass about. She was too different. As an adult, she could also understand her mum had every right to see who she wanted and when. Lolita was sex positive. She expected to be treated with respect and no man entered their house if he wasn't a good guy. It wasn't like Cass had been exposed to creeps. Lolita was a great mum, who happened to have a high sex drive and didn't see having a child as a reason to stop living her own life.

Back then, of course, the idea of a woman being sexually liberated was frowned upon. Their neighbours thought she was a cheap tart. Lolita was nothing of the sort. But in the court of public opinion, the truth rarely mattered.

Their house was a living embodiment of everything that made Cass uncomfortable. They had books on sex. Art that would make a nun blush adorned their walls. Lolita had no issues talking about sex with Cass. Not Lolita's own experiences, of course. That boundary was never crossed. But she felt it was her job to open Cass's mind to the wonders of the human body. All it did was make Cass retreat and hate everything to do with sex.

Cass knew she wasn't exactly adventurous, but Kendal had never complained about their love life throughout their marriage. People called it vanilla, but what was wrong with that? Why did sex have to be vulgar and in your face?

She knew there had been times Kendal wanted to try new things, but it was like a wall slammed down and Cass couldn't cope, which in turn caused Kendal to stop asking. She was so lovely about it and never forced the issue. Kendal was one of only a handful of people who understood where Cass's issues came from and didn't expect Cass to "get over it."

"The oven is making a weird sound," Kendal called the second Cass stepped into the café kitchen. "I've checked all the usual things, and I'm stumped. Should I call Sean to come and check it out?"

"Sure," Cass answered, her head buzzing.

"Oh, Harriet stopped by earlier."

Well, that got Cass's attention. "What? Why?"

Kendal shut the oven door and came to stand by Cass, who leant against the counter, shoulders slumped. "I invited her for coffee the day we met and she came to collect. It was nice. She's nice."

"Right."

"Hey," Kendal said softly, gently knocking Cass's shoulder. "What's going on?"

Cass rubbed both hands down her face. "I just had a session with Dr Herman."

"I didn't know you were still seeing Herman."

Cass shrugged. "I needed a chat."

They fell quiet. The only sound was the hiss of the coffee machine in the other room. "You can talk to me, you know," Kendal tacked on. "About anything."

"Are you seeing someone?" Cass blurted, and then immediately cringed.

Kendal chuckled. "Ah, you figured it out, huh?" Another shrug. Jesus, was she fifteen again? "Cassandra, look at me, please."

"I'm being ridiculous, I know," she groaned, turning to look at her ex-wife, who was wearing a sincere smile.

"You're not. I wasn't keeping it from you, Cass. It's relatively new and I wanted to see if it was going somewhere before I introduced you."

"I shouldn't have made you tell me. Ugh, Herman would be so disappointed." Cass chuckled. "Sorry, Ken."

"Don't sweat it. Come on. Let's have a coffee and talk. About anything, or nothing. Up to you."

Knowing the café was in safe hands with Billie, their resident hipster, Cass felt okay with taking a bit more time off. Plus, Kendal was owed an explanation for Cass's recent behaviour.

"I may have felt a little spirally lately."

"Elaborate," Kendal said seriously.

"No! It's creepy you're so good at mimicking our therapist."

Kendal smirked. "I practise in the shower sometimes."

"Of course you do. Anyway..."

Cass did herself proud by opening up and spilling all her inner thoughts. She even managed to get through the conversation she'd had with the doctor about her mum. Kendal squeezed her hand at that point.

"So, now you know it's less about Harriet and her shop, and more about..."

"My issues."

"*No*, your experience. Are you ready to give Ero-Tea-Ca a chance?"

"Let's not get ahead of ourselves, Ken."

"Alright, alright. But how about you at least come to this friends and family opening on Monday?"

"You can go for us."

Cass might have had a breakthrough with Dr Herman, but Rome wasn't built in a day. Going to the soft opening sounded horrendous. Cass couldn't think of anything more humiliating and uncomfortable than spending the evening in a tea shop with naughty art, toys, and God knows what else.

No way. Out of the question.

7

Harriet

T he teas were stocked, toys displayed, and the tables set. The small issue with the electrics had been sorted after a mini breakdown and a very helpful electrician Kevin knew. Everything was ready for Ero-Tea-Ca's soft opening. Everything except Harriet. Her uniform was on, and physically she looked set to open the doors for the first time, but emotionally, she was a mashed potato. Tears kept popping up in her eyes and rolling nausea swept through now and then. Ero-Tea-Ca was Harriet's baby, and in a few minutes, people were going to come in and judge the hell out of it, and her.

"Five minutes!" Nabi called through the toilet door.

Shit, five minutes! Harriet had to clean up and look presentable. Lip sweat did not a confident businesswoman make. Tucking her black short-sleeve shirt further into her black slacks, Harriet regarded herself one more time in the mirror. She gently ran her fingers over the Ero-Tea-Ca emblem stitched over her pocket. The only thing left to do was tie on her apron, and voila! Harriet Kirkwell, business owner, was ready.

Instead of milling around chatting, Harriet planned to wait tables and serve behind the counter. She might be the owner, but she wanted to show everyone how hard she planned to work. Harriet wasn't the type of person to have her employees do the dirty work. She'd be right there with them, serving and dealing with customers, pleasant and difficult.

Summoning her brightest smile, Harriet sauntered to the serving area. Manifestation was a wonderful thing. She would will herself to succeed, and that started with a show of confidence. Spotting Nabi fixing a table setting so it was perfect, Harriet gave her a thumbs up before unlocking the entrance door. With a big breath in, and a slow release out, she opened it to find several friends already waiting, gifts in hand and adoring smiles on their faces.

"Welcome," she called, accepting hugs and cheek kisses. Her face hurt from smiling so much, but the discomfort was worth it. Genuine happiness was rare in the world, and Harriet swore to hold on to hers. Because she *was* happy.

Her nerves in the loo had dissipated the second she had her friends and family surrounding her. Several minutes later, two of the Shop Owners' Guild rocked up, looking apprehensive but open-minded. They shook Harriet's hand and proceeded to take a look around. Nerves pitter-pattered their way through Harriet's chest again, but she kept them to a minimum. Nothing would pop her bubble.

Diane arrived with her husband, Mitchell, and their eldest, Robbie, who'd turned eighteen a few weeks ago. Robbie was the spitting image of Harriet and therefore her favourite. Diane's other kids were just as precious, but she couldn't help but have an extra-special bond with her mini-me.

"Guys, thank you so much for coming," Harriet called as she embraced them all. Robbie held on a little longer, squishing her ribs. "Aunt Harriet, this is so cool," Robbie gushed. Her eyes were wide with wonder. Doing what Diane did for a living meant her kids weren't taken aback by sex or anything related to the human form. Robbie came out at thirteen. She had "The Talk" at sixteen when she got her first girlfriend, but it wasn't the horrifying shit show most teens endured when discussing sex with their parents. There was nothing in Ero-Tea-Ca that Robbie would find scandalous.

Harriet insisted her other niblings adhere to the 18+ policy, though, much to their irritation. Milly and Parker were only eighteen months shy of becoming legal adults, but Harriet wouldn't endanger her business.

"It really looks fantastic, sis. Well done," Diane said, giving Harriet another bone-crushing hug.

"Let's be honest, I couldn't have done it without you and Kevin," Harriet replied sincerely. They'd been her rock, both emotionally and monetarily. If not for their sizeable investments, the tea shop would never have happened.

"We helped, but this was your brainchild. You did this, Harriet, and I am so very proud."

A lump the size of Jupiter formed, threatening to choke her up. Batting her sister away with a playful punch to the arm, Harriet inhaled deeply. *No more tears.* "Anyway. Why don't you sit. I'll get Nabi over to take your order."

Seizing the opportunity to step away for a moment, Harriet leaned on the office door frame, taking it all in.

People were laughing, some were in deep discussion, and others were checking out the display of toys. All seemed happy, including Mandeep and Shirley from the Shop Owners' Guild.

There were only a few people missing—notably, her parents, but they'd been adamant they couldn't support her in this, so no surprise they'd kept to their word and stayed away. The other two people Harriet hoped would show were Kendal and Cassandra. Cass. Could she use the shortened version yet? Ugh, whatever. It was still early, though. Plenty of time. Harriet was determined to become friends with every shop owner, miserable café owner included.

"Harriet!" Kendal's excited voice filtered over the chatter. She really was a striking woman. And she was alone. Damn it.

"Kendal, thank you for coming," Harriet replied, giving Kendal a cheek kiss. She felt comfortable enough to do that, and something told Harriet she and Kendal were going to be great friends.

"This place is amazing!"

"Thanks. I'm really happy with it. I hope everyone else feels the same way."

"If all the smiling faces are anything to go by, I'd say so."

"Can I get you a drink? We have Champagne, or...tea. Lots of tea," Harriet said with a smile and a chuckle.

"I'll take a flute of bubbly before perusing the tea. I've never seen so many varieties. It's impressive."

"We have a tea for everything. There's a reason it's been consumed for thousands of years."

"And the teapots," Kendal gasped. "Who made them? The art is exquisite!"

Harriet beamed. "All local artists. I'll introduce you. The glass toys are made by my brother and a friend."

"I love the gift boxes. Very clever."

"So...no Cassandra, huh?"

Kendal sighed. "She said she might come. That's more than I expected after she flatly refused the first time I asked her."

"Better than nothing, I guess. Now let's go talk to some fabulous artists."

And talk they did. Kendal slotted in seamlessly with Harriet's friends, the majority of who were clearly experiencing a tiny crush. Understandable...Harriet might have one herself. Still, a small blip of disappointment hovered like a tiny cloud over Harriet's sunshine-filled day.

What did she have to do to get Cass here? Why couldn't the woman just give Harriet and the shop a chance?

"Why are you frowning?"

Harriet turned to face Nabi. "Cassandra didn't come."

"Who?"

"Cassandra Beaufort. The coffee shop owner."

"Well, Kendal's here and she's fifty percent of The Beanery, isn't she? So, I don't think we'll get any more shit."

"That's not the point," Harriet stated.

"M'kay. So, what's the point?"

"Just...well...I don't know, but it's important Cass gets on board."

"Right. Okay, I'm gonna leave you with all that and carry on serving. We've already sold three glass dildos and four teapot gift boxes." Nabi danced away, leaving Harriet with a choice: she could wait in vain for Cass to turn up, or she could make it happen.

Giving a swift glance over the room, Harriet slipped out the door and raced over to the café. It was closed, but she could see Cass behind the counter. With a jaunty tap, Harriet smiled brightly. Cass looked up and furrowed her eyebrows. A few seconds passed before Cass huffed and beckoned Harriet inside.

"Hi," Harriet called brightly. "How are you?" She shut the door and skipped over.

Cass regarded her with what could only be seen as contempt. "What are you wearing?"

Harriet looked down in confusion. "Um…my work uniform." Wasn't that obvious?

"You can't wear that. Take it off!"

"Wow, you could buy me dinner first." Harriet laughed. Cass either didn't get the joke or didn't find it funny.

"I'm serious. That can't be your uniform."

Hopping onto the closest stool, Harriet rested her chin on her hand. "And why's that?"

"Because it looks too much like The Beanery's uniform. Clients will get us mixed up and think we're connected," Cass spluttered.

"But the logo's different," Harriet mused. She felt something unexpected stir in the pit of her stomach—laughter. Now she knew to expect Cass's prickly demeanour, it was starting to feel more amusing than off-putting.

"Unless someone's staring at it, they won't see the difference!" Cass shrieked.

"Hmm. But I also have teapots on my apron. They're smiling—look." Harriet stood up on the stool's crossbar. Her apron did, in fact, have smiling teapots on it. They made Harriet's day every time she looked at them.

"It doesn't matter. Your shirt and trousers are exactly like mine. You have to change it."

Harriet whistled. "Sorry, Cassandra, no can do."

Cass growled—actually growled. "Ms Kirkwell—"

"Harriet."

"Harriet. You cannot—"

"Did you try the tea I gave you?"

Cass's retort died in her throat. "What?"

"The tea? The one that aids sleep?"

"I...no, why? I sleep fine."

"Just wondering. It tastes great. I tried the coffee you brought over. It's great."

"It's Peruvian Gold."

"It tastes golden," Harriet replied sweetly.

"How could it possibly taste golden?"

"You know. It's the feeling you get when something is delicious. Golden."

Harriet stifled a laugh when Cass pinched the bridge of her nose. "That's the most ridiculous thing I've ever heard. Although I shouldn't be surprised a young whippersnapper like you would think what you've said makes perfect sense."

Holding up a hand, Harriet snorted. "Did you just use the word *whippersnapper*?"

"What's wrong with that?"

"Well, nothing. It's just I've never heard someone younger than eighty use it. Just took me by surprise. Sorry, I interrupted. Please continue."

Another frown from Cass and Harriet was feeling happier than ever. "I can't remember what I was saying."

"Oh, you were telling me to take off my uniform."

"What? No."

"I distinctly remember you telling me when I came in to take it off."

"Harriet—"

"Cassandra."

"Ugh, you're infuriating."

"Are you finished working?"

"Why?"

"I want you to come to my opening."

"No thank you."

The back and forth was dizzying, but Harriet was up for it. She liked a good verbal spar. "I'll take off my uniform for you if you come over."

"I don't want you to take off your uniform!" Cass cried.

"I absolutely remember you asking me to take it off, Cassandra."

"I didn't mean it like that!"

"So, you want me to keep the uniform on?"

"Yes."

"Glad we got the uniform issue sorted. Now, why won't you enter my shop?"

"It's...I...I'm busy."

Harriet knew she had Cass on the ropes. "You just told me you finished working and I'm only asking you to come over for a few minutes. Just so you can see the shop isn't what you think."

"I have a cat!" Cass declared. She even raised her index finger in exclamation.

Harriet grinned. "Oh, I love pussy...cats. I'd love to meet them. Do you live close by?"

"Well, yes, but..."

"I could meet your kitty and then you could come over to the shop for a cup of tea. Mandeep is there."

"He would be," Cass grumbled.

"So, shall we?" Harriet jumped off the stool and headed for the door. Clasping both hands behind her back,

Harriet rocked on her heels, smiling at a slightly confused and stunned-looking Cassandra Beaufort.

Silence descended, but Harriet's patience and overtly sunny nature finally won out. Cass was grumbling to herself the entire time, but she still threw off her apron, grabbed her purse, and headed out.

Casting a quick glance towards Ero-Tea-Ca, Harriet concluded everything was going okay. A quick wave to Nabi and the returned *rock on* sign cemented it. She had to go double speed to catch up to Cass, who seemed to be race walking. Maybe she was trying to get away. The thought made Harriet quietly chuckle. They remained silent the entire time. Harriet was more than happy to go along with the flow. Oxford was gorgeous and there was always plenty to see.

"I live here," Cass murmured.

"Is that your cat?" Harriet asked with a gasp. The sweetest looking cat sat at the window, staring at them.

"Yes. That's Mr Whiskers."

"Cute name."

"He came with it from the shelter."

"It's still cute."

Cass didn't reply. She just pushed through the gate. Harriet followed, her eyes straying from the cat to Cass's backside. The trousers were really working for her.

"How long have you lived here?" Harriet took in the decor, which was...plain. Everything seemed very orderly.

"Years," Cass mumbled.

Jesus, the woman wasn't giving her much to work with. "So, can I look around?" A shrug. Was that even a valid way to answer? Leaving Cass to feed Mr Whiskers, Harriet wandered aimlessly. The living room was stark. A few nondescript prints hung on the walls. The rug was nice. It at least had a colour in it.

"I'm done." Cass stood in the hallway, hands on hips.

"That was fast. Are you ready to head back?"

"You didn't actually meet Mr Whiskers."

Harriet bit her lip. "You're right. I'll do that now."

Slipping past Cass, Harriet inhaled her coffee and slightly floral scent. *Nice*. Mr Whiskers had his back to the room, happily munching on his fresh bowl of food. Crouching, Harriet gave him a scratch behind the ear, earning her a low rumble. He even stopped eating to butt his head in her hand.

"Huh."

Harriet turned around. Cass was there, frowning. "Everything okay?"

"He doesn't like people."

"He seems to like me."

"Hence the *huh*," Cass replied, rolling her eyes.

Standing, Harriet straightened her shirt. "Ready to go?"

Cass shifted on her feet. It was her tell. Harriet knew what was coming next. "I never actually agreed to come back. I've got laundry to do, and paperwork. Plus, it's going to rain."

"Hmm. It's true, you didn't agree to come back with me. And it *is* going to rain, which means I could get wet on the way back. Maybe I should stay here with you a little longer. We could discuss the uniforms a little more."

"I'm ready to go."

"Wow, you find the idea of spending one-on-one time with me that disconcerting? Should I be offended, Cassandra?"

"Yes. Now do you want me to come or not?"

Oh, Harriet was going to enjoy this. One perfectly shaped eyebrow raised, and Cass went red. "I'd love you to come."

"I didn't mean...that wasn't...oh, for God's sake, why does everyone your age insist on turning everything innocent into something sordid?"

Holding her hands up, Harriet chuckled. "I don't know what you mean. Now, shall we go?"

"Fine."

Harriet beamed. She'd done it. She'd convinced the resident grump to come to the shop. That was the hard part, right? Surely everything else would take care of itself as soon as Cass entered Ero-Tea-Ca. After all, it was a wonderland of delicious tea and fantastic art. What could Cass possibly have against any of that?

8

Cassandra

Unbelievable! The gall of the woman to play Cass so well. How dare she confuse Cass so effortlessly? One minute, she was behind the counter finishing up for the day, and the next, she'd been coerced into visiting the blasted porn tea shop by a living embodiment of happiness.

How was Harriet so perky? After their previous interactions, the woman should be angry at Cass, not bloody smiling. And certainly not visiting Mr Whiskers and talking about taking her uniform off. What in the world had happened? Cass genuinely couldn't understand how she'd gone from point A to point B. More infuriating was

Cass's inability to stop, turn around, and go home. There was no reason she should be following Harriet to...*that* shop. It was the last place she wanted to be and one she'd sworn never to visit. Ever.

Yet here she was, fifty metres from the entrance. The frosted glass did its job well; however, Cass still knew what lay behind that door: Filth! And lots of other people, by the sounds of it. Great, Cass was going to flush red in front of her fellow shop owners, ex-wife, and random hippies.

"I promise you'll like it, Cassandra." Harriet's earnest words did little to quell her anxiety.

"Highly unlikely," Cass responded. Her heart rate spiked, and she felt a cold sweat form at the base of her skull.

Harriet stopped shy of the tea shop door. "Look, if after this visit you're still not on board, I'll leave you be. I just don't want you thinking I'm here to do damage. The shop's success is my entire focus. That goes for other shops on the street too. We all know how hard it is to run an independent business no matter what we sell. I wouldn't purposefully open a shop that could damage the sales and reputation of others."

"And what if, in the long run, it does? Negatively affect other businesses, I mean?" Last night's nightmare came to mind again, causing Cass to shiver. She'd watched her beloved café go down in flames while Ero-Tea-Ca thrived. Mr Whiskers had woken her with a face bump to the chin and Cass had let a few tears fall. Her anxiety over the fate of her business was getting out of hand.

Maybe visiting Harriet's shop would help. The tea shop was like a mythical beast at the moment. Something to be scared of, which seemed ridiculous for a woman in her forties. Cass couldn't continue letting it affect her like this.

"It won't. I'm that confident."

Crap, Harriet *looked* confident. Sighing, Cass caved. "Fine. I'll give it a chance." Cass held up her hand as Harriet bounced on the spot, excitement dancing in her lovely eyes. "But if I still hold the same opinion after, you promise to leave me alone. I won't interfere with your shop, and you won't bug me. We get on with our lives. Separately."

Harriet nodded. "But what if you do like it? Does that mean we can be friends? Help each other out?"

"You can be friends with Kendal."

Harriet rolled her eyes, which was cute. Everything about the woman was cute, and Cass didn't like it one bit.

Wiping her now sweaty palms over her slacks, Cass painted on the best smile she could convincingly get away with. It probably looked more like a grimace, but it was all she could muster.

Harriet pushed open the door. The noise grew exponentially louder. Cass tensed, waiting for the assault of vulgarity to strike. It didn't. Where was all the red and neon? She'd imagined something closer to a shop in the Red-Light District, not an actual tearoom. The place looked so...tea shop-y. Huh. In fact, it was lovely. The old-style counter, tables, and display case were gorgeous. So where was the erotic bit?

Harriet bumped her shoulder. "So far, so good?"

Cass grunted. She was busy casing the joint, looking for stuff she knew would ruin her experience and validate her dislike of the place.

"Cass, you're here?" Kendal sounded suitably surprised.

"Not voluntarily," she grumbled.

"Harriet, did you kidnap my ex-wife?" Kendal laughed.

"Not quite." Harriet grinned. "Cassandra, would you like a glass of Champagne?"

"No, thank you." Her reply was gruff, unnecessarily so, but Cass couldn't shake the disbelief of how wrong she'd gotten the situation, and the tea shop. And then it happened. Her eye caught something on the back shelf behind the counter. A glass...good Lord.

"Ah, I see you've found the toys we sell," Harriet said quietly and far too closely. Cass's face burned with embarrassment.

"I..." Cass's eyes then travelled to the teapots on every table. She looked closer and studied the pattern. Christ on a bike! Were they Kama Sutra inspired? Who would want one of those sitting on their kitchen table?

"Aren't the teapots brilliant?" Kendal said.

"I..." Cass couldn't come up with words. Yes, the erotic part of the shop was subtle, but it was still there. All she could see was the glass "artwork" sitting on the shelf, staring at her. "I'd like to go now. Thank you for the invite. I've seen all I need to. Good night."

Pushing through the crowd, Cass stepped into the street and pulled in a big lungful of air. All she wanted was to get home and snuggle with Mr Whiskers.

"Cassandra, wait!"

Shooting a glance over her shoulder, Cass gritted her teeth as Harriet came scuttling over. "I'd like to go home, Ms Kirkwell."

"No need to last name me. It can't have been that bad."

"I held up my end of the deal." Cass wouldn't cause trouble for Harriet. The shop wasn't overtly sexual, so she was confident the café wouldn't be impacted that much. That didn't mean she had to like it, or that she had to endure another minute inside.

"Cassa—"

"Look, each to their own, okay? I visited, and yes, I'll concede it isn't what I thought. We'll co-exist without drama. Now, can I go home please? I have an early start."

The crestfallen look didn't suit Harriet at all, but Cass couldn't lie. Ero-Tea-Ca would never be a place she'd feel comfortable with.

Harriet nodded and gave a small smile. "Sure. Thank you for at least checking it out."

"You're welcome. Good night."

The walk home was short, thank God. Cass burst through her door, shed her clothes, and jumped in the shower. Her skin felt weird and her head buzzed. Would she ever get to a point where the mere mention of sex wouldn't send her into a spiral?

The glass dildos swam across her mind. They were beautiful if you took away their purpose. A nice ornament, possibly—if you liked that kind of thing, but did people really enjoy using them? It's not like they were true to life. Their shape sort of looked like a man's thing. Ugh, Cass couldn't even bring herself to use the anatomically correct name. Was this just her character or had her mum's lifestyle broken something inside? Why did she have to be so damn awkward?

Shuffling to the couch in her fluffy slippers and silk camisole, Cass took a large swig of the beer she'd nabbed on her way to the living room. What a day. Thankfully, she had tomorrow off. It would be good to put a bit of distance between her and Harriet.

A sliver of guilt surfaced. Just the look on Harriet's face when Cass all but ran out the door was awful. Harriet, the new resident bundle of joy, whom Cass had upset. Again.

"How was your day off, Cass?"

Cass popped her purse under the counter and headed for the coffee machine. "It was fine. Went to Sainsbury's."

"Wow, hardcore."

"They've put Tetley tea bags up again. Ten pence more now," Cass grumbled.

Kendal leant against the worktop. "Good job you only have to buy a box every blue moon when your mum's finished it off. God knows how you'd afford to live otherwise."

"Mock all you want. It's still bloody outrageous to spend that amount of money on a bag of mediocre tea."

"A whopping one pound fifty. Yeah, I understand."

"Well, I didn't have a choice." Cass sighed. "I woke up yesterday morning with my left hip aching."

"Ah, the prophetic ball joint."

"Again, you can mock, Ken, but you've witnessed it enough to know the truth."

Kendal laughed. "True, true. So that means..."

"Mum will be visiting soon. I just need to wait for the message."

"What's a prophetic hip?"

Cass stilled. When had Harriet arrived? She definitely wasn't in the café when Cass walked in.

"And, hi, guys. I just came to get my morning pastry."

Turning with her espresso, Cass scowled. "You can't bring your own drinks in here, Harriet." Not only was she in here, when her own shop served pastry-type food, the woman had brought in a travel mug of what Cass could only assume was tea. "How would you like it if your patrons waltzed in with their own beverages?"

"Cass." Kendal sighed.

"What? How am I in the wrong?"

"No, you're right. I should have left the tea behind. I won't do it again. I just got excited about the thought of your Danishes. We don't serve the same foods, which you'll be happy about. No competition."

Cass snorted. "As if it'd be a competition."

"Wow." Kendal chuckled. Cass flushed. Harriet grinned.

"Anyway, what's a prophetic ball joint?"

Cass glared at Kendal. It was her signature "Don't say a word" look, but of course it didn't work, or Kendal blatantly ignored it.

"Since the day Cass left home, she developed a gift. Whenever she woke up with an aching left hip, her mum would show up."

"Like an early warning system," Cass added.

"Oh, don't you get on with her?" Harriet asked, settling on a stool. Cass wanted to tell her to leave because she smelled really good, and her smile lit up her face to the point of distraction.

"We're just different."

"Polar opposites," Kendal interjected. "Chalk and cheese. Night and day."

"I think she gets it, Ken."

Harriet was nodding knowingly. "I totally understand. That's how it is with me, my siblings, and our parents."

Cass stared. "What? You're telling me your parents aren't liberal hippies like their kids?"

"Cassandra," Kendal admonished.

Harriet threw her head back, laughing. "Not at all. In fact, I think you'd get on really well with them. Do you like snooker?"

"Um..."

"What about *Antiques Roadshow*?"

"I'm not that old!"

"No, but you act it," Kendal supplied.

"And how do you know my siblings are liberal hippies?"

"Just a guess."

Harriet chuckled. "Well, I suppose you're right. Kevin is an artist. He helped make the glass...ornaments in my shop."

Cass flushed again and looked away. "I need more coffee."

"And my sister," Harriet ploughed on, "is a sex therapist to celebrities."

Cass fumbled her espresso cup, almost dropping it to the floor.

"Diane is lovely," Kendal replied. "Kevin, too. He's so funny."

"Don't tell him that, he'll be insufferable."

"Kendal, we have customers," Cass bit. This conversation needed to end.

"Where?" Kendal replied.

Dammit. Everyone was sitting down, happily sipping their coffees. "The stock needs counting."

"You do it then. I'm having a five-minute break to talk to my friend."

"Fine," she shot, slamming the cup down far too hard before stalking off to the back to count the stock that didn't need counting. "God, first expensive tea bags, and now a distracting strumpet with hippy siblings."

"Who's a strumpet?"

Cass clutched her chest. "Don't sneak up on me."

"Are you talking about Harriet?" Kendal leaned on the door frame.

Cass pretended to count the wooden stirrers. "Who's watching the café?"

"Our employees. Now, come on, why did you randomly shout *strumpet* in the stockroom?"

"Never mind."

"Do you know the meaning of the word? Because if you were by chance referring to our lovely new neighbour as a strumpet, then you're being quite offensive."

"I...no, I didn't mean..."

"Strumpet is a woman who has many sexual encounters."

"Oh, so my mother," Cass replied.

"Jesus, you're salty today. Do you need another day off?"

"I didn't mean any offence."

"So, you *were* talking about Harriet?"

"I..."

"You know...just because she runs an erotic tea shop doesn't mean she sleeps around. And even if she *did*, that's not for you to judge, Cass. I get you have strong opinions on this kind of stuff, but you can't go around being like that to people. She doesn't deserve it."

"I meant to say *seductress*," Cass blurted, "not strumpet. I didn't mean that. I got my words confused." Oh Jesus, she was in a full-on panic.

"You think Harriet is a seductress?"

"No!"

Kendal pushed off the door frame with a giant smile. "Oh, Cass. You like her."

"I do not!"

"I can see why. She's gorgeous."

"She's too young."

"Ah, so you've thought about it?"

Raking both hands through her hair, Cass slumped against the storage racks. "Kendal."

"Cassandra."

"Look, she's pretty. But she's young, and not my type at all."

Kendal hip-checked her. "Maybe that's a good thing. Change it up a little."

Cass shook her head, trying to formulate a rebuttal.

"Before you completely shut the idea down, just think about it. I want you to be happy, Cass."

"Whoa, whoa. I admitted she's pretty, let's not get carried away. And for your information, I'm very happy."

"No, you're plodding along. Have an adventure. Get a little naughty."

"I don't want to get naughty. I want to run my café and live my life exactly as it is without—"

"A seductress turning your head?"

"You're insufferable!"

"Cassandra, my love?" Lolita Beaufort called from the front of the shop. Cass closed her eyes and breathed deeply. Today *really* sucked.

"Wow, the Lolita Hip strikes again." Kendal grinned.

"I told you. It's foolproof."

"It's never been that quick, though. You usually get at least a week to prepare."

"The universe hates me. It's karma for reporting Harriet."

Kendal tilted her head. "That's fair."

Taking off her apron, Cass headed to the door. "Please tell me Harriet left."

"Yeah, as soon as you walked off in a strop. Don't worry."

Ha! 'Don't worry.' Hilarious.

All Cass could do was worry. She'd developed a weird crush-type thing on a woman too young and too different, and now her mother was here. It was only a matter of time before she'd want to drag Cass to Ero-Tea-Ca and then her world would collide with Harriet's again. It was going to be an embarrassing horror show, and Cass was helpless to stop it.

9

Harriet

The soft opening had been a roaring success, and Harriet had accomplished the seemingly impossible by getting Cassandra to step foot in the tearoom without passing out.

Then again, she'd run out of there pretty damn fast. That was disappointing. Harriet couldn't understand what had triggered the flight response, or the icy attitude when they'd spoken outside. After meeting Mr Whiskers, Harriet believed they were getting somewhere. Clearly not.

As usual, though, Harriet had put a smile on her face and returned to the tearoom to celebrate with everyone. She couldn't let Cass's reaction dampen the rest of the evening. They'd all put too much work into getting Ero-Tea-Ca up and running. They deserved a night to honour that.

Instead of avoiding the café, which Harriet was sure Cass would prefer her to do, she'd toddled over for her usual Danish, where she had a weird conversation about a hip joint before Cass got the hump over something and ran away to the stockroom. It was difficult to pinpoint all the things that set the woman off. At this rate, Harriet would need to make lists of conversations and topics that were bound to make Cass lose her temper.

With the Danish consumed and tea drunk, Harriet set about cleaning the tearoom. She and Nabi would have a confab later on. Their friends and family had been kind enough to fill in a short form reviewing the service. It was imperative Harriet and Nabi worked out any kinks before the grand opening on Friday.

"I've just had an amazing idea!" Nabi shouted, rolling into the room. Literally.

"Are you wearing skates?" It was an unnecessary question. Nabi was gliding around the tables, picking up trash and teacups.

"Yes. I was tidying my room and found them under the bed. I was so happy!"

"And you just *had* to wear them to work?"

After a rather impressive twirl, Nabi skidded to a stop. "Of course. Lolly?"

Harriet regarded the neon yellow blob of sugar. "No, thanks. It's 8 a.m. I've not long cleaned my teeth."

Shrugging, Nabi did another spin. "So, back to my wonderful idea, that frankly, I'm mad at myself for not thinking of earlier because it's so good."

"Hit me," Harriet replied, sitting down.

"Book clubs."

The thought had occurred to her, but she'd had more important things to think of at the time. Maybe they could organise it now. "Yeah, I like it. We could put a package together. Um...free sandwiches, or the second pot of tea half price."

"Yes!" Nabi beamed, clapping her hands. "There must be loads of book clubs around here."

"Let's make a poster. How about Sunday afternoons?"

"I'm happy with that. It's nice and quiet, and could offer people an alternative to sitting at home with the Sunday blues. Do we leave it to the group to decide the book, or should we be more involved? Like the book comes with the package deal?"

Tapping a finger against her chin, Harriet hummed in thought. "How about we offer several books to choose from?"

"That could work. What if the group already has a system they use?"

Harriet shrugged. "That's cool. They can purchase the package, sans book."

"Can we have queer nights, too? If we're thinking of creating packages, why not look at offering different options? Once a month we could do a...oh, a Queer-Tea-Be Here."

Laughing, Harriet bobbed her head. "Totally. We might need to mull over the name a little more, but the premise is good. Let's not do too much too soon, though. We still need to go through the reviews and work out any problems. I don't want to overload us. The next few weeks are going to be nuts. As soon as we're in a routine and comfortable, we can look at properly organising events."

Nabi stuck two thumbs up. "Oh, I went through the notes this morning. All good. No issues. The only complain—"

"There was a complaint?" Harriet all but shrieked.

Nabi held up her hand. "From Gogo. They complained there weren't enough dildos on the shelf. Bear in mind, this was after their fifth glass of Champagne and not accounting for the fact we'd sold a bunch of toys."

"Oh, well, okay then." Harriet's heart returned to its normal rhythm.

Chuckling, Nabi grasped Harriet's face. "Honey, we rocked it. Everyone was happy. Even those Shop Owners' Guild-y people."

But not everyone was happy. Harriet's mind naturally flitted to Cass walking out flustered. "Yeah. Okay, I'll relax. That means that we have the rest of the week to do one last deep clean."

Pushing away, Nabi rolled back a few feet. She tipped her skate, effectively putting on her brakes. Putting a hand on her hip, she wiggled the index finger of her free hand. "Nope! Not happening. I'm kidnapping you."

"Nabi!"

"You know it's the right thing to do. I get you want to make this place successful. I do too, but I'd be a terrible best friend if I let you shackle yourself to it twenty-four seven. Work-life balance, baby. It's a thing. Now, I know you have dinner with the 'rents tonight, and for that, I'm truly sorry. But tomorrow morning, we'll be on a train to London for an impromptu getaway. And before your blood pressure spikes, it's just for two nights."

Harriet relaxed. The thought of getting away sounded pretty good, actually. "You're the best, you know that, right?"

"I do." Nabi grinned, twirling on the spot.

"But you still can't wear roller skates in the shop, Nabs."

Two hours later and without a skating Nabi, Harriet did one last sweep of the tearoom. She still had time to kill before she dragged herself to her parents for an evening of condescension, disappointment, and dried-out roast pork.

"What to do?" she murmured to herself.

The overwhelming urge to go back to The Oxford Beanery decided that for her. Cass would absolutely scowl at her, but Harriet kind of liked it. Was that weird? She'd never been attracted to someone so moody. Harriet's usual type had a sunny disposition like herself. Cass was the opposite in every way, but for whatever reason, Harriet was very attracted to her.

She'd figured it out after that morning's run in. It was somewhere between the confusion of her prophetic hip and the chat about their parents that Harriet felt it hit. The "Oh crap, I like this woman" zap, straight to the heart.

It was no longer about getting Cass to like Ero-Tea-Ca. Harriet wanted Cass to like *her*. There were layers to Cass which Harriet wanted to peel back. It was becoming clear her aversion to the shop and anything remotely to do with sex went deeper than a general stick up her bum, and Harriet wanted to know the truth. She wanted Cass to feel comfortable enough to open up to her.

She was on an impossible mission, for sure. Harriet wasn't convinced Cass liked her in any capacity. How was she supposed to get the woman to see her in more than a friendly light?

Exposure therapy. Harriet would make herself a part of Cass's everyday life. Sure, she could grab a bun from her own display case, but The Oxford Beanery really did have amazing pastries. All Harriet had to do was make visiting the café a part of her daily routine. As long as she didn't make another faux pas as bad as the one this morning, Cass had no reason to stay mad at her. She should've known better than to take her tea into the café.

The only problem now, though, was Harriet had already visited The Beanery today. What reason could she come up with to go back? Scanning the tearoom, she spotted the teapot Kendal had all but drooled over.

"That'll do," she said, grinning. Nothing wrong with a new neighbour offering a gift in the pursuit of friendship, right? Honestly, she and Kendal were already well on track to becoming great mates. That was neither here nor there, though. Not when Cass refused to get with the program.

Doing a rush job on the wrapping, Harriet tucked the newly gift-wrapped teapot under her arm and headed for the café. Upon entering, she saw neither Kendal nor Cass. There was, however, an older lady manning the counter. Her hair was dark and short, styled into messy spikes. She wore large, hooped earrings and bright eye makeup. Her smile lit up the entire room as she chatted with a patron.

Waiting for her turn, Harriet strained her neck, trying to see through the door which led to the back of The Beanery. No luck.

"Hello and welcome to the one-and-only Oxford Beanery. Best coffee in all of England, guaranteed," the woman exclaimed with vigour. Harriet couldn't help but return the energy.

"Wow, that's one hell of a greeting. I love it! I'm Harriet. New to the area. Is Kendal or Cassandra around?"

"They've just popped out. New to the area you say?" The woman scanned Harriet from head to toe. "You aren't by any chance the owner of that fantastic new tea shop, are you?"

Harriet jiggled on the spot. It was so refreshing having a person praise the shop rather than bemoan its existence. "I am indeed."

The woman clapped and shrieked. "Oh, you wonderful woman. I was over the moon when I read about it in the council's newsletter. What a delightful idea. It's about bloody time we got something new and invigorating in the area. When do you open?"

"Officially, Friday," Harriet replied. "I'd be happy to give you a tour, if you want. Do you work here part-time? I haven't seen you before."

The woman waved her hand. "Oh no, dear. My daughter owns this fine establishment."

Her daughter. Oh my God, the weird hip prophecy was real. "You're Cassandra's mum, right?"

"The one and only," she replied. "I'm Lolita Beaufort."

Harriet took the proffered hand. "Harriet Kirkwell. It's lovely to meet you."

"Mum, we're bac— What are you doing here?" The tone was as lethal as ever. Harriet pasted on her sincerest smile and turned to Cass, who'd stumbled through the café door, weighed down with bags. Kendal followed soon after.

"Cassandra Beaufort, you don't speak to people like that!" Lolita admonished.

"Oh, hey, Harriet," Kendal called, ignoring the tension between mother and daughter.

"Hey. I wanted to give you this," Harriet said, ignoring Cass's scowl, which was firmly aimed at her.

Kendal waddled past with her mountain of bags, dumping them behind the counter. "You've brought me a gift?"

Harriet shrugged. "It's a *thank you for being so welcoming* gift." Her eyes flitted to Cass, who had the decency to look guilty.

"You daft sod. I don't need a gift."

"Well, you're getting one. Take it." Kendal took the box and began unwrapping it. Shit, Harriet didn't think she'd open it in the café. Great, Cass was going to throw another fit. "Um...maybe save it for later," Harriet quickly added.

"Nonsense, I want to open it now." And that was what she did. Harriet expected Cass to start growling, but she was suspiciously quiet. It was Lolita that made all the noise. As soon as she spied the teapot, she whipped it out of Kendal's hands to inspect it.

"Oh, wow, look at this! That's just gorgeous. The artwork is sublime."

"My brother is in charge of sourcing local artists to paint the pots. He also adds his own art."

"He's done a fine job. I've never seen doggy-style look so fancy!"

Lolita brought the teapot closer for a more thorough inspection. Harriet noticed several customers were looking over. This was not what she'd envisioned. Risking another peek, she looked at Cass, whose eyes were firmly on the ground, her face red. Crap.

Kendal took the pot with a chuckle. "Harriet was right. I can look at it later."

Harriet saw Kendal look at Cass. Something flitted over her face. "Sorry, I should have waited until you were ready to close."

"Oh, don't be silly," Lolita interjected. "Everyone here is an adult. It's only a bit of erotica between friends."

Harriet cringed. Lolita wasn't being exactly quiet. Waiting for Cass to finally lose her temper, Harriet was more than surprised when she simply passed by them all and went into the back. Kendal closed her eyes briefly. Yeah, Harriet had fucked up. Again.

"Don't worry about Cass," Lolita said. "She's always been a big prude. I don't know where she gets it from. Certainly not me."

Now *that*, Harriet could believe.

Pointing to the backroom door, Harriet caught Kendal's attention. "Should I…"

"No, don't worry. I'll talk to her later." Kendal was speaking at a fraction of her usual volume. Was she hoping Lolita wouldn't overhear?

"I'm sorry," Harriet replied just as quietly.

Shaking her head, Kendal placed a reassuring hand on her forearm. "Don't be. She'll be fine."

"I'm going to head out for an hour, girls," Lolita called, entirely unaware of the tension. "I'll meet you at the pub later for dinner, Ken. Let Cass know, would you?"

"Of course, Lolly."

"Harriet, would you care to join us?" Harriet would've loved to have dinner with them, but after this,

Cass definitely wouldn't want her there, and her parents would only give her more grief if she bailed on them.

"Thank you for the offer, but I have a prior engagement."

"Next time then. I've got so much I want to talk to you about. Maybe I could pop by the shop tomorrow? Are you there in the day?"

Harriet smiled. "Not tomorrow. I'm going away for a few days before Ero-Tea-Ca opens to the public. A bit of a recharge."

"Good thinking. You must look after yourself. Okay, well, if I'm still here next week, I'll come in."

"I look forward to it."

Kendal and Harriet watched Lolita leave the café. "She's...something," Harriet murmured.

"Oh yeah," Kendal replied with an affectionate grin.

Turning from the door, Harriet looked Kendal square in the eyes. "How badly have I just messed up with Cassandra?"

Kendal's face softened. "It's not you."

"It seems to be," Harriet replied, her shoulders slumping.

How did she keep messing up? Maybe the universe was sending her a very clear signal that what she wanted to happen with Cass would never materialise, no matter how much Harriet tried to manifest it. Maybe she should have Nabi do a reading for her. Tarot was a reliable way to decide if Cass would eventually stop hating her, right?

Sighing, Harriet gave one last look towards the back door. "Okay. Well, I'll leave you to it. I need to get over to my parents."

"Please don't let it get you down, sweetie. Cass will come around."

"Is it sad I want her to like me?"

A glint of something sparkled in Kendal's eyes. Was that a grin she was trying to hide?

"Oh, don't worry. I think you'll win her over."

10

Cassandra

Cass had hoped the morning would be a new start, maybe a break from the string of shitty circumstances which had befallen her recently. Yesterday had been a doozy, completely embarrassing herself in front of Kendal with her word vomit about Harriet being a seductress, her mother turning up, and then her worlds colliding spectacularly while the entire café listened in as Mother Dearest yapped on about doggy-style drawings on a sodding teapot.

She'd gone through an agonising dinner with Lolita and Kendal. All she'd wanted to do was stay hidden away in her house, but that wasn't a remote possibility when her mum was in town. After dinner, they'd all gone back to Cass's place, watched crap telly, and gone to bed. It was fine. In fact, it was the best way to end the terrible day; however, because Cass had clearly pissed off the gods or something, she had to listen to the distinct buzzing emanating from the spare room. Her mother was utterly shameless.

So here she was, preparing the café for opening, praying to anyone or anything listening to grant her a day of reprieve, when the oven in their tiny kitchen started making a weird noise. Sean, the maintenance worker, had assured Kendal he'd fixed the blasted thing, but clearly not. It was making such a racket, Cass was reluctant to put anything in to bake. The way her life was shaping up, the bloomin' thing would set fire, or something equally hazardous.

Snatching her mobile off the counter, Cass jabbed the screen until she found Sean's number. He was about to get an earful. *Fixed, my arse!*

"Cass, what can I do for you at this very early hour," Sean practically yawned through the phone. Instead of speaking, Cass held the phone close to the oven. After several moments, she retreated back to the café.

"That's our supposedly fixed oven, Sean."

"It was fixed, Cass."

"Well, it's not anymore. I can't bake in it while it's making that noise. God knows what will happen."

"Alright, I'll come in. Give me an hour."

"Fine." Cass jabbed the screen again, ending the call. Now what was she supposed to do? Her loyal customers expected their Danishes freshly cooked. As she was mulling over her predicament, a wave of gold hair zipped past the window. Harriet. Harriet, who had an oven. Harriet, who had witnessed her mortification yesterday. Actually, Harriet, who was the cause of it. Again.

Cass was still ticked off Harriet had brought the teapot into the café. Why couldn't she have waited until the end of the day? Even better, why couldn't she have found Kendal's address and given her the sodding thing at home, far away from Cass and the café?

Torn between staying mad and forgoing Danishes for the day or putting on a smile and heading over to the tea shop, Cass flexed her hands, which curled into furious little balls.

Unable to disappoint her customers, Cass snagged the tray of uncooked pastries and slipped out the back door. Harriet's rear entrance was only a few feet away, but it felt like Cass had to bridge more than that to get over the discomfort wriggling in her belly.

Clearing her throat and donning her very best professional face, she rapped on the door three times, waited for three seconds, and repeated. Banging sounds reverberated through the steel door, followed by some profanities. Eventually it swung open, and a dishevelled-looking Harriet stood there half irritated, half pleased.

"May I use your oven?"

"You know, I didn't even realise there was a door here. We've only ever used the front entrance, so thanks for that. Although, the mountain of stock I just had to shift puts me well over my weekly exercise quota. I should thank you for that too, I guess. Now I can have a second Danish, which I'm guessing are what's on that tray you're holding."

Ignoring the fact she found Harriet's long-winded sentences cute, Cass simply nodded. "Indeed. The oven's on the fritz. I daren't use it until Sean has inspected it."

Smiling brightly, Harriet beckoned Cass inside with a flourish and a small bow. "My oven is at your disposal."

The Danishes were cooking well, and Cass was running out of reasons to look through the oven door. She either did that or entertained a conversation with Harriet, and she'd rather drink Starbucks swill than look at the woman right now.

Harriet had tried to make polite conversation but eventually begged off to do something elsewhere. Now Cass was sweating in the heat of the tiny kitchen area, wondering if she could slip back to the café and come back when the food was ready.

"Would you like a cuppa?" Harriet's chirpy voice sliced through Cass's latest mind meltdown.

Wiping the sweat off her forehead as discreetly as humanly possible, she shook her head. "No thanks. These will be done shortly and I need to get back. Sean will be over soon, and I guess Kendal will start wondering where I am."

"No worries." Harriet was smiling again, and Cass didn't know where to put her eyes. The young woman was so effortlessly lovely, and it was becoming harder for

Cass to ignore it. She internally scoffed. She hadn't ignored *anything*. Cass knew full well she'd entertained one too many thoughts about Harriet. Not all pleasant, because she was, after all, opening this damn shop. But mostly they were nice—some even risqué. A few dreams may have occurred that left Cass a little breathless in the morning light.

The second the oven bell rang, Cass let out a sigh of pure relief. Harriet cocked her eyebrow but remained silently watching from the doorway. Feeling like her skin was itching from Harriet's gaze, Cass bundled the hot pastries onto a serving dish she'd had the foresight to bring along.

"Thank you for this."

"Anytime," Harriet replied. "That's what friends are for, right?"

Biting the inside of her cheek, Cass bypassed the remark, sending a tight-lipped smile back, and then slipped out of the kitchen. The morning air was a welcome balm to her now clammy skin.

Kendal was in the kitchen with Sean. "There you are!"

"Harriet was kind enough to let me use her oven. We have pastries."

Kendal sidled over and leaned her body into Cass's side. "Harriet, huh?"

Clenching her jaw, Cass did her level best not to take the bait. She should have known Kendal wouldn't let yesterday's slip-up go.

"Well, I didn't think Doris in the haberdashery would have an oven, so yes—Harriet."

"And how is our delightful neighbour?"

Don't bite, Cass.

"Working, I presume. I was a little too busy cooking to pay attention."

Kendal shot a look over her shoulder to Sean, who was bent over inspecting the oven and had his butt crack showing. "She didn't try and seduce you, did she?"

The humour in Kendal's voice grated, but Cass was stronger. She wouldn't entertain another second of her ex-wife's mocking.

"I'll put these in the display and open up. I presume my mother will be here soon. Would you mind if I took a half day? I'd rather take her shopping than have her here all day."

Sensing Kendal was about to delve into something Cass had no time for, she pushed through the door and began her routine in the café. There were several locals already milling about outside, looking grumpy due to caffeine deprivation. That suited Cass just fine. Maybe her day could be salvaged after all.

Flopping on the sofa, Cass growled out loud. It was a cathartic growl, a cleansing growl after an afternoon spent with Lolita. It saddened Cass a little that her mother didn't know her at all. Or maybe she did, and simply didn't like the person Cass was: too quiet, too ornery, too introverted.

No matter what Cass did or said, Lolita followed her own path, regardless of how it made Cass feel. At least their visits were only a few times a year. That was the only saving grace. Surely Lolita would be packing her bags again soon, off on a cruise or something similar, to sow a few more seeds.

At least she had the rest of the evening to herself. That was one advantage of Lolita's sex drive. She soon homed in on the closest single male and that was that. Cass would unfortunately hear all about it tomorrow, no doubt. But, for tonight, she could have a nice hot soak, stick a microwave meal in, and then watch telly. She might even find the time to write another letter to the council. This one would outline Cass's irritation with the local busker who insisted on playing nothing but Ed Sheeran songs.

If she had to listen to one more rendition of "Perfect" she was going to drown herself in the discarded coffee grounds. The man couldn't possibly think he was going to become a successful musical sensation that way. The only thing he was succeeding at was playing on Cass's last nerve. Gordon wholeheartedly agreed, so Kendal couldn't tell Cass she was being difficult.

With a smile on her face at the prospect of her evening being nothing short of perfect, Cass's eyebrows furrowed the second her doorbell chimed. If the person disrupting her night was anyone but an official from the Lottery informing her she'd won a gazillion pounds, Cass was going to unleash hell. Nothing would ruin her night.

Stomping to the front door, Cass ripped it open. Instead of a tirade, she fell mute. Harriet stood there in a cute, flowing dress, her hair pinned up in a high ponytail.

"Can I come in?"

"No, you cannot come in," Cass wanted to shout. Instead, she stood aside and opened the door further. Harriet brushed past her, smelling like a summer breeze...again.

Closing the door, Cass followed Harriet to her living room, where her guest immediately found Mr Whiskers and began scrubbing under his chin. The cat was in heaven and Cass was in hell. What did Harriet want? Why was she here?

"He's so adorable," Harriet cooed. Mr Whiskers' purr motor ramped up a few more notches.

"I agree. Now, what can I do for you?"

Placing the cat down gently, Harriet turned all her attention to Cass, which Cass found slightly alarming. She felt a wave of heat rise from her feet, definitely to do with the menopause, or *something* hormonal.

"Would you sit down?" Harriet asked. She laced her fingers together and waited. Cass wanted to say no, but once again, her body did the opposite.

The air suddenly felt close. What on earth could Harriet possibly have to say? "Harrie—"

Cass was silenced by a petite hand rising up in a *stop* sign. "Cassandra, I'm a forward person. If something is on my mind, I like to talk about it, no matter how difficult."

Cass cleared her throat but didn't speak.

"I like you, Cassandra, and for the life of me, I'm not sure why. You're a sourpuss."

"And you say I use outdated terms," Cass scoffed, which only led to Harriet smiling at her.

"I thought you'd appreciate it," she said with a grin. "Anyway, as I was saying, you're a sourpuss who tried to get my shop shut down before it even opened. I should dislike you. But I don't."

"Okay," Cass replied, not sure what else she could add.

"At first, I thought I just wanted your approval. The thought of having any animosity with my neighbours was awful, so I put my need to know you down to that. But then, I quickly realised I wanted to get to know you, regardless of your opinions. I'm attracted to you—physically and emotionally. After this morning, I knew I just had to have a conversation with you. So here I am. Having a conversation. A one-sided conversation at the minute, but I'm hoping you'll chime in any second."

The silence spread over several painful minutes as Cass tried to process what Harriet had just said. Maybe she'd misheard. "Sorry. You like me, as in..."

"I'd quite like to take you out on a date," Harriet clarified with astonishing ease.

Cass stood abruptly, no longer able to stop herself from pacing. After another few agonising minutes, she stopped and turned to Harriet, who was casually leaning against the fireplace. "You're too young. We're far too different and I'm not interested in dating. I don't do one-night stands. I'm sure it's very uncool of me, but casual...anything, isn't what I want. If I wanted anything, which I don't, because as I said, I'm not looking to date. Anyone."

"Okay. Thank you for telling me where you stand on the matter. Although, I'd like to point out I'm only eleven years younger than you, and opposites attract. They tend to balance each other out. But if you're not interested in dating, that's cool. I'd like us to be friends, though."

"Why?" Cass just didn't understand. She'd been horrible to Harriet from the get-go, and she still had the odd bout of irritation towards her, even now.

Harriet shrugged. "I can't answer that. I just know that's what I'd like."

"Friends?"

"Just friends. I've told you how I feel, and I respect your answer so I wouldn't dream of pushing you. I think we could be good friends, Cassandra."

"Cass. You can call me Cass."

The elation on Harriet's face stole the air from Cass's lungs. "Great. That's great. But before we move on, I'd like to apologise for yesterday. I shouldn't have brought the gift into the café."

Why did she have to bring that up? "It's fine," Cass said as calmly as possible.

"No, it's not. You were upset and embarrassed. It won't happen again. I'd really like a clean slate between us."

Fidgeting on the spot, Cass nodded. "Okay." She just wanted this over with. It would take her a little while to process and acclimatise to the new dynamic in their...friendship. The word felt weird, like it wasn't quite enough to describe them. But Cass was sure she didn't want to date. After Kendal, she knew she was unlikely to find another human who would put up with her eccentricities. She'd dated a few women, post-divorce, and every time left her feeling a little more shitty about herself. No, she was better off alone. Friendship she could handle...maybe.

"Clean slate. I can do that. But you should know I'm not the type of friend who likes shopping or gossiping about the latest celebrity drama. I like reading, coffee, and quiet."

Harriet took a step closer, and Cass had to fight the urge to retreat. "I can handle that. I'm not a shopper unless it's for food, and I have no idea about celebs. I think I'll surprise you, Cass Beaufort!"

Cass wanted to tell her she'd already succeeded. Instead, she nodded and offered her a cup of coffee. Harriet politely declined, which Cass was grateful for. She desperately needed to sort through all the tumbling thoughts in her head.

Maybe they could be friends. Harriet seemed to understand what Cass needed without having to be told. That was a good start, right?

When Harriet had gone, with a promise to see Cass in the morning for her Danish, Cass abandoned her bath and lay in her bed, staring at the ceiling. She'd made a new friend, one that made her uncomfortable for so many reasons. But instead of dread, something else flickered in her belly. An ember of...excitement? Huh, that was new.

11

Harriet

Nabi was right: London was just what Harriet needed. The break from constantly thinking about tea bags and the aesthetic look of dildos on a shelf was a welcome one. It had been way too long since Harriet jumped on a train and headed into the capital.

Camden Market was, without a doubt, Harriet's favourite place in London. Nabi, being the bestest friend in the world, booked them a hotel close by so they could shop, eat, and wander to their hearts' content. And boy did they ever.

Eventually, they agreed to wander a little further afield. Nabi wanted to go to the M&M's shop—even though Harriet was sure Nabi was made up of ninety percent sugar already—so they hopped on The Tube after getting their Camden Town fix. They'd bought several large vintage sweet jars, and it was their intention to fill them with M&M's. Nabi wanted to make a rainbow-style jar, which then led her wanting to make several other Pride flag-themed sweet pots. It was an extremely expensive trip.

As they filled bags with M&M's, Harriet thought of Cass when she spotted Caramel Cold Brew flavour. Friends gave each other gifts. She'd given Kendal a teapot. Cass couldn't get upset over a few bits of chocolate, right?

She'd done her level best to put her confession and subsequent rejection from her mind, although Harriet didn't believe Cass had rejected her because there wasn't a spark. Oh, no, they were sparking alright. Cass just wasn't ready yet, and that was fine. Harriet would wait. She'd happily be a friend until Cass felt comfortable enough to take things further.

It was going to be hard, because now Harriet had opened the floodgates, her crush was turning into something a lot more serious. There was no stopping the feelings which suddenly coursed through her body. And honestly, Harriet didn't want to stop them. But that was her problem. Cass needed time, and even then, she may never want to take their friendship any further. It would suck, but Harriet would support her decision. How she'd get over it was a separate issue.

"The train is in half an hour. We should get a move on," Nabi said, startling Harriet. They were both weighed down with bags, and Harriet definitely needed to sit down.

"Sure, let's go." Harriet saw Nabi giving her side-eye. She wanted to ask why Harriet had zoned out, which she'd done a few times recently and Nabi hadn't pried. Obviously, Nabi was done holding back.

"Okay, out with it. You're a complete space cadet at the minute."

"Just tired, Nabs."

An obnoxious buzzer sound fell from Nabi's mouth. "Wrong, try again."

"There's nothing going on."

"Do you promise? On the fate of the teashop?"

Harriet sucked in a breath. That was a low blow. Harriet might not be as superstitious as Nabi, but there was no way she'd put that kind of energy out into the universe. "That's not fair!" she protested.

"So there *is* something. And I appreciate you not lying and fucking up the energy flow between us and the shop."

Harriet rolled her eyes. "You're welcome. Okay, I have a thing for Cass, and I sort of told her."

"Cass. As in, Cass, our grumpy next-door neighbour who seems to want to be our nemesis?"

"Yes, that's the one." It wasn't like Harriet was purposefully keeping things from Nabi. She'd already confessed she wanted Cass's approval. She just figured there was no point telling anyone anything until she had something concrete to tell. Maybe when she rocked up to a party with Cass holding her hand or something.

They shoved through the weekday crowd, bouncing their many bags off of dawdling tourists. "I can't believe you didn't tell me," Nabi finally replied.

Harriet laughed. "Nabs, there isn't anything to tell."

"Of course there is," Nabi shot back over her shoulder. They were about to enter St. Pancras, which teemed with travellers. "We'll continue this when we're on the train."

When they were finally settled in their pre-booked seats—which had turned into a right old drama when Harriet had to ask a woman and her kid to move because they were occupying their seats—Nabi didn't waste any time interrogating Harriet about Cass.

"But she's like super mean, Har."

Shaking her head, Harriet dipped into her private stash of M&M's. "No...well, sort of. Yeah, she's prickly at times, but the more I get to know her, the more I understand. Most of what you see is a mask."

"Prickly," Nabi cackled. "Sweetie, she tried to get us shut down!"

"And she's apologised for that."

"Oh, that's okay then," Nabi scoffed.

Harriet turned in her seat. "If you're gonna get sarcastic we're not talking about it anymore."

"Sorry, sorry. Okay, I'm all ears."

"I like her, a lot. I don't know why, but I do. There's more to her, and I want to get to know her. I want her to feel comfortable enough with me to open up. Like I said, I don't know why. She's not my usual type, but maybe that's a good thing. Anyway, she said she doesn't date, so for now, I'm just going to work on a friendship."

Nabi threw a handful of chocolate in her mouth. She chewed for an excessively long time, all the while looking at Harriet as if she were trying to solve a puzzle. "Okay," she said after finally swallowing, "I'll give her a chance if you feel this way. I only want to see you happy, and if Cass could one day be that happiness, I'll back you one hundred percent."

"Thank you."

"But," Nabi continued before Harriet had a chance to add another word, "how are you going to get her to see you as date material when the woman won't step foot in Ero-Tea-Ca? We're all chained to our shops. You'll never see each other unless you make the effort. A relationship, whether platonic or romantic, needs to be equal. You can't be the one constantly making an effort, Harriet."

That was fair. Harriet didn't mind waiting and letting Cass take the lead, but eventually, Cass's issue with the teashop would cause barriers to pop up between them.

"I hear you, and I promise I won't be a sucker. Cass's problem with the shop is deeper than we think. I just have this gut feeling it's not about the reputation of the street or The Beanery."

"Gut feelings are real," Nabi stated plainly. "If you think there's more going on, there probably is."

"Hmm. I just have to work out how to get her to open up to me. Maybe it's good we're starting with friendship first."

"I'll collect some crystals together. Scatter them around her place if you can. It'll help unblock her."

"Nabi, I guarantee she will *not* appreciate me spreading crystals around her house."

Rolling her eyes, Nabi produced a lollipop from her coat pocket. This one was neon blue and smelled of chemicals and bubble-gum. "That's why you need to hide them, dumbass."

"I'll think about it." Harriet wouldn't think about it. Cass needed trust, and sneaking around, planting crystals without her knowledge, was just asking for trouble.

"Oh, that reminds me!" Nabi exclaimed, far too loudly for a quiet train carriage. "Cass actually gave me an idea."

"Really?"

"Yes. CBD."

"Okay, fill in the gaps because I'm lost." Harriet loved this about Nabi. Her thought patterns were often chaotic, and she'd blurt out random things.

"Okay, so after Cass accused me of smoking weed in the shop, it hit me—CBD. We should stock it. It's legal and would add to the chill vibe of the teashop."

Harriet scrunched up her face. "How does it fit in with what we're doing, though?"

"CBD tea, Harriet."

"Oh! Well, yeah. Okay."

"We could bake it into some of our cakes, too. The point of Ero-Tea-Ca is to provide a safe space. Somewhere people can visit to relax. Nothing wrong with adding a bit of the green stuff to our repertoire."

Harriet immediately thought of Cass's reaction. She'd explode with ire, and Harriet kind of wanted to see it happen.

"Fuck it. Let's give it a shot. I'll need to look into any paperwork or licences we might need. Have you got a supplier?"

Nabi was all but vibrating in her seat. Her signature buns were jiggling as she danced erratically in her chair. "Leave it to me!"

Patsy Kirkwell's voice filled Harriet's place as she replayed the answerphone message. She shouldn't have pressed play. Or she should have waited more than ten seconds after she'd got home, maybe when she was well lubricated with alcohol.

It was the same old shit; her mother begging her not to open the shop and save the family from eternal social damnation. Harriet deleted it the second it was over.

As time went on and she got closer to officially opening the door to Ero-Tea-Ca, Harriet became less bothered by her parents' limited views. It was their problem, not hers. She had the support of the people who were the most important, and that was good enough.

Casting a quick look at the clock, Harriet hesitated. Cass would probably be working and possibly wouldn't appreciate Harriet disturbing her. But Kendal was also a friend, and she'd be happy to see her. Plus, Harriet was in need of a Danish.

Ten minutes later, Harriet pushed in through The Oxford Beanery door. It was always so cosy inside. The smell of coffee and pastries was simply divine. The view wasn't too bad either. Cass was at the enormous coffee machine. Her hair was in its usual style, but with a few wispy bits sticking to the side of her face. She continued without slowing down, despite being flushed. They'd clearly had a rush, and Cass had been front and centre for it.

"Hey there, lovely people," Harriet called.

Kendal whipped her head round with a bright smile attached to her face. "The wanderer returns. How was London?"

"Excellent. I spent way too much money."

"I thought you didn't like shopping?" Cass said without stopping. Harriet wanted to grin, but she didn't.

"Correct, Cass. I do *not* like shopping unless..." She let the sentence hang, hoping Cass would fill in the blanks. If she did, then Cass had definitely begun processing Harriet's sudden confession.

"Unless it's food," Cass whispered, but Harriet heard her. Harriet's stomach did a tiny roly-poly. Yeah, Cass was thinking about her. She was sure of it.

"Absolutely. I spent way too much money on food."

Kendal was looking at Cass with a cocked eyebrow. If Harriet had to guess, she picked up on Cass's insider knowledge and was wondering what the hell was going on.

So, Cass hadn't told Kendal about Harriet's visit. Interesting. Was that because she'd dismissed it and didn't think it important enough to tell her ex-wife, or was it the opposite? Hopefully, it was the latter. Harriet had given Cass something to mull over, and she wasn't ready to share her thoughts yet.

"Why don't you tell Cass all about it on her break,"
Kendal not-so-subtly suggested.

"I'd love to!" Harriet beamed. "What do you say,
Cass? Coffee and a chat?"

She almost felt sorry for Cass, who was chewing her
lip, looking confused. Her eyes darted from Harriet to
Kendal. All Harriet had to do was wait her out.

"Okay."

One word that made Harriet's heart leapfrog. "I'll
take a cappuccino then, please," she said to Kendal, who
was grinning like an idiot.

"Sure. Cass?"

"My usual." The growing scowl was becoming
Harriet's favourite Cass facial expression.

Turning, Harriet headed for a free table. She was
having a coffee with Cass. Would wonders never cease?

"I brought you something," she blurted as soon as
Cass's bum hit the seat.

"Why?"

Chuckling, Harriet lifted the bag of Caramel Cold
Brew M&M's to the table. "Well, Kendal got a teapot, and
I thought it only fair you got something too, in light of our
new friendship and all. Here, they have coffee in them."

Cass regarded the bag with suspicion.

"Do you not like chocolate?"

"Pfft, who the hell doesn't like chocolate?" Cass shot.

"Lots of people, actually."

"They're idiots."

They were verbally sparring again, and Harriet loved it. "I'm sure they'd disagree. What if it's due to allergies?"

"Then it's nothing to do with liking chocolate but the inability to consume it."

"Two coffees," Kendal said, placing the cups on the table. Harriet hoped she didn't stick around. She could already see Cass withdrawing. "Enjoy."

Breathing a small sigh of relief, Harriet sipped her cappuccino. "So, you like M&M's?"

"Yes." Monosyllabic or not, at least Cass was here. Progress. "Are...are you ready for tomorrow?"

Ero-Tea-Ca would officially open at 7 a.m. tomorrow morning. Instead of being consumed by nerves, Harriet felt only excitement filling her body. They'd worked hard, and the place looked great. All indications showed they'd created enough of a buzz to have a packed-out place tomorrow. There was nothing more to be done, and Harriet had to believe it would work out.

"I think so. I can't wait to officially cut the ribbon and open up."

"You've got a ribbon?" Cass's espresso was almost to her mouth, causing Harriet to stare for a second too long. Dropping her eyes to stop anyone from getting uncomfortable, she shrugged.

"Nabi and Kevin thought it would be fun. We've even got a giant pair of scissors."

"So, are you having a ceremony or something?"

"Sort of. Whoever is waiting to come in will see it. It's not like I invited the mayor or anything." Harriet smiled.

Cass placed her espresso down and nibbled her lip again. "Maybe...maybe Kendal and I could be there. As a show of support."

If Harriet wasn't already sitting down, she'd have fallen to her bum. This was huge. Her instinct told her not to make a big deal about it. Cass's body language was screaming vulnerability and Harriet didn't want her to retreat.

"That would be lovely."

"Okay."

A beat went by until Harriet remembered the CBD conversation with Nabi. "Oh, I wanted to let you know something I don't think you're going to be a hundred percent happy with." Cass didn't reply. She just bored holes into Harriet's irises. "So, remember when you accused Nabi of smoking pot in the shop?"

"Yes."

"Well, she got an idea I support."

Cass adjusted herself in the chair, sitting up straighter. "Go on."

"We plan to sell CBD products."

"Is it legal?"

"Entirely. I need to double-check there aren't permits or something, but yeah...that's the plan."

"Why are you telling me, Harriet?"

Oh, she loved hearing her name slip from Cass's plump lips. "Because I wanted to be transparent. I told you I'm a forward person. I didn't want it to cause an issue between us. Not when we're just figuring our shit out."

Cass cocked her head. "Is that what we've done? Figured our shit out?"

Harriet shrugged. "Sure. We're friends now, right?"

Another lip bite before Cass answered. The simple act was going to be Harriet's undoing. "Yes. We're friends."

Victory! Cass admitting they were friends was a massive leap forward. Now all Harriet had to do was battle through the seemingly endless layers of scepticism, bullishness, and irritation to get to Cass's gooey centre. A challenge she happily accepted.

They'd covered some ground today, and Harriet knew it was time to pull it back. If Cass felt pressured, she'd revert to being a spiky asshole. Harriet was learning the ways of Cassandra Beaufort, one conversation at a time.

"So, how's Mr Whiskers?"

12

Cassandra

According to the thermometer, she didn't have a fever. After a thorough body check, no rash was found. Sinuses were clear, and no headache. Diagnosis? Cassandra's recent behaviour was not because of a malady. No, she just had to accept Harriet was wearing her down. She made Cass softer, more pliable, and it was utterly unbelievable!

Shocking, actually. Even Kendal agreed when she learned Cass had signed them up for the ribbon-cutting event. And it *was* an event. People lined the street, waiting to get their first look at Ero-Tea-Ca. Harriet had looked overwhelmed and Cass had to physically hold on to the drainpipe to stop herself from going over and taking Harriet into her arms. What was *that* about?

If she hadn't had her own place to run, Cass might just have gone into the tea shop. Voluntarily! Strange things were happening, and Cass didn't know how to proceed.

After Harriet's confession, Cass was finding it more and more difficult to shut out the voice telling her to give it a go; ridiculous when her original reasons for not giving Harriet false hope were still valid. Harriet *was* too young. Eleven years wasn't insurmountable, the little voice whispered, but Cass couldn't let go of the idea that eventually, like many others, Harriet would come to see her as an old curmudgeon. Or a fuddy-duddy—even her ex-wife thought that.

There were glaring differences between them. Cass was set in her ways. She had peculiar habits, likes, and dislikes, which led to her third and final reason for shutting Harriet down: No woman would put up with her, and Cass was tired of feeling shitty about herself, so it was better not to date at all.

And yet, with all those things still very valid, Cass's heart was straying from its set path. She'd get a glimpse of

Harriet, and it was like a fizz of excitement would dance in her chest.

Two weeks had passed since Ero-Tea-Ca had officially opened and Cass was more than a little disappointed with how little she saw Harriet. Sure, every morning, like clockwork, she'd come into The Beanery and order a Danish, but their conversations were often short because Harriet had a million and one things on her mind or a list as long as her beautiful hair to complete.

What should it matter, though? Cass only wanted to be friends, and a friendship was what they had. Cass could get on with her life, just the way she liked it, because that was what she wanted, right?

"Ugh," Cass sighed into the mirror. No, it was not what she wanted. She wanted to kiss Harriet Kirkwell. She'd dreamed about it several times and woken up panting. Mr Whiskers regarded her from the hallway. It was delivery day and Cass always went in super early because she'd badgered the deliveryman to drop her stock off first. He didn't like her very much, but she'd worn him down.

Deciding to leave her hair down until she arrived at work, Cass surveyed herself one last time. Had she started wearing a little mascara? Yes. Had Kendal noticed and given her an amused look? Of course. Cass found *herself* ridiculous, but it was like she'd been possessed. That bloody voice in her head made her do things she'd never dream of doing...like dressing a little nicer and adding a bit of perfume, or wearing her hair down. All of this for the attention of Harriet. Utter madness.

There had even been times when Cass had wanted to go to Ero-Tea-Ca. Not for tea, or the other things in there, but just to get a look at Harriet in her element. The teashop was brimming every day, and it didn't look like it would settle down anytime soon. But as much as she wanted to see her little ray of sunshine, Cass just couldn't bring herself to go there.

It was the proverbial bucket of cold water on her overheating feelings. The shop, and Harriet's attitude towards all things saucy, would be a big problem, and Cass couldn't see a way around it. They were fundamentally different where sex was concerned.

Her meandering thoughts carried her all the way to The Beanery. Mark, the delivery man, was already there and looking miserable. "Mornin'," he gruffed.

"Mark." Cass opened the back door and began moving stock. It was a simple and quick process which suited them both. Mark shoved the invoice in her hands and left the second she'd finished penning her name.

"Hey, Cass," Kendal called an hour later. "Delivery all sorted?"

"Yes. Want an espresso?" Cass was already moving to the machine.

"Please." Kendal dropped her belongings in the back and then wandered over to where Cass was skilfully making their coffee. People thought it was as easy as shoving some ground coffee in the press and hitting a button. Excellent coffee needed a gentle hand.

"So," Kendal began, "I'd like you to meet Shauna."

Cass's hand froze midway to the machine. "Shauna? The woman you've been seeing?"

Kendal nodded, before taking her cup of espresso from the drip plate. "Yes. It's going somewhere, Cass. You're my best friend and I want you to meet."

Wow, okay. Cass knew the day would come. She just wasn't expecting it to be so soon. Taking her own cup, she gestured for Kendal to follow. They settled down in a set of comfy chairs. "Of course I'll meet her, if that's what you want."

"Would this weekend be okay?"

Cass swallowed a lump. It would give her several days to process the news. That would be sufficient. If Kendal thought it was important they meet, Cass had to try to get over herself. She couldn't help the pang of sadness. Kendal getting serious meant they were really over. Not that Cass wanted to reunite with Kendal. They were much better as friends.

"I can make that work."

Kendal dropped a hand on Cass's knee. "Thanks, Cass. This means a lot."

"Does she make you happy?"

Kendal's cheeks blushed delicately. "She does."

Cass cleared her throat. "And does she want what you want?" It was the politest way to ask if Shauna was okay with not having kids.

"She doesn't want children. Like me, she's happy to be a fun aunt, but that's it."

"Good." Cass had a million and one questions, but she didn't want to come across as interrogating. "What time should I come over?"

"How about seven? I'll cook."

"Perfect. Okay, let's get set up."

They went about their morning routine in comfortable silence. Kendal knew Cass needed quiet, especially when she was thinking. She tried to imagine meeting Shauna. Would it be awkward? What if they didn't like each other? Shit, would she have to sit there while Kendal and Shauna got all gooey over each other?

In addition to the voice harping on about her feelings for Harriet, Cass now had to contend with all the questions and feelings meeting Kendal's new lover raised.

By lunchtime, Cass had to get out of the café. She usually ate in the back room, but the sun was shining and she needed some fresh air, away from Kendal, who kept shooting her worried looks. Did she think Cass was that fragile?

Taking her panini, Cass headed to the local park. It'd been a while since she'd visited and already she felt lighter. Sitting on the bench, she watched dogs run around chasing sticks and balls. Kids were playing on the field with parents.

"Hey."

The soft voice made her jump and choke on the last bit of food. A sudden *thwack* landed on her back, dislodging the bread. After several moments of coughing, Cass looked up through watery eyes. "Hi."

Harriet was smiling her usual disarming smile. "I didn't mean to almost kill you."

"You just startled me. What are you doing here?" Cass really had to work on her delivery sometimes. Why did she always sound pissed off or accusatory?

Chuckling, Harriet sat on the bench next to her. "Taking a break. The shop is non-stop."

Cass brushed some crumbs off her trousers. "You're certainly doing well."

"Thanks," Harriet beamed.

Together they sat watching the world go by until Harriet turned her body. "Are you okay? You look like you've got something on your mind."

Ugh, Cass wished she didn't wear her feelings on her face all the time. "Fine," she replied. Harriet didn't push. She never did. Suddenly Cass blurted out her reason for needing some space. She told Harriet about Shauna and the fact Kendal wanted them to meet, how it was making her anxious because of what it meant and all the ways it could go wrong.

Cass never opened up like this. It took Kendal years to pry open the vault doors, but with Harriet, it felt so natural.

"That sounds difficult," Harriet said once Cass finished.

Cass blew out a long breath. "But it shouldn't be. I mean we've been divorced for years. We love each other but we're not *in* love. I want her to be happy."

"May I ask why you got divorced?"

"Kids," Cass replied. "I wanted them and Kendal didn't. We saw a therapist and knew it wasn't something either of us could compromise on."

Harriet nodded. "Understandable."

Cass glanced at Harriet. Was she really about to admit she still saw a therapist? "I still see our therapist sometimes."

"Good. I mean, if they help."

"She's nice. For a long time, I felt like I'd failed Kendal. If I could just stop myself from wanting children, we would probably still be together."

"Is that what you want? To be with her?"

Cass didn't miss the hint of disappointment in Harriet's voice.

"No. But she's my normal, you know? The one person in this world I feel comfortable with, and who knows me—grumpiness included. It's completely selfish on my part, I know that. Kendal deserves all the happiness in the world."

Cass looked down when she felt a hand on her arm. "You do, too," Harriet whispered. "You both deserve to be with someone who wants what you want, Cass."

With a self-deprecating laugh, Cass shook her head. "I'm better off alone. No one wants to put up with my shit. Trust me."

Another arm squeeze. "I'd like to try. Even if it's just as a friend, Cass. You can open up to me, if you want. I'd like to know you, grumpiness and all."

A sharp laugh left Cass's throat. "You would, wouldn't you? I actually believe you."

"I don't tend to say things I don't mean," Harriet said with a smile.

Turning towards Harriet, Cass let her defences drop a little more. "Would you come with me?"

"With you?" Harriet asked, looking confused.

"To Kendal's on Saturday, to meet Shauna? I know it's a lot to ask. Yeah, too much, just forget—"

"Hey, it's not too much and I'd happily tag along. Don't take the offer back."

They were sitting closer than before. Who had shifted? Cass shook the thought away. "Are you sure?"

"Would it make things easier for you?"

Cass nodded. It would take the pressure off her. She was sure of it. There would be less of a third-wheel feeling, and she knew Harriet would help her through any tough spots.

"Then, I'm sure. What time should I be ready? I can come to your place first if you want? Maybe we can have a pre-game drink. Nothing takes the edge off like a nice glass of wine."

"Okay," Cass heard herself say. "Why don't you come 'round about six. It will be super casual, so don't worry about getting dressed up."

"I look forward to it." Harriet playfully bumped against Cass's shoulder. "Now, I suppose I should head back. Nabi and Kevin are in charge, and together they usually get into trouble."

"Yeah, me too. Thanks...you know...for this," Cass said.

Another award-winning smile. "Anytime. I mean it. I like getting to know you, Cass."

Swallowing, Cass smiled back. "Me too."

They walked back in comfortable silence. Harriet gave Cass a little wave before disappearing into Ero-Tea-Ca. Taking a cleansing breath, Cass went back to work. The lunch rush was about to start, and she had to focus.

When Saturday arrived, Cass was a bag of nerves. Not only because she was going to meet Shauna, but because, in less than ten minutes, Harriet would arrive. They were going to have a glass of wine and Cass was going to do her best not to kiss her. That was where her head was at nowadays. They hardly knew each other, and yet Harriet pulled Cass like a magnet. It was infuriating.

A knock on the door ramped up her nerves by a factor of ten. Only it wasn't Harriet standing on her doorstep.

"Cass, darling," Lolita said, pulling her in for a kiss. "I couldn't find the key. Are you off out?"

Lolita had done one of her famous disappearing acts. Cass hadn't seen or heard from her mother since, unfortunately, hearing buzzing coming from her spare room. It was typical Lolita, though. Cass would bet she'd met a nice man and had her way with him for a couple of weeks before getting bored. Cass also knew she'd return at some point, considering her luggage was still taking up space in her spare bedroom.

"I'm going to Kendal's," Cass replied. There was no point in asking why Lolita didn't think to let her only daughter know where she'd been.

"Oh, hi," Harriet said from behind Lolita. She was dressed in tight-fitting jeans and a light sweater. Cass wanted to rush them out of the house and far, *far* away from Lolita, but it was too late. Her mother pivoted in place until she was face to face with Harriet.

"Harriet, my love. Oh, it's lovely to see you. Are you here for Cass?"

"Yes, we're going to Kendal's for dinner."

"Together?"

"Yes, Mother. Together. I'm meeting Kendal's girlfriend—"

"And you wanted Kendal to meet yours? How wonderful."

"No, Mum. Harriet and I are just friends."

Lolita spun back around. "Why on earth aren't you together?"

Cass gritted her teeth. "Are you coming in or what?" she shot back. Lolita rolled her eyes, but stepped through the door. Harriet followed behind. This was not going at all the way she'd hoped.

"I'm not staying," Lolita called. "Henry is picking me up in five. We're going to the Lake District. I'll call when we arrive."

So the mystery man had a name. "Sure, Mum," Cass replied, her eyes still on Harriet. What was she thinking?

"Okay, my lovelies. Cass, I'll come back soon. Harriet, I'm so sorry I didn't get to see your beautiful shop. Next time."

"Absolutely," Harriet said, allowing Lolita to draw her into a hug. After seeing her mum out, Cass let out a deep breath the second the door was shut. Her mother could be exhausting.

"By the looks of it, you're ready for that glass of wine now," Harriet said with a laugh.

Spinning around, Cass nodded. "More than one, probably."

13

Harriet

Well, this was a turn up for the books. Harriet was on a friend date with Cass. Purely platonic. No lusty feeling whatsoever. *Not a date, not a date, not a date.*

After witnessing Hurricane Lolita for the second time, Harriet wasn't at all surprised Cass avoided talking about it once her mother left. They'd shared two glasses of wine over a surface-level conversation. Mr Whiskers—whether he liked it or not—was centre stage. He gave them the perfect bridge to step over the gaping chasm that was Cass and Lolita's relationship.

Harriet knew a thing or two about strained family bonds, so she spotted the discord between Cass and Lolita a mile off. Sadly, it didn't seem Lolita saw the problem. It was Cass's body language that shone like an emergency flare, giving it away. But not to Lolita. She was happily ignorant of her daughter's feelings. Or she was wilfully ignoring them. Harriet hoped it was the former.

At some point, Harriet wanted to ask Cass about it. She wanted to delve into the hard stuff to gain a better understanding of this complex woman. Every little piece she chipped away revealed more answers and ramped up her curiosity; however, Harriet knew Cass's life wasn't there to serve her interests. She'd have to approach things delicately, allowing Cass to open up when comfortable.

Speaking of comfortable, Harriet was the absolute opposite as she sat at Kendal's kitchen breakfast bar. Cass had frozen up the second she'd stepped over the threshold. It was like a switch had flipped. Harriet had done her best to carry the conversation as they were greeted, but it was painfully clear Cass was struggling.

Shauna was lovely, as far as Harriet could tell. She was tall, blonde, kinda ripped, and harboured a smile that could power a small county. She'd shook Cass's and Harriet's hands, made them all drinks, and chatted politely. Cass had become more rigid as the minutes went on and Harriet didn't know what the hell to do. Normally, she'd try to lighten the mood with some smutty humour, but that would be a huge mistake.

"I made spinach and ricotta ravioli," Kendal said as she stirred the pasta. The smell wafting from the stove made Harriet's mouth water.

"Delicious," Harriet replied, giving a sincere smile. She watched Cass regard Shauna as she helped Kendal. They touched at every given moment. There was an ease between them Harriet thought to be lovely. Cass, on the other hand, frowned and then gulped several large mouthfuls of wine. It was going to be a long night.

"So, Cass," Shauna began, her mega smile in place. Cass visibly flinched, which broke Harriet's heart a little. Going on gut instinct, she gently placed her hand on Cass's knee. It took a second, but she felt the leg muscles unclench a bit. "Kendal says you're a coffee nut."

There was a minute clenching of her jaw. Harriet held her breath, hoping Cass wasn't going to be rude. "I'd hope so. Otherwise opening up a café was a bad career choice." Cass's delivery was so dry, Harriet wanted to hide under the table.

Shauna wasn't put off, though, as she laughed. "She also said you had a dry and sarcastic wit."

"Mmmm." Cass didn't even look at Shauna, instead focusing on her glass of wine.

Jesus, this was painful. Harriet was a natural empath. She was used to soaking up the energy of others and right now it was a mix of anxiety, irritation and impatience. They were just Cass's emotions, though. If Kendal's over-the-shoulder scowls were anything to go by, she was less than pleased with Cass's behaviour, which was fair.

Shauna still seemed okay. It was obvious she wanted to make a good impression, which was nice. She understood Cass's role in her girlfriend's life and wanted to foster a decent connection. Harriet somehow needed to get Cass onboard, otherwise she was pretty sure they'd be thrown out before dessert.

"Cass, can you show me where the bathroom is?" Harriet didn't give Cass the chance to say no as she hauled them off the stool and towards the hallway.

"The loo is just there," Cass said irritably. Harriet continued to drag her until they were safely locked in the downstairs toilet.

"Harriet?"

"Okay, you gotta do better, Cass."

"I beg your pardon?"

"We're friends. And friends tell each other when they're being a dick. And you, my dear, are being a dick. Shauna is lovely and she's really trying."

"I've not done anything," Cass argued, becoming defensive.

Harriet mirrored her posture, adding a cocked eyebrow into the mix. "You know what you're doing, and you're upsetting Kendal. Is that what you want?"

Cass broke eye contact and looked to the ground. "No, I don't want that."

"Good. So this is what's gonna happen: We're going to go back out there, get you another drink, and you're going to fake it if you have to. You're going to show Kendal you support her by getting to know Shauna. Then, after we've had a pleasant evening, we can go home, open one—or ten—bottles of wine, and you can vent."

Cass rubbed her head and then nodded. "Okay."

"Great." Harriet clapped. "Let's do this."

Back in the kitchen, Shauna was holding Kendal as she strained the ravioli. They were smiling and laughing. Cass faltered in her step but steadied herself with a supportive hand squeeze from Harriet. She pasted on a smile, sat back at the breakfast bar, drank half a glass of wine, and then entered into polite conversation. Harriet wanted to breathe out a sigh of relief, but she kept her game face on. She did, however, get a small nod and smile from Kendal.

The dinner was sublime. All in all, the evening had turned out to be a lot of fun. The more Cass drank, the lighter she became and the more she spoke to Shauna, who, in solidarity, matched the amount of wine Cass poured down her throat. Harriet sat back in her chair, chuckling at the pair. She noted Kendal doing the same thing, and it sent a wave of familiarity down her spine, like this was something they did regularly as a foursome: Kendal and Shauna. Harriet and Cass. Two couples spending the evening laughing and eating.

But the feeling was false, despite being a desire Harriet so desperately wanted to make a reality. She could absolutely see them double-dating. A whole different life flashed through her mind as she watched Cass double over with laughter at something Shauna said. She wanted this. Wanted Cass to be her girlfriend, wanted them to have nights like this with friends.

"Okay, you lot. Time to break it up," Kendal shouted over the din, breaking Harriet from her daydream.

"Booooo!" Cass shouted. That was Harriet's cue.

"Come on, Cass, you need water and sleep." She laughed as she hauled Cass from the seat. Surprisingly, Cass voluntarily draped her arm over Harriet's shoulder. After a few quick goodbyes and uncoordinated hugs, Harriet stumbled with Cass down the street. Thankfully, they didn't have far to walk.

"You smell nice," Cass slurred, "like summer." Harriet had to bite her tongue as Cass sang "You Are My Sunshine" at the top of her lungs. She had quite a nice voice, but Harriet wasn't sure the neighbours would give a monkey's about that, considering the hour.

It took several minutes to get Cass's front door open because the woman staunchly refused to give Harriet her keys. When they'd fallen to the floor for the third time, Harriet whipped them from the ground and shoved the key in the lock. A laugh burst out of her when she turned back around to Cass, who was pouting—hard.

"Let's go," Harriet said quietly, hoping Cass would keep her volume down.

In the living room, Cass flung herself on the couch, dislodging a very pissed off Mr Whiskers. Checking everything was in order, Harriet draped a blanket over Cass and headed for the door.

"I'm not tired," Cass suddenly announced as she sat up with vigour.

"Right," Harriet said with a sigh. "Do you want some water?"

Cass shook her head, and then seemingly changed her mind. "Yes. Probably a good idea."

It was definitely a good idea. Cass was going to be hurting in the morning. Armed with a pint of water and some painkillers, Harriet stepped back in the living room. Cass was on her feet, staggering to the record player. "I want music," she declared.

Soft jazz filtered through the speakers. It was nice. Cosy. Harriet settled on the couch and waited. She had a feeling Cass was about to spea—"Shauna's nice," Cass blurted with a hiccup. She waltzed back to the couch and sat next to Harriet. Actually, she almost sat *on* Harriet. "Do you think she's nice?"

"I do. She's lovely and clearly likes Kendal a lot."

Harriet wasn't expecting her answer to cause Cass's face to crumble. Before she knew it, tears streamed down Cass's face.

"Hey, hey, what's wrong?" *Oh Jesus, what had she said?*

Cass buried her face in Harriet's neck and sobbed. A part of her knew this was the booze talking. But another part of Harriet wondered if Cass really wanted Kendal to herself.

"I let her down," Cass wailed.

"Let who down? Kendal?" *What on earth?*

Cass nodded. She continued to cry for a few minutes more until she was out of tears. Sitting back with bloodshot eyes, Cass wiped her face. "I should have known Kendal was settling with me," she rasped.

"Cass, you're not making sense. Have some water and just take a second to calm down."

When the tears were finally dry and Cass was less agitated, Harriet gave her an encouraging rub on her lower back. Cass sighed deeply. "Shauna's great. She's the absolute opposite of everything I am and look how happy Kendal is."

Harriet measured her words carefully. "She is happy. But that doesn't mean she wasn't happy with you."

"She was never that happy. I...I couldn't give her the things she wanted."

"The kids thing?"

Cass shook her head. "No. Lots of things. I've got too many weird habits and odd boundaries. Kendal must have hated being married to me."

Oh, my Lord, this was awful. Harriet hated hearing Cass speak so low of herself. "No way, Cass. Kendal loved you. She still loves you. You wouldn't have the relationship you have today if she hated any part of her life with you."

Cass shrugged. "But I'm not upbeat or sunny. I'm miserable and stiff. I need routines and hate change."

"And Kendal knew all that before she married you."

"I feel broken, Harriet. Like there is something wrong with me. Why can't I be like everyone else?"

"You're perfect the way you are, because you're authentic."

"I'll be alone forever," Cass cried.

Okay, this was interesting. So much for Cass *wanting* to be alone. She'd certainly given Harriet the impression she didn't want a partner.

"But you don't want to date," Harriet replied, hoping she wasn't pushing too much.

Cass cackled. "Because there's no point. Women leave me because I'm weird and inflexible. It hurts too much, so I just stopped."

Argh, how should Harriet respond? A large part of her wanted to remind Cass that *she* wanted to date her. But Cass was seriously intoxicated, and it wouldn't mean anything if they had that conversation right now.

"I think the right woman will love you for all that you are, Cass."

Harriet stifled a laugh as Cass blew a raspberry. "Then where is she?" Cass asked loudly.

I'm right here.

"She's out there, Cass. You just have to be brave enough to try."

"Yeah. But then when I can't give her what she needs...you know, in the bedroom," Cass whispered, "then she'll be off."

Swallowing, Harriet felt her heart beat hard. What was Cass talking about? "What do you mean?"

Cass shook her head. "It doesn't matter. I'm too fucked up to properly satisfy a woman. Too rigid and grumpy. I'll be a spinster with Mr Whiskers."

Rolling her eyes, Harriet grabbed Cass's shoulder, effectively turning her until they were face to face. "Cassandra Beaufort, what a load of shit. You will not be a spinster. You *will* have Mr Whiskers, though."

"You smell nice," Cass murmured, her eyes cast to Harriet's lips.

"You already said that," Harriet replied. Oh boy, she was in trouble.

"Seductress," Cass whispered.

Harriet laughed. "What did you just call me?" This was a very interesting conversation, indeed!

Cass looked up. "I said you're a seductress. You keep pulling me in."

The smile left Harriet's face in an instant. She could see how serious Cass was, but the fact she was still drunk gave her pause. Knowing Cass, she'd retreat in the morning and Harriet didn't think she could handle it if they shared something as beautiful as their first kiss, only for Cass to backtrack and get upset the next day.

Pulling back, Harriet gently cupped Cass's cheek. "I'd like to talk about this tomorrow if that's okay?"

Cass frowned slightly, looked back to Harriet's lips, but remained in place. "O-okay."

"Time for you to sleep, sweetie."

Helping Cass off the couch, Harriet propped her up as they ambled up the stairs to Cass's bedroom. It was the first time Harriet had gained entry, and to be honest, it wasn't quite how she'd envisioned it. But after that little conversation, she had renewed hope. Cass was interested, for sure. She saw the lust in her eyes and felt the pull. Harriet knew for a fact, if she hadn't pulled back, they would've kissed; however, their first kiss needed to be savoured and done when sober.

Laying Cass on the bed, she helped take off her trousers and top. God, she had a gorgeous figure. Instead of creeping, Harriet put on her caregiving hat and helped Cass dress in pyjamas and snuggle under the duvet.

By the time she returned with the pint of untouched water and paracetamol, Cass was snoring. Mr Whiskers jumped on the bed and curled himself into a ball. Harriet wanted nothing more than to slip in and pull Cass close. Maybe one day.

For now, Harriet would have to be content with what they had. In fairness, though, that was becoming less clear the more time they spent together.

Knowing Cass wouldn't appreciate her presence in the morning, Harriet slipped out of the room, giving Cass's sleeping form one last look. "Good night, sourpuss."

Tomorrow would be interesting. Harriet had no intentions of shying away from Cass's revelations. She didn't want Cass to get defensive and shut down, which she'd surely do the second Harriet reminded her of their evening. But they'd had a breakthrough and Harriet felt it in her bones that Cass needed to unload. She needed someone else to understand, and that person was Harriet.

"One day at a time," she said to herself as she stepped into the street.

14

Cassandra

Cass huddled in bed until Mr Whiskers grew so impatient he attacked her face. Having a ball of fluff almost suffocate you brought things into perspective. Last night was bad, but not *deserve to die by feline* bad.

Dragging herself to the kitchen, she ignored the fact she still wore her underwear from last night because Harriet Kirkwell undressed her and put her in jammies. She'd compartmentalise the crap out of yesterday evening, allowing herself time to process and react with one thing at a time.

First, she had to feed her starving kitty before he really got mad and started shitting in all her shoes. She'd learned her lesson long ago where Mr Whiskers was concerned. Second, she needed a shower to wash away the wine still seeping from her pores, followed by three or four pints of water and some more painkillers.

Then the real work started. Even though it was Cass's day off, she'd have to go to The Beanery and apologise to Kendal. Once again, this came in stages, too. First, for acting like a brat at the beginning of the night. Harriet had every right to call her out on her behaviour. Second, for then getting Kendal's new girlfriend drunk. It wasn't the plan, but after Cass relaxed, she'd found it really easy to talk to Shauna and one thing led to...many open and drunk bottles of wine.

If Kendal forgave her, Cass would then have to unpack her beautifully compartmentalised mind and figure out how the hell she was supposed to ever look Harriet in the eye again. For once, Cass wished she'd got blackout drunk. But oh, no. She remembered everything clearly: How she'd told Harriet she smelled of sunshine. She remembered the singing. Oh, God, the singing. Her neighbours would be pissed, too. She'd called Harriet a seductress. To her face! And lastly, the almost kiss. Cass remembered *that* vividly.

Not forgetting the word vomit she'd so beautifully upchucked. What the hell must Harriet think of her? No way the confident young woman would still want to date her. Not that Harriet planned to ask her out. Ever. If last night proved anything, it was that Cassandra Beaufort is a hot mess who should be alone for the sake of everyone else.

For once, Lolita's usual disappearing act didn't even register on the list of problems Cass had. Maybe she'd finally accepted her mother just the way she was. There was no changing her. It was the job of her new man to put up with her now. *Until the next time.*

With Mr Whiskers fed and bribed with double the amount of kibble, Cass took her shower, taking twice the amount of time to scrub herself clean. She dressed in comfy jeans and a T-shirt, opting to leave her wet hair down.

The walk to The Beanery was brisk. Nothing got rid of a pesky hangover better than a bit of exercise—if you could call fast walking exercise. Whatever. It would have to do, because Cass had no plans of doing anything else after she'd prostrated herself in front of her ex-wife.

It was close to lunch by the time she arrived. The café was nearly full. Kendal smiled over when Cass entered, which had to be a good sign. Or she was lulling Cass into a false sense of security and would rip her head off when she least expected.

In the staff room, Cass dumped her bag and willed herself to go back out and make a cup of coffee. She'd just summoned up the courage and energy when Kendal bustled in with an espresso of Cass's Peruvian Gold.

"You look like you need this."

Cass took the cup happily and inhaled. "Thank you." After a long draw, she put the cup down and looked at Kendal. "Ken—"

"It's fine." Kendal laughed. "You and Shauna were extremely entertaining."

Groaning, Cass cradled her heating face in her hands. "How many bottles did we get through?"

"Too many!" Kendal continued to laugh. "Feeling a little green?"

Sitting at the table, Cass gestured for Kendal to join her. "Not as bad as I thought. I do need to apologise, though, Ken. For my behaviour, pre-wine."

"Ah, yes." Kendal crossed one leg over the other and waited.

"I acted like a dick. Harriet's words. She was right, though. I behaved badly and I'm sorry. I'd like to apologise to Shauna also."

"There's no need, Cass. I knew it would be hard. On both of us. Shauna really enjoyed getting to know you. I'd prepared her for a frosty reception."

Oh, Christ. That felt awful. Kendal had to pre-warn people about Cass's tendency to be an arse. Ugh. "I'm still sorry."

"Do you want to talk about the reason you acted that way?" Any other time, Cass would talk to Kendal, but after last night, things shifted. Kendal had a relationship to nurture. Her attention had to be on Shauna, not her ex-wife. Plus, Cass immediately thought of Harriet. It was she who Cass wanted to talk to about things. Not just her shitty behaviour or issues, but about everything.

"No, I'm good."

Kendal furrowed her brows ever so slightly. "Okay."

"I'd really like a do-over, though. With you and Shauna. Without copious amounts of alcohol. How about next Sunday? I'll cook."

She could see Kendal trying to work out what was happening. This wasn't Cass. Cass didn't invite people over for lunch. She didn't care what people thought. And yet, she was trying.

"I'll ask Shauna, but I'm sure it'll be fine."

"Excellent. Now I need about four more espressos and I think I'll be functioning normally."

Before Cass could fully stand up, Kendal took her arm. "She's good for you, Cass." No need for Cass to pretend she didn't know who Kendal was referring to. "She really is."

Cass nodded but didn't answer. She couldn't. Harriet was all she could think about, but it was more complicated than asking her out. Cass had baggage she had to work through before she subjected someone as lovely as Harriet to it. She needed the friendship to work. If, and it was a big if, Cass could get over some stuff, maybe she'd think about asking Harriet out. Only time and lots of therapy would tell.

In the café, Cass settled on a barstool, quite content to inhale several strong coffees and a couple of Danishes. She felt Harriet before she saw her. A wave of embarrassment and warmth washed over her.

"Hey, I was just about to grab a coffee and come over to your house." Harriet hopped on the stool next to Cass, looking fresh-faced.

"Morning," Cass choked out. The Danish was now taking an excruciating amount of time travelling down her oesophagus. "I needed coffee."

"Well," Harriet replied, looking Cass over. Her eyes paused on Cass's flowing hair. "You don't look too worse for wear."

"I think I have you to thank for that. The water and paracetamol saved me."

"Standard care package." Harriet smiled. "Do you want to have lunch?"

"She'd love to," Kendal interjected.

"Cass?"

"Yeah. That'd be nice. I pay, though, as a thank you for looking after me last night."

"Deal. How do you feel about tapas?"

"I love Spanish food."

"Excellent. Let's get another espresso down you first and then we'll get off."

Smiling, Cass flicked her eyes to Kendal, who gave her a warm smile and a playful wink, causing Cass's face to heat again.

She was having lunch with Harriet. As a friend. Maybe.

Why hadn't Harriet brought up last night? Since leaving The Beanery, they'd chatted about things. Nothing of consequence. Certainly not Cass's confessions. Maybe she didn't want to talk about Cass's baggage. Or she was too embarrassed.

Cass did her best to get through lunch without having an anxiety attack, but it was getting harder as time passed. They paid the bill and somehow arrived at Cass's house. "Um...do you want a drink?"

Harriet smiled. "Sure." She was so laid-back Cass couldn't get a grip on the situation.

As with every other time Harriet had stepped foot in Cass's house, she immediately scooped Mr Whiskers into her arms and cooed into his face. It was cute and at least gave Cass a few moments alone. She set about making tea for Harriet using the tea she'd been gifted. Deciding more caffeine was probably a bad idea, Cass settled for some lemon water.

"Here we are," Cass announced. "One cup of weird-smelling tea for you."

Harriet giggled. "It's not weird smelling. You're just used to having the smell of coffee permanently up your nose."

Shrugging, Cass sat on the couch next to Harriet, who plonked a disgruntled Mr Whiskers on the floor. The air seemed heavier suddenly and Cass felt her skin become uncomfortable.

"Cass, relax." Harriet was leaning towards her. "I can feel your anxiety. Please take a breath. You're safe with me, okay?"

Wow. Cass had to swallow several times. "About last night," she began. "I said some things."

"You did. And I'm here if you want to talk about them a little more."

Cass cast a quick look at Harriet's face. She couldn't detect any deception or forced sincerity. "Why? I mean, you must see what a mess I am. You don't need that."

"How about you let me decide what I want." Harriet shifted a little closer. "I like you, Cass. A lot. I know you're not ready for more. Hopefully, one day, but if all we have is friendship then I'll be the best damn friend you've ever had.

When you opened up a little to me, I felt like I was getting to see the real Cassandra."

"It's hard to talk to people." Cass felt ridiculous. She was in her fourth decade of life, and she still felt like a lost child. "I think you, of all people, will find my issues silly."

Harriet shook her head. "That's not fair. First, I don't know the full extent of your experience, so I can't form an opinion. Second, I only want to create a safe space for you. There will be no judgement, Cass. I swear."

Was she really contemplating telling Harriet about her life? Fully? No holds barred? Since Harriet came into her life, Cass was doing things she'd never ordinarily consider. She might as well go along with the flow because it didn't seem she had much control over her actions where Harriet was concerned.

So, over the course of half an hour, Cass took Harriet on a nonstop tour of her childhood. She opened up about her lack of confidence and how anything sexual left her feeling awkward and uncomfortable. How that led to pressure in the bedroom with partners. Kendal was the exception, but even then, Cass explained how she felt guilty for not being able to give her ex-wife what she needed.

At one point, Harriet asked if Cass knew about the term *ace*. She did, but it wasn't a term she felt identified her. She felt sexual desire. She experienced sexual attraction towards people. It was all a mental block.

Never once did Harriet laugh or make snide comments. Not that Cass expected her to, it was just a fear. Cass's experience with people understanding her was never positive. Even her own mother couldn't get her head around why Cass was the way she was.

"So, there you go. My story." God, Cass felt knackered.

"Thank you for sharing with me."

"I'll understand if you want to run away screaming." Cass laughed humourlessly.

Harriet simply shook her head and took Cass's hand in her own. "I'm not going anywhere. In fact, I have an idea. Well, more like a proposition."

"A proposition?"

Harriet nodded. "I'd like for you to work in Ero-Tea-Ca."

Cass choked on her own spit. "I beg your pardon?"

"Hear me out. A swap. Nabi will work at The Beanery, and you will work in the tearoom."

"Why on earth would I do that? Did you not just hear everything I said?"

"I did," Harriet replied calmly. "And that's why I think it's a good idea. Exposure therapy, in a safe space, with no judgement."

"But...how? I mean..."

"Just think about it. No pressure, I promise. I just thought it could be a way for you to be around people who are more comfortable with sex. You'd be in the vicinity of erotic art and toys without it being in your face. I know you'll find that hard to believe, but I promise the tea shop isn't about peddling sex. Ninety percent of my customers simply sit and enjoy learning about tea."

Cass wasn't entirely convinced.

"Not everyone comments on the toys, or the teapots. Ero-Tea-Ca is a haven for everyone. A lot of people just want to spend time surrounded by their own people. As you can imagine, there are a lot of queer people who visit because they feel welcome and safe. Sure, there are a few customers and groups who want to talk about erotica, but I know them and wouldn't expect you to interact. Plus, Kevin works part-time, and he loves running any events like that."

Could she do it? Work in Ero-Tea-Ca? Cass's first instinct was to withdraw, even bite back at Harriet for suggesting something so far out of her boundaries, but she wanted to be different. Cass needed things to change. If she ever wanted a chance at love again, she needed to face her fears.

"I need to think about it, Harriet. It's a big ask."

"Like I said, no pressure. Maybe you could talk it over with Kendal."

Cass shook her head. "No, I'll talk to my therapist."

"Whatever you need, Cass. And that includes me backing off. The idea just popped into my head, but I'm fully aware I might have just crossed a line. If you want me to leave, I will. Whatever you need."

Cass didn't know what she needed. Thoughts of walking into Ero-Tea-Ca played on a loop. It's not like the tearoom was anything like what she'd expected. Sure, the toy had tipped her over the one and only time she'd entered the shop, but now she knew what to expect. Could she take it a step further? Expose herself to something that made her skin feel itchy? All in the name of growth?

Because Cass had to grow if she didn't want to become a spinster with a million cats. Overcoming her sex issues wouldn't guarantee a great love, but at least she'd feel capable of offering a partner everything she had, without holding anything back.

There was a lot to consider.

"I'm going to go," Harriet murmured. Cass realised she'd been sitting silently for an uncomfortable amount of time. Harriet probably thought she was upset.

"No. Don't go. Sorry, I was just processing."

"Understandable."

Cass took a few deep breaths. "Would you like to watch a film or something?"

She waited as Harriet assessed the situation. Was she expecting Cass to have a breakdown or something?

"I'd love to. Although, if you haven't got popcorn, I may rethink my decision."

A weight lifted from Cass's mind. Harriet's natural ability to make things comfortable was a godsend.

"Of course I do. I'm not a monster. Salted or sweet?"

"Both. I like a bit of variety."

Cass grinned. "Me too. Do you trust me?"

"Yes," Harriet said with such ease.

"I'm gonna blow your mind," Cass replied. "My popcorn is legendary."

"I look forward to it." Harriet's smile was almost shy.

Cass bit her lip. If she took this chance and worked at Ero-Tea-Ca for a little while, she'd get to be close to Harriet. That was definitely worth it.

"I'll do it," she blurted.

Harriet cocked her head. "The popcorn?"

"No. I'll work in your shop. If Kendal and Nabi agree, I'll do it."

"I thought you wanted to discuss—"

"I don't. I'll do it."

15

Harriet

"Thanks for coming in early," Harriet said, wincing slightly. Kevin and Nabi looked half asleep and kept shooting her pointed looks.

"Early? Early! This is still nighttime. Why couldn't we have the meeting after hours? You know, when we've all had a full night's sleep." Kevin promptly dropped his head to the table after his outburst.

"Yeah," Nabi echoed, her eyes falling closed.

"I didn't want to wait until this evening. Look, I have an idea I need you to get behind."

Nabi blinked rapidly, trying to will her eyes to stay open. "You know we'll more than likely love it."

"It's not what you think," Harriet replied. Ever since Cass agreed to work at the teashop, she'd mulled over the idea. It was a spontaneous offer at first, but the more she thought about it, the more perfect a solution it became.

Cass needed a low-pressure environment to face her fears. Was fear the right word? Harriet pondered for a second. Yeah, she guessed fear was the right descriptor. Cass was afraid of sex because she'd rejected any thought of it. The subject held too many negative connotations.

So, yes. Cass having some time to be around people who were comfortable with themselves, and artwork that was salacious but discreet, was the absolute best way to help. Harriet was sure of it, until a creeping doubt flittered in. She wasn't a therapist. What if her suggestion was the complete opposite of what Cass needed? Maybe even suggesting it was a major overstep?

"Sis, you look constipated."

Harriet punched him in the arm. "And you look like a unicorn threw up on your head. What is that colour, anyway?" Kevin's new hairstyle was...a choice.

"Gogo wanted to experiment. This was the result."

"I hope they paid you for your time and possible damages."

"Damages?" Kevin's hands shot to his dry-looking hair. "What damages?"

Nabi plucked several broken ends off in her hand. "They over-bleached, my friend. Your hair is crispy."

"Fuck," Kevin growled. "Why do I let them do it?"

Harriet knew why. Kevin had a crush on Gogo that spanned many, *many* years. He'd never summoned the courage to ask them out, even though they'd be a great couple.

"Anyway. Back to my idea."

Two pairs of eyes snapped to Harriet. "We're all ears," Kevin replied, still fingering his hair with a scowl.

"For reasons I can't fully explain because it's not my place or story, I'd like Nabi and Cass to swap shops for a week."

Silence. Kevin looked bewildered. "Cass? You mean the bitch from next door?"

"Don't call her that!" Harriet fumed. "She's not a bitch."

Keven sat back, hands in the air. "Okay, chill out. But didn't she—"

"Yes, but it's water under the bridge. We're friends now and I'm trying to help her with something."

Kevin nodded and shrugged. "It's entirely up to Nabi. If she's cool, so am I."

Harriet turned a hopeful gaze to her best friend, who was in the process of unwrapping a lollipop. "Kendal's cool. I can work with her. When do you want to do it?"

Giving Nabi a high five in appreciation, Harriet told them she'd like Cass to start next week. "Because we're dark on Sunday afternoons—"

"Only until the week after next," Nabi reminded her. "After that the Dommes are taking over," she said with utter delight.

Amazingly, Nabi had found a book club full of Dommes. They'd formed over seven years ago, meeting in one another's living rooms every month. As soon as Nabi put the flyer up offering the tearoom on a Sunday afternoon, exclusively for book clubs, the Dommes called in, reserving one Sunday every month, starting next week.

"How could I forget? In fact, I wanted to run some theme ideas by you both."

"I can only deal with one thing at a time," Kevin complained. "It's too early for multi-tasking."

"Here," Harriet said, thrusting a muffin towards him. "It's blueberry."

While Kevin devoured his muffin, Harriet poured them all tea. "Are you sure you're okay with this, Nabs?"

"Yeah, why not? It'll be fun. Although, I'm really surprised. Cass all but scaled the walls to get out of here last time."

"I know. I wish I could tell you more, but it's up to Cass and I'm not going to betray her trust."

A quarter of a muffin hit Harriet square in the head. "You like her," Kevin declared.

"Fuck! Why did you need to throw food at me?"

"I got excited."

"You know how he gets," Nabi added. "His motor functions take on a life of their own."

"Whatever," Harriet grumbled as she picked crumbs from her hair. "Yes, I like her. But we're just friends. She needs that more than a relationship."

"But you think she'll change her stance later down the line?" Nabi surmised.

Sighing, Harriet nodded. "I hope so. She's like no one I've met before."

"You mean emotionally repressed," Kevin shot.

"No, she isn't. She's the absolute opposite actually. If anything, I think she feels too deeply. Is this going to be a problem, Kev?"

"Hey, no need to get snippy."

"No need to run your mouth," Harriet shot back. "I like her, Kevin."

"Alright, alright. My lips are sealed. You know I only want you to be happy. I'm a little worried, is all."

"So why get so excited?" Nabi asked. Harriet could always rely on her to have her back.

"Because it's been ages since Harriet liked someone."

"It has, but can we not hyperfocus on it, please? And do not make any stupid comments to Cass. I'm serious, Kevin. I need you to promise me."

"Jesus," he snorted. "I'm not that bad. I'll be nice as pie. I guess we'll work together at some point?"

Harriet nodded. "You'll have a shift next Thursday. I'll need you to take point on any toy sales or enquiries about the art and teapots."

"So, Cass is literally just here to serve tea?" he stated.

"Yes."

"Okay then. Now can I go back to bed?" Kevin was already standing and putting on his coat. "I'm still pissed at you for dragging my arse here."

Harriet stood and pulled him into a hug. "I appreciate it, bro. See you at Mount Doom."

Nabi cackled. "Do the 'rents know you've baptised their house Mount Doom?"

Kevin grinned. "No, but even if they did, the reference would be lost on them."

"Completely lost on them," Harriet reiterated.

"Okay, beautiful people, I'll see you later."

Harriet started the job of preparing for opening. The chairs were already placed under tables, and they'd cleaned the night before. Just the food needed to be cooked and displayed.

Nabi hopped on the kitchen counter. "So, you and Cass?"

"There is no 'me and Cass'. I'm happy to be her friend."

"Okay. And this swap is really about helping her through something? Not just a way for your fragile gay heart to spend some quality time with her?"

Harriet laughed. "My heart is not fragile. And spending extra time with her is a perk of the situation. But really, this is about helping Cass. That's my number one priority."

"And you can't tell me what it's about? Even though I have a vague idea."

Harriet shook her head. "No. Sorry, Nabs."

"Fair enough. So, this Sunday, you're gonna what? Let her roam the teashop?"

That's exactly what Harriet intended. Hopefully, a day with no customers would give Cass the chance to process and acclimatise. "Yes, that's the plan. I've got plenty of paperwork to do, so Cass can have the run of the place."

"To do what?"

"Whatever she needs. Now, enough of the third-degree. Get the croissants in."

Harriet didn't go in for her usual Danish. She thought it wise to wait for Cass to come to her. Before leaving Cass's house the night the decision was made, she'd said she'd chat with Nabi this morning and Cass said she'd do the same with Kendal.

But Cass hadn't contacted her all day, and now she was en route to Mount Doom. An evening with Patsy and

Ronald was low on the list of things she wanted to do, but Diane insisted they try to keep some semblance of a family unit.

Mentally scrolling through the different takeout restaurants she'd hit up once the night was over, Harriet pulled up alongside Diane's car. Kevin opted to grab a lift from her instead of on the back of Harriet's scooter. He said it was too cold, but Harriet knew he just didn't want to put the helmet on in case it further damaged his already wrecked hair. She had visions of him removing the headgear, only to find all his hair stuck to it and a nice shiny bald head. She snorted at the thought. It would keep her going through the evening, a bright spark in the pit of darkness her parents no doubt intended to cast over the disappointments that were their children.

Diane called a greeting from the kitchen. Kevin waved from the living room, which was deadly quiet. Only the glow of the muted TV gave any clue of life. Placing her bag and coat by the door, Harriet dragged her heels. God, she already felt the oppressive judgement of her parents weighing her down.

"Well, if it isn't the family's madame," Patsy sneered.

Great start.

"Mum," Harriet murmured, bypassing her to hug Diane.

"Don't listen to her," she whispered in Harriet's ear.

The rest of the evening followed the same trajectory. One or both parents slipped in jibes and insults about Ero-Tea-Ca. They were disgusted she was still in business. Apparently, they'd heard things about the shop from their friends and couldn't believe Harriet was disgracing the family like that. Diane tried in vain to interject, but they were on a roll.

Even Kevin, who usually found their parents' rants funny, sat silently. Harriet tuned out completely. Her mind wandered to Cass. She thought of their upcoming week together, which brought a smile to her face.

"And what exactly do you have to smile about, young lady?"

The vitriol in her mother's voice was enough to bring her crashing back to the doily-lined table.

Oh, right, I'm still in hell.

Looking up, Harriet stared down her mother and father. *"Enough of this shit,"* a voice whispered in her head. "I have plenty to be happy about. I'll smile whenever I please."

"Harriet Kirkwell—" her father began.

Slamming her cutlery on the table, Harriet rose from her seat. "Don't '*Harriet Kirkwell*' me. I've had it." Casting her gaze to Diane, she smiled regretfully. "Sorry, Di, I can't keep doing this. None of us should. We come here out of duty because we're blood-related, but that's it. I will *not* have my mental health suffer just for the sake of blood ties. None of us are good enough. You're the only one with any redeeming qualities and that's because you have kids. But I'm sitting here, time in and time out, getting verbally abused and putting up with it. Not anymore. Mother, Father, this will be the last time I step foot in this house until you can offer me some modicum of respect. I am a business owner—a successful one at that. My life is rich and full of love. Your approval is no longer needed."

Pushing out her chair, she bent to hug a stunned Kevin, and then Diane. "I'll see you at work, Kev. And I'll see you when you're free, Di. Just give me a call. Night."

In a storm of indignation, Harriet walked past her parents without sparing them another second of her time. Only on the ride home did the realisation of what she'd just done hit her. But she didn't regret it. Actually, she felt bloody brilliant. It was amazing how much of a weight her parents' criticisms and outright disdain weighed on her. But now she felt liberated.

Instead of driving home, Harriet parked the scooter outside Cass's place. The curtain twitched. No backing out now. She could see Cass's silhouette moving from the window.

The door opened before Harriet had a chance to knock. "Hi, sorry to turn up unannounced."

Cass shrugged. "It's fine. Want a tea?"

Harriet liked this. Cass was so much more comfortable with her, and the fact Harriet could turn up without getting scowled at was great.

"Hey there, little man," she cooed. Mr Whiskers wound himself around her feet until he was scooped up and cradled.

"You're both ridiculous," Cass teased.

"You're just jealous."

"Mmm. Biscuit with the tea?"

"God, yes, I'm famished." On cue, her stomach growled.

Cass went wide-eyed. The noise was impressive. "Um, I think you might need more than a Hobnob. I'll order pizza."

And just like that, Harriet was having dinner with Cass.

"I spoke to Kevin and Nabi. They're both on board if you still want to do the swap thing."

Cass didn't answer right away. She finished tapping their food order into her phone and poured the tea. "I spoke to Kendal."

Harriet settled Mr Whiskers on her lap. "Okay. Would you like to talk about it?"

"Nothing to talk about. She's fine with the idea. Ken knows me well enough not to push. I just told her it was something I needed to try, and she was completely supportive."

"So, we're doing it then?"

Cass looked at her for the first time since sitting down. She swallowed nervously, but allowed her mouth to curl a little. "We are."

"Everything at your pace, Cass. I thought it would be an idea to start on Sunday, when we're closed."

Cass nodded. "I thought the same thing. Maybe if I have time to orient myself and process, it'll help when there are customers."

"You're just serving tea, remember. Nothing more. No pressure."

"You keep saying that." Cass laughed.

"Because it's true. And if you *do* feel it's too much, just nip out the back and take a breath. You can also talk to me, too. About anything."

"I can't believe I'm doing this," Cass murmured to herself. Harriet needed to have some kind of contact. She settled her hand on Cass's thigh.

"You can back out. But I hope you don't because I think what you're doing is very courageous."

Cass scoffed, "I think it's ridiculous. A forty-one-year-old needing to be schooled on…sex. How pathetic."

"You aren't being schooled, Cass. You're working through trauma to make your life easier."

Cass wiped her face. "Whatever the reason, I wish I didn't have to do any of it. I just want to be normal."

"Whoa. Okay, I don't want to hear you say things like that. Cass, you *are* normal. As normal as any of us can be. It's a horrid term. You are you. That's all you can be. We go through life, changing and learning. It never stops. That's all you're doing. You're growing. It's a beautiful thing, okay?"

They looked each other in the eye, and that overwhelming desire to capture Cass's lips surged through Harriet's body.

This was going to be harder than she thought.

16

Cassandra

"Just knock and walk in...that's all you have to do. It's not difficult." Cass paced the back garden of Ero-Tea-Ca. "You're being an idiot. Just knock!" She was getting pissed off with herself. It was Sunday afternoon. There was no one else here except Harriet. Why couldn't she just knock on the bloody door?

A steely determination formed in her chest when she thought of Harriet inside, waiting for her. This was the reason she'd agreed to the shop swap—this crippling, absurd fear that stopped her legs from taking her over the threshold of a shop. Ero-Tea-Ca triggered her, and she was entirely sick of it.

Still warring with herself, Cass eventually got her legs to move in the right direction. Her fist shook as she lifted it to knock. Sweat formed along the base of her back, making her feel sticky. Blimey, was she about to have an anxiety attack?

"Hey, you're here!" Harriet pushed open the door with a bright smile that instantly soothed Cass's nerves. Taking Cass's hand, Harriet rubbed soft circles on her palm. "I'll prop the door open. Come in when you're ready."

Cass watched Harriet turn and leave. Taking a few calming breaths, she forced her feet to move. She'd been in this part of the shop before without incident. The kitchen area was fine, and the small breakroom didn't cause any concerns.

There, she'd made it inside and the world hadn't ended. Now what?

Spotting a coat rack, she whipped off her jacket and placed her purse on the table. So far, so good. The stockroom was just through the next door. That might be more of a hill to climb, knowing what Harriet had in there.

Cass imagined boxes upon boxes of glass toys and her face flushed.

Rustling and key tapping came from the office. Should she check in with Harriet? No, if she did that, she'd want to stay in there all day and that would defeat the purpose. A coffee pot—that looked suspiciously brand new—stood on the side, already bubbling away. A plain mug with a Post-it note grabbed her attention. It read: "Look—you get your own mug!" Cass smiled. The rich aroma wafting from the pot could only be Peruvian Gold.

Taking the full cup, Cass took tentative steps towards the main tearoom. The office door was closed, so she had complete privacy. Only the secondary mood lighting illuminated the room, creating a warm glow. They really had done a lovely job with the restoration. Even though it still felt a little raw to have lost out on buying the place herself, Cass had to admit Harriet and her team had done the place proud.

Wandering to the traditional-style cash register, she simply stared for a while. It was a thing of beauty, and she couldn't wait to play with it. That childish curiosity she thought long dead poked its head up every time she found something new to admire.

Although the display case was empty, it was still magnificent. She could picture all the delicious cakes and sandwiches Harriet put out every day. Her mouth watered at the thought of fresh scones with jam and clotted cream. Oh, it'd been ages since she'd indulged in something as lovely as that.

Whipping out a granola bar from her back pocket, Cass grumbled with every disappointing bite. She should have had a bigger lunch.

As she circled the hardwood tables, she could sense them watching her—the things that made her splutter and flush. The toys. Placing her now half-empty mug on the closest table, Cass shook out her limbs. "You're a grown woman for goodness' sake. They're bits of glass. Pull yourself together."

As pep talks go, it wasn't the best, but it did the job. Cass practically marched over and stood eye to...tip? With the...*dildos.* Even the word made her hot, and not in the way intended.

If she detached herself from what they were, Cass could absolutely appreciate the artistry. Glass blowing was an impressive medium to master and whoever blew these...whoever *made* them, was very talented. The mix of colours and shapes was very impressive.

Her curiosity overrode any awkwardness, allowing Cass to pick one up. She surveyed it as an ornament. Nothing scandalous there. Until a thought crossed her mind. *What would it feel like?*

By this point, Cass would usually be heading for the door in a foul mood. She'd be ranting and raving about decency and decorum. But not today. Today, Cass would take the dildo by the shaft and gain some control.

Her stubbornness was often seen as a negative trait, but today it would propel her towards growth. Instead of running away, Cass was determined to stay and learn. Even if she couldn't voice the questions yet, she'd take note of anything she wanted to learn about.

Placing the toy back on the shelf, Cass took the notepad she used for coffee orders and jotted down her question. Satisfied, she moved over to the teapots. Immediately she spotted the pattern Harriet had gifted Kendal. Picking it up, she studied each drawing. Once again, the artistry was extraordinary. Each position was skilfully painted. The detail was incredible. Turning it in hand, she saw the doggy-style part of the scene her mother had so openly loved. Cocking her head to the side, Cass took it in. One woman was on all fours as another woman knelt behind her with a hand on hip and the other in her hair.

Cass pulled the teapot closer. The woman kneeling had some sort of...oh, it was a harness. Of course. Cass rolled her eyes. It was a strap-on scene. She might find sex difficult to talk about, think about, and generally navigate, but that didn't mean she was completely out of the loop.

Turning the pot again, she came across two women in a sixty-nine position. Another turn and...well, she didn't know this one. Taking her notepad, she jotted down a reminder to learn about sexual positions. If she looked at this as more of an assignment, she might just come out the other side.

Walking over to a table, Cass sat down, placing the teapot in front of her. She wanted to understand what Harriet's customers experienced. If you didn't look too closely, it was just a teapot on a table. Cass imagined sitting with a friend, enjoying an afternoon of tea and sandwiches. Yes, she could do that without feeling weird. Unless someone pointed out the design, that was. That might cause her some embarrassment. Hmm, maybe she should ask Harriet to sit with her, like a test run. "Maybe another day," she murmured.

Once satisfied she'd learned the layout of the tearoom and could handle seeing the toys and teapots, Cass headed for the stockroom. Walking in, she chuckled to herself. It was practically identical to her own. Boxes lined each shelf. A small ladder stood propped up. All this time, she'd had it in her mind the room would be some sort of sex dungeon, filled with more naughty things that would make her feel awkward and would justify her fears that Harriet was indeed here to sully the reputation of the street. Of course, she knew that wasn't true. It never had been, but irrationality was a weird thing.

Still chuckling to herself, Cass knocked on the office door. "Come in."

Harriet was a sight for sore eyes. Cass firmly believed the woman constantly exuded happiness. It was like a warm light being cast over the darkest shadows. Harriet just made things better.

"Ah, you found the coffee?"

"I did. Thank you."

Harriet scoffed playfully. "I can't have an under-caffeinated employee."

Cass smiled. "I'm surprised you didn't insist I drink tea."

"Oh, I will eventually. We have so many choices, it'd be wrong not to sample some."

Stepping into the room a little more, Cass looked around. It was the mirror image of her own office except Cass's was organised and tidy, whereas Harriet's space was piled with papers and all other manner of things. Cass's left eye twitched as she noticed more clutter.

Harriet's laugh started off small until it was a full out bellow. "Oh my God, you should see your face, Cass. I think your left eye is about to pop!"

Cass grinned. "I don't know what you're talking about."

"Sure. So, my office space doesn't make you want to claw your face off, then?"

"It's..." Cass sighed. "Fine, this is an appalling mess. How on earth do you get any work done? There's no way you know where everything is. Are you a hoarder?"

Shaking her head, Harriet leaned back in her chair. "No, I'm not. However, I will admit paperwork bores the shit out of me, and I tend to get distracted easily, so nine times out of ten, I end up spreading things around because I can't be bothered to put them back properly. This is the result."

"Can I organise it?" Cass was deadly serious. She couldn't work here knowing this monstrosity lurked behind the door. She'd have nightmares.

"You want to organise my office?"

"Very much so!"

Harriet running a hand through her hair was momentarily distracting.

"Cass, I didn't ask you here to do that."

"I know. But I've done what I needed to feel more comfortable. I know the layout and I'm sure learning the cash register won't take long. We can have a tea-making session later. But, Harriet, if I don't sort this," she gestured to the desk, "I'll not sleep. It will haunt me, and you wouldn't want that."

Biting her lip, Harriet smiled from her eyes. "No, I wouldn't want that. Okay, have at it. What do you need me to do?"

Cass was already picking up paperwork. "Show me where your files are and I'll start sorting these out."

Pushing back, Harriet stood and pointed to a small cabinet under her desk. "It's there. I'll make us some more tea and coffee. How about a snack?"

"You don't by any chance have scones left over, do you?"

"I'll see what I can do."

Cass was in her element. She'd sorted the paperwork into piles, organised them by subject matter, and was happily filling them away. The place looked so much better. The desk was clear, and the floor no longer posed a tripping hazard.

"Coffee number four," Harriet announced.

"Great." Cass barely lifted her gaze. That was, until a hand pulled the latest batch of invoices from her grip.

"Break time, Cass."

"Sorry. I tend to get hyper-focused sometimes."

Harriet sat in the chair opposite. "And it's done wonders for my office."

"Can you try and keep it this way?"

"I'll do my best, but I can't promise. It might get messy again."

Cass squinted. "Is that your way of getting me back over here?"

Harriet smiled. "Maybe? Would it work?"

Cass shrugged. "If I can't see the mess, it won't bother me."

"Hmm. What if I accidentally sent you pictures?"

Cass laughed. "Yes, that would do it."

They smiled at each other over the rims of their cups. This was nice. Cass felt extremely comfortable, and if she wasn't mistaken, a little flirting was going on.

"So..." Harriet began, "how's it been?"

Cass put her cup down. "Being here?" Harriet nodded. Blowing out a breath, Cass leaned back. "Not nearly as bad as I thought."

"That's good to hear. Can I ask what you thought it would be like?"

She sighed. "I tend to believe things will be a lot worse than they are. You know, building a situation up until I've convinced myself it's going to be terrible."

"Yeah, I get it. But it's not been as bad as you imagined?"

"Not at all. The tearoom is delightful. I can't say I'm one hundred percent comfortable, but I'm not bolting for the door."

"Progress."

"I'm still worried about tomorrow."

Harriet put her cup on the desk and placed both elbows on it, resting her chin in her palm. "What's freaking you out?"

"Customers asking me things. I'm sure you've noticed my face flushes. It's not something I can control."

"Okay. That's no problem. You can do stock take in the morning, give yourself a bit more time. Then when you're ready, you could serve or be a runner between the kitchen and the cash register. Whatever you want."

Cass bit her lip. "Why are you doing this?"

"Because I can. We're friends, and you're struggling with something I can hopefully help with."

The woodgrain on the desk became suddenly interesting. The sincerity in Harriet's voice took Cass by surprise. She felt a lump in her throat. "Thank you." It came out as a whisper and her voice cracked. She heard Harriet's chair scrape back and felt arms wrap around from behind.

"I'm here for you, Cass. Anytime."

As soon as Harriet pulled back and sat down, Cass missed her touch. She was getting used to Harriet's tactile nature and was growing to like the little touches. She was growing to like a lot of things.

For the first time in years, Cass was regretting her stance on dating, or not dating, in her case. But could she really trust herself with someone as lovely as Harriet? There was still the eleven-year age gap. Cass wasn't worried about what people thought in the sense of an older woman being with someone younger. She was more concerned about her proclivity at acting like a bitter old crone.

Harriet was in the prime of her life. Surely she liked to go out to the pub? Maybe even clubs? Cass couldn't think of anything worse. And Harriet's friends? They'd certainly tell her she'd lost her mind for dating the bitch next door.

Did they have anything in common? Did Cass want to find out? Well, she would eventually. If they remained friends, they'd naturally get to know each other.

And what if Cass couldn't fully overcome her issues with sex? Or what if she did, and they started dating, but then Harriet realised Cass had so many other quirks it was too much?

How she wished it were possible to have a personality transplant. Cass would take it in a second. There was only so much growing she could do. Even if she won this battle, her character wasn't great. Who the hell wanted to stick around a person with mood issues? No, they weren't even issues; it was all just her natural character.

"You know, you get this little wrinkle between your eyes when you're thinking hard."

"That's just old age," Cass snapped back.

"No, that's called overthinking."

"It's just my face."

Harriet stood. "Come on."

"Where?" Cass still stood and followed. Her ears were buzzing.

"We're taking a walk. It's a lovely afternoon."

"But—"

"But nothing. Let's go, Beaufort. Time's a-wasting and I want to feed the ducks."

17

Harriet

Operation Duck Pond Distraction worked a treat. Every second Harriet got to know Cass better, the easier it was to spot her negative thoughts starting to manifest. It was like a cloud descended on her face, drawing in her eyebrows and causing frown lines to appear.

Instead of asking what was wrong, Harriet knew the best course of action was to get outside, away from whatever was causing Cass's irritation and anxiety.

They spent a good hour walking around the pond, throwing oats on the ground. Cass's entire face lit up when a mum duck waddled over with her stumbling ducklings.

It was in that moment, Harriet knew she couldn't remain just friends with Cassandra Beaufort. The enigmatic, frustrating, and wonderful woman had entirely captured her heart.

They'd left each other with a friendly hug. As much as Harriet had yearned to spend the rest of the evening with Cass, she knew her *friend*—ugh—needed space to process today and prepare for tomorrow.

When her alarm clock jolted her from a saucy Cass-filled dream, Harriet had to take an extended cold shower. Cass needed her to be a support system today, not a letch.

She'd compiled a list of tasks for Cass, all of which allowed her to stay relatively invisible, if that was what she needed. Monday was delivery day. Cass could put the stock away. Maybe Harriet would ask her to organise the shelves? Other jobs included cooking the pre-made pastries.

Arriving at the teashop, Harriet went about her daily routine. It was strange to think of Nabi rocking up to The Oxford Beanery in all her chaotic, sugar-loaded glory, and not Ero-Tea-Ca. How would Kendal handle her? The thought brought a smile to her face. Oh, God, Harriet would put bets on Nabi placing crystals around the place.

Laughing to herself, she didn't hear the back door open and close. Only when she sensed a presence did she turn and scream like a banshee.

"Jesus, fuck!" she yelled.

Cass stood frozen with wide eyes, clutching her purse. "S-sorry."

Harriet shook her head. "No. My bad, I was daydreaming and didn't hear you. Phew, that got the heart pumping." She laughed.

Cass stood in her usual uniform, hair in its neat low ponytail. "I knocked."

Harriet waved her hand. "It's cool, but we have a slight problem."

She saw Cass clutch her purse even harder. She was really wound up, and Harriet momentarily thought she was about to bolt out the door.

"W-what's the problem?"

"You're not working at The Beanery this week," Harriet answered, gesturing to the logo on Cass's shirt. "We need to get you in the proper attire."

"I figured."

"There's a shirt on the back of the toilet door. I'll grab you an apron."

Cass wrinkled her nose. "Does it have smiling teapots on it?"

Harriet grinned mischievously. "It does not. It has smiling teacups instead."

The eye roll must have given Cass a headache. It was that hard. "Fantastic."

Patting Cass's shoulder, Harriet pointed to the loo. "Oh, stop being a sourpuss. Smiling teacups are cute. Now, get changed and I'll get you set up for the day."

While Cass changed, Harriet accepted the delivery and began shifting boxes to the stockroom.

"There, I'm appropriately dressed. What's next?"

As much as Harriet wanted to stare at Cass in Ero-Tea-Ca apparel, she needed to stay in boss mode. "Can you sort out the delivery?"

"Sure. Do you have a system?"

"Not really. The only thing I ask, if you change things, is not to touch or move any crystals."

Cass stared, her eyebrow cocking. "Really?" Her tone was a little mocking, which Harriet could understand. Few people believed in crystals and their power. She wasn't entirely convinced herself, but she respected Nabi's beliefs and wishes.

"Seriously. It's the only rule."

Cass shrugged. "Okay. I'll get started then."

They went about their mornings separately. Harriet ensured the tables were set to her standards. Of course they were. She was the only one who set them up. But in the infinitesimally possible scenario where the tables had suddenly changed overnight, Harriet had to check.

Flipping the sign to *Open*, she unlatched the deadbolt. Her regular customers filtered in with warm smiles and uplifting energy. Unlike the café, her customers didn't look like they wanted to commit homicide before their first caffeine hit of the morning.

Her phone buzzed several times. Normally she had a "no phone outside of the staffroom" policy, but with Nabi being in a new environment, Harriet wanted to stay close to her mobile, not that she foresaw any issues. And to be fair, Nabi was literally next door, so if there was a disaster, she was a thirty-second walk away.

Whatever. Harriet felt better having a phone nearby. Sneaking a quick peek at the messages, she couldn't stop the snort of laughter when she flipped through several photos Nabi sent. She was already hiding crystals. There was one of Kendal laughing as Nabi made a *rock on* sign as the coffee maker dribbled out espresso. And last but not least, Nabi's foam cock art she'd drawn in a cappuccino.

At least her friend seemed to be settling in and having fun. Harriet thought of Cass in the stockroom. She really hoped this experience would be as fun for her as it was for Nabi. *One day at a time.*

Time passed quickly. It always did when Harriet was in the zone. She chatted and laughed with regulars. There were several new clients who needed hand holding. It was quite normal. Everyone expected Ero-Tea-Ca to be something it wasn't. Thankfully, it didn't take long for new customers to settle in with a good pot of tea. Harriet prided herself on her knowledge. She loved using what she'd learned to help people find their perfect tea. It wasn't all about selling gift sets and sex toys. Her first passion was the tea. Always.

"Harriet, my sweet cherub!" Ronnie, Harriet's oldest and most beloved customer, shouted as she shuffled in the door.

"Ronnie, it's good to see you. I missed you on Friday."

"Had a bloody doctor's appointment. I swear the man doesn't know an arse from an elbow."

Harriet chuckled. Ronnie was a character. "Everything alright?"

"Oh, yes. Just a spot of eczema. Anyway, I have some wonderful news!"

Putting Ronnie's favourite tea in to steep, Harriet pulled out a Cherry Bakewell and placed it on a tray. Ronnie was a creature of habit.

"Oh, do tell."

"Well," Ronnie began, "you know how I hoped Tori would come out to me before I kicked the bucket?"

"I remember." Harried laughed. Tori was Ronnie's adult granddaughter—a lovely woman who definitely had queer vibes but identified as straight. Until now, apparently. Ronnie never believed her interest lay in men and often spoke to Harriet about it. Clearly, her intuition was spot on.

"She finally did it! Saturday night. She came over all nervous looking. At first, I thought she had the shits or something. I even offered her some Imodium. Well, she got all flustered and said her bowels were fine, which was a good job really, because I was low on loo roll."

Harriet's shoulders shook with silent laughter. A story from Ronnie usually took several wrong turns until she got to the point.

"So, there she was, looking like death warmed up. When I was sure she wasn't about to soil my couch, I started to worry something was up with my Cheryl." Cheryl was Tori's mum, who Harriet had yet to meet.

"I take it Cheryl's fine?"

Ronnie waved a dismissive hand. "If you exclude the fact she's married to a fat slob, then yes, she's fine. But I didn't know at the time and Tori was looking more upset. I asked if her mum was okay and she just burst out crying. Well, I didn't know what to do, so I made her a cup of tea and laid out some Jammy Dodgers—her favourite. She used to dunk them in milk as a kid. Anyway. After a few minutes of sobbing, she finally squeaked out she had something to tell me, and she hoped I still loved her afterwards."

"Poor Tori," Harriet sympathised. Coming out was awful and the emotional toll was overwhelming, even to those whose parents were cool with it.

"Then I knew it was finally happening." Ronnie was practically bouncing on the spot. Her walking aid made rhythmic thumps on the floor as she moved. "It was so hard just sitting there. I wanted to tell her I already knew, but I didn't. That would've stolen her thunder."

"Well done for holding back." Harriet smiled.

"It was like a Mexican stand-off. We just sat staring at each other for ages until finally, *finally,* she all but shouted she was a lesbian."

"Ah, that's great, Ronnie."

"Isn't it just? I want to throw her a coming out tea party. Here, on Sunday afternoon. I know you said it's for book clubs, but I was hoping I could twist your arm."

"No arm-twisting needed. I'd love to help." This was what Ero-Tea-Ca was all about. "Just tell me what you need."

Cass stepped out from the back with a box tucked under her arm. Her face was wary, as if she expected an orgy to be taking place. She visibly relaxed when she noted the lack of anything exciting. Weirdly, the shop was full of people drinking tea. Who'd have thought?

Harriet smiled to herself. She ignored Cass, not out of malice, but she felt drawing attention to her would make things uncomfortable. Plus, Ronnie was still happily jabbering away. "I'd like to invite her friends. She told me she's met a lovely bunch of people. They're all queer, you know. I bet one of them is sweet on my Tori. She's adorable. Say…you're a single lesbian, right?"

Harriet heard the box hit the floor behind her, and Cass mumbled an apology. "I'm a lesbian and currently single, yes."

"Would you be interested in Tori?"

Several tea packets hit the floor this time. Harriet desperately wanted to look over her shoulder, but fought it.

"Tori is lovely, and in other circumstances I would happily ask her out, but I have my eye on someone, so…"

Ronnie nodded. "Fair enough. Thought I'd ask. What about you?" Ronnie shouted, her eyes on Cass.

"Um…I…"

"Not a lesbian?" Ronnie asked.

"I don't think that's any of your business," Cass bit out.

"Oh, sorry, love," Ronnie replied, not looking in the least bit sorry. She'd told Harriet once that she'd long gotten over upsetting people. She asked awkward questions and gave her unsolicited opinions no matter what. She'd said it was the only positive aspect of getting old. "No potential here, then. Bugger."

Harriet removed the tea bag from Ronnie's pot. "Here, have a cuppa."

"Thanks, cherub. Back to the party. Would you make those delicious French Fancies?" Ronnie pointed to the stack of cakes in the display case. "But instead of the normal icing, can you do them in the colours of the lesbian flag?"

"Sure. How many people are you expecting?"

Ronnie tapped her chin. "Let's say twenty. You, Nabi and Kevin will come, right?"

"I can't speak for the others, but I wouldn't miss it."

"Obviously, you'll be running it," Cass mumbled behind her.

"And what about you, grumpy arse? Wanna come to a coming out party?"

Cass cleared her throat, and Harriet finally allowed herself to look. She was red-faced and her eyes darted from Harriet to Ronnie. "I..." Harriet wanted to jump in and save her. But Cass was a grown woman. She could speak for herself. "Okay."

"Fantastic," Ronnie exclaimed. "So, the French Fancies are sorted. Can you do a selection of sandwiches? I'd also like to purchase some gift boxes. Tori's eyed up the Ancient Greek porn pot every time we've been in."

"It's not a porn pot." Harriet laughed. The teapot in question had Ancient Greek replicated scenes of women getting busy painted over it.

"You know what I mean. I want that to be her present. Also, a dildo of her choice."

Harriet could feel Cass's face radiating heat. Surprisingly, though, she'd not stormed out. "That can be arranged. But maybe wait until Tori is alone before offering her that. You don't know where her comfort level is yet."

Ronnie nodded. "Good point. Okay, we'll leave that bit until the end."

"I'll make a list of everything and send you an invoice."

"Perfect. Right, I'm going to take my tea and leave you lovely ladies to it. Ta ta, for now."

Instead of immediately checking on Cass, Harriet wiped the counter and rearranged the display case. Cass would talk to her when she was ready.

"Wow, she's something."

Harriet closed the case and spun around. "She's great. I love her. Tori is a sweetheart too. I'm so pleased she felt confident enough to come out."

"So, you do events?" Cass continued to fill the shelf. Her eyes darting to Harriet's now and then.

"Book clubs, yes. We've never done a coming out tea party before. Should be fun." Harriet paused. "You...you're really going to attend?"

Cass looked back to the box in her hand. "If that's okay?"

God, Harriet had the urge to hold her again. "Of course it is. I think you'll really enjoy it."

"Then I'll come." They continued for a little while in silence until Cass had no more tea to put out.

"You can take a break now if you want." Harriet didn't want Cass to go back to the stockroom. She wanted her at the counter next to her. But this whole thing wasn't about what *she* needed.

"I'm okay, for now. I was wondering if you'd teach me to use the till. It's gorgeous."

A warmth filled Harriet's chest. "Sure. Put the box in recycling and come back out. It won't take long."

Cass came back, looking more determined than ever. Did this mean she was feeling less anxious about being in the main serving area? It only took Cass a few tries before she was a whiz on the vintage machine. Her eyes lit up every time she got it right.

"Want to take over for a bit? I can make the tea and wait the tables."

Biting her lip, Cass cast a glance around the room. "Okay. Yeah."

They worked seamlessly together until there was a lull. Harriet made them both a pot of tea and plated two French Fancies. "Did you make these?" Cass licked off a blob of cream from her lip and Harriet swore she whimpered out loud.

Clearing her throat, she took a bite of her own cake. "Yes, I love baking."

Cass's eyes went wide. "You made all of this from scratch?"

The display case was jam-packed, full of delicious treats. Harriet made the majority of them. Baking helped calm her racing thoughts. It was easy to get lost in a recipe.

"Not everything. I don't make the crumpets."

Cass scoffed. "But everything else?"

Harriet nodded.

"Wow. They're delicious. Where on earth do you find the time? I can barely cook pre-made croissants."

"Mostly I stay after the shop's closed and bake. It doesn't take long. Nabi and Kevin do the sandwiches."

Chewing the last bit of cake, Cass sighed. "You're impressive, you know."

Harriet smiled shyly. "Thanks." It felt good, too good, to have Cass compliment her. She was so, *so* screwed. Cass was going to run away with her heart, and Harriet had no intentions of stopping her.

18

Cassandra

Well, Cass just felt stupid. After getting herself into such a state over Ero-Tea-Ca's existence, imagine her humiliation when everyone in the place just...drank tea.

It didn't take a genius to know she'd projected her warped view of sex onto the new tea shop and Harriet. And all the people associated with her. The presence of toys and erotic art still sent a wave of unease up her spine, but even after just a few hours in the environment, she felt better.

The day started with putting the shop's standard order away, which helped Cass settle into her new role. It didn't stop her mind from racing, but she did her best to focus on the job at hand, a job that turned out to be bigger than first predicted because the second Cass saw the stockroom's disorganisation, she knew the rest of the morning would be spent rearranging it. She'd got the okay from Harriet, as long as she didn't touch the crystals. Cass definitely rolled her eyes a few times at that.

Satisfied with a job well done, Cass filled the shelves in the tearoom. It was the first time she'd entered with clients occupying tables. There was a low hum of chatter, but other than that, it was peaceful, bar the old woman talking to Harriet about a coming out party. She'd not expected to get dragged into the conversation, but it'd happened and Cass felt strangely okay about it all. Alright, she may have gotten a bit snippy when the nosy old sod asked her to label her sexual orientation. That was a little too forward, in Cass's opinion. But then she was suddenly going to the aforementioned coming out party and was actually looking forward to it.

Once Busybody Ronnie had waddled off, Harriet taught Cass the ins and outs of the cash register, which Cass thoroughly enjoyed. Every time she made the machine ping, a giggle wanted to slip out.

Standing behind the counter, taking money and writing orders, hadn't been scary either. So far, nothing about the experience was as bad as she'd feared it would be. Now Cass decided to face her fear head-on, and she was more determined than ever to soak up as much as she could.

The majority of soaking up arose when she volunteered to swap with Harriet. Cass wanted to wait tables for a while. It meant she would interact more with customers, and even though that came with the possibility of awkward conversation, Cass was dead set on doing it.

So, she weaved her way through the tearoom, stacking teapots and teacups on trays and wiping away cake crumbs and half-eaten sandwiches. As she worked, her eyes roamed and took note of several books clients were reading, all sapphic by the looks of things.

She listened in—discreetly—to a group of four friends who were chatting about their relationships, sex included. Cass's ears flamed, but that was as far as it went. What really surprised her was the lack of...well, to be blunt, the lack of debauchery. Cass had been convinced the customers would be people like her mother: loud and brash, wanting the entire world to hear about their conquests. Okay, that wasn't entirely fair to Lolita. Yes, she was loud and brash, but she didn't tell strangers her business. It just felt like that to Cass at times.

The four friends were discussing a sex position one of the women had never done before. By all accounts, the woman's new girlfriend wanted to spice things up, and it was causing her to feel uncomfortable. Cass hovered as the friends talked her through it, offering support. No mocking or silly jibes. It was refreshing to hear and made Cass feel like there was hope for her after all. She wasn't alone. There were other people out there who weren't as experienced as some, but they wanted to learn. Cass could do that.

By the end of the day, she was feeling reinvigorated. She'd made a list of things to research. Homework, of sorts, starting with a trip to the bookstore.

She left the shop with a quick goodbye to Harriet. They'd spent a lot of time together this afternoon and Cass needed some space. All this talk of new sex positions had Cass's mind going to some inappropriate places. She couldn't help it.

At one point, her befuddled brain came up with a scenario where she asked Harriet to help her with the physical aspect of her education. Cass wanted to get over her shit, and she would by researching. But, at some point, she'd need practical experience, someone to test her newfound confidence—or the confidence she hoped to gain over the next week.

Of course, she quickly dismissed the idea as absurd. Harriet would think her pathetic, plus she wouldn't want Harriet to feel used. Cass still couldn't commit to anything more than friendship. Not until she was positive she'd moved on from her issues.

Cass would also read up on the different types of tea Harriet offered. This whole thing couldn't revolve around the erotic part of the business. Cass wanted to make sure she was offering the clients a well-formed knowledge of all things tea. It would be a steep learning curve considering how many varieties Ero-Tea-Ca stocked. A week didn't feel like enough time. Could she ask Harriet for an extension?

Shaking her head, Cass headed into the bookstore. She had three titles in mind, all of which she'd seen in the shop today. With a successful book-finding mission complete, Cass was keen to get home. There was no time to waste. Her phone chimed. It was Kendal checking in. No time. There were subjects Cass needed to Google anonymously.

She was three hours down the rabbit hole when her doorbell rang. Cass's eyes were glassy from staring at her laptop screen for so long. The bell sounded again, and then twice more in quick succession, which finally tore Cass from her digital world of all things sexy, and back to reality.

Stumbling to the door, Cass blinked several times. "Harriet?"

"Hey, can I come in?"

Letting Harriet by, Cass scrubbed her face. "Everything okay?" she called, closing the door. Harriet was already heading for the kitchen. Thank God Cass had the sense to close her laptop lid.

"I wanted to ask you the same thing."

Cass headed for the kettle. "I'm fine, why?"

Shedding her coat, Harriet settled at the kitchen table. "You left abruptly. I was worried it'd been too much for you."

Cass winced. In her hyper-focused state, she hadn't realised Harriet had taken her departure as anything but what it was: a need to get her homework started.

"Sorry. No, everything was fine." Harriet didn't look convinced. "Honestly. The day was fun. Nothing like I imagined."

"And you still want to come back tomorrow?"

"Absolutely. If you're still happy with that?"

Harriet smiled brightly for the first time since arriving. "Of course I want that. But don't feel pressured, alright? I know Ronnie was a bit forward today, and I can't guarantee we won't get other customers like that."

"Do you want to stay for dinner?" Cass needed Harriet to stop rambling. She needed her to know just how okay she was feeling. Maybe it was more than okay. It felt more like excitement.

"Um...sure?"

Cass chuckled. "It's not a trick question."

Harriet sat back in the chair, assessing. "Something's different. I was expecting my sourpuss and am facing someone entirely different."

Her sourpuss. Cass's chest swelled with pride. Oh, dear. Taking some time to make their drinks, Cass weighed her options. Tell Harriet how she was feeling about today? The truth of it all or keep it to herself? Hmm, that might be where she'd gone wrong in the past.

Cass only had one true confidant, and that was Kendal. She was the only one to know Cass's fears and anxieties. Maybe if Cass had opened up more, this whole sex thing wouldn't have amounted to the giant problem it had become. Sadly, that just wasn't in her nature, though.

Being timid and shy with personal things wasn't an option. It was ingrained in her character, so there was no point thinking of the what-ifs. The fact of the matter was, Harriet had wormed her way under Cass's skin. She now felt comfortable enough with Harriet to talk, even though a part of her screamed not to, because Harriet felt like more than a confidant and what she had to say could lead to a world of embarrassment.

Steeling herself, Cass sat opposite Harriet and placed their cups on the table. "The truth is, today was wonderful. I can't explain it, and I'm sure I'll need to unpack some of it with my therapist, but I feel like I have knocked down a barrier."

Harriet leaned forward. "Okay. Will you explain that to me?"

Cass nodded. "I'll never be the type of woman to be openly secure with sex. It's just not who I am. But today proved I don't have to be so scared. The only way I can explain it is..." Cass huffed. "It's like a weighted blanket, but not the comforting kind. That's how anything sex-related felt. Like it was a constant pressure on me. I understand part of it is my personality and part because of my experience with my mother and her behaviour. The two, combined, created this seemingly insurmountable thing I didn't think I could overcome. I didn't want to, if I'm honest. But then you came along and installed a shop that brought all my fears and anxieties to the surface." Harriet opened her mouth to comment, but Cass leaned over and rested her hand on Harriet's. "That's not an accusation." Cass laughed. "Well, not anymore. It's just fact. The thought of seeing something that made me so uncomfortable, every day, was awful."

"Made? As in past tense?"

Cass shrugged. "Not entirely, but after today my perspective has shifted. I felt comfortable. There were conversations that made me blush, but instead of wanting to run, I listened. And...I realised I'm not the only one. Everyone has questions and is still learning. I might be a little older than most, but then again, maybe not. What about women who come out later in life and have to navigate sapphic sex for the first time at fifty? Or people who are in new relationships trying to learn how to be intimate with a new partner?"

"Wow, Cass. That's...just wow."

Cass smiled shyly. "It's going to be a process, but I want to learn. That's why I rushed out of Ero-Tea-Ca this evening. I had a list of things I wanted to research."

"Can...can I ask what you were looking up?"

Cass nibbled on her lip. "Open the laptop."

Instead of diving in, Harriet watched Cass for a moment before slowly opening the laptop lid. The tab, still open, was about dildos—glass ones, to be specific. It was both informative and quite exciting.

"I figured I should learn about them in case I get asked a question. I thought I'd be less embarrassed if I had some facts to offer."

Harriet didn't answer at first. Instead, she kept her eyes on the screen. Cass took a sip of her tea, unease creeping in with every silent minute. Finally, Harriet looked at Cass. "I'm blown away."

"It's not that big of a deal."

"I think it is," Harriet replied, shutting the computer lid. "You've come such a long way over a really short amount of time. I mean, you've only been in the shop a day." She grinned. "I thought for sure you'd be mad as hell when I turned up tonight."

"Normally I would be." Cass just had to say it. "But you, Harriet, make me feel like I can do this. It's utterly your fault."

"My fault?"

"I can't say no to you. I wanted to hate you when you barrelled into my life. Instead, you've cracked me wide open, and for the life of me, I don't know how. Everyone knows I'm hard to get along with. Hell, it took Kendal years to get me to open up. And then you showed up, with your shiny hair and infectious positivity, and I found myself unable to say no."

"But you *did* say no," Harriet stated. "You said you didn't want to date me. Or anyone."

Cass breathed in. "Because I can't offer you what you deserve, Harriet. My quirks go beyond what most people want to put up with."

"So then why do all this?" she replied, nodding to the laptop.

"Because no matter how much I try, I can't help but want to do better...for you."

Running a hand through her hair, Harriet huffed. "You're being quite infuriating right now, Cassandra. On the one hand you're telling me we can be nothing but friends. And then you say things like that."

"I know. See? I'm a pain in the arse. A miserable pain ninety percent of the time."

"But you like me?"

Cass rolled her eyes. "Have you seen yourself?"

"I don't mean my looks, Cass."

How the hell had the conversation veered off so spectacularly? Oh, right. Cass opened her mouth. That's how. "Yes, I like you for more than your looks. I...you..."

Harriet was on her feet before Cass had a chance to formulate the rest of her sentence. She towered over Cass, causing her to rock back in her chair. "I'm going to kiss you, Cass. Is that okay?"

Where were all the words? Cass's mind was totally blank. All she could process was the tantalisingly tiny distance between her and Harriet's lips. She felt her head nod, and that was all it took. Harriet descended on her. Their lips crashed together, causing a surge of adrenaline to pump through Cass's system.

They were kissing, and it was sublime. Minutes passed as Harriet consumed Cass. She'd never been so thoroughly kissed in all her life. By the time Harriet pulled back, they were both panting. Cass still couldn't construct an eligible sentence.

Clearing her throat, Harriet stood straight and adjusted her shirt. "I'm going to leave now so you can process this. Just know, I've wanted to do that since the day we met, and I'd like to do it more. The ball's in your court, though, Cass."

Cass watched, dumbstruck, as Harriet popped on her coat, gave her a sweet kiss on the cheek, and left. Today had definitely not turned out the way Cass thought it would.

Blindly reaching for her phone, she hit speed dial.

"Cass, it's rude to ignore messages, you arse. I've been trying to get hold of you for hours."

"Kendal, I need you to come over."

"Cass, what's wrong?"

"I'm fucked. That's what's wrong."

There was some shuffling on Kendal's end. "Are you hurt?"

"No, but I'm pretty sure I'm going to be."

"Alright, enough of the riddles."

"I looked up glass dildos, bought three spicy sapphic books, and kissed Harriet."

Kendal whistled down the phone. "Christ. I'm on my way. I'll bring emergency provisions. Just stay put and don't do anything stupid."

She'd just *done* something stupid. Or magnificent. She couldn't tell yet. Either way, things had changed. Cass was on a path she swore she'd never travel. Harriet wasn't just a woman you dated. She was forever material, and Cass was terrified she wouldn't be enough to be the one to keep Harriet in the long run.

19

Harriet

Harriet was baffled. Cass's behaviour was baffling. An agonising day passed, and nothing, not one word, had been uttered about their kiss. A kiss that shook Harriet's foundations and had her running out the battery of her favourite toy when she got home that night.

Was *she* supposed to mention it? Cass didn't seem likely to. Although, Harriet surmised Cass was still processing, and after all, the ball was in her court, right?

What if Cass didn't want the ball in her court? What if she wanted to forget there was a ball at all? Crap, Harriet was spinning out. The confidence she'd valiantly summoned to give Cass what turned out to be a life-altering kiss had waned somewhere around twelve hours post-snog.

When she told Cass the ball was in her court, she kind of thought it would be a two-to-ten-hour kind of timeframe. I mean, who knew a person could share a kiss like that and then completely ignore it? Because that was what it felt like Cass was doing.

The morning after—with no communication from Cass—Harriet assumed she'd be confronted with a surly Cassandra Beaufort. She waited—yes, with bated breath, like a walking cliché—for Cass to turn up. When she did, they'd shared their usual morning greeting, all very normal and completely confusing. Cass was entirely her usual self. Not a hint of...anything!

All day, Harriet waited for the other shoe to drop, for Cass to storm out or tell Harriet the kiss had been inappropriate and there had to be boundaries because they were colleagues. She'd expected Cass to retreat to the stockroom, only to emerge when the tearoom suffered a rush.

But Cass didn't storm out *or* retreat. She happily stood side by side with Harriet, serving customers, asking questions about the different teas, and baking pastries. It was infuriating! Harriet felt like crawling out of her skin by the end of the day, especially when Cass laid a gentle hand on her arm and wished her a good night. What the bloody-chuffing-hell was that?

Of two minds whether to go to Cass's house and force a conversation, Harriet locked up Ero-Tea-Ca for the night. Her mind was buzzing, and the likelihood of sleeping tonight seemed slim.

"Hey, bestie! Miss me yet?" Nabi's voice was like a rush of warm, comforting water over her cold bones. Swirling on the spot, Harriet grabbed Nabi by the dungaree shoulder straps and pulled her in for a mammoth hug.

"I've missed you so much!"

Feeling Nabi's arms tighten, Harriet sunk further into the embrace. "So, shit's going down then?"

"I don't know what you mean." It came out a mumble as Harriet spoke into Nabi's neck.

"Yeah, okay. Want a movie and beer night?" Harriet simply nodded. She couldn't be alone with her thoughts right now. She'd end up doing something stupid, like stand outside Cass's place with a boombox and a sack of coffee beans as a sort of desperate lesbian mating dance.

With provisions bought, Nabi hopped on the back of Harriet's scooter. They were only two minutes away from a night of frozen pizza, Belgian beer, and *The Goonies*.

Nabi refrained from asking any questions until they were appropriately situated on the sofa. She had a lollipop sticking out the top of her dungaree pouch pocket, a red swizzler rammed into the back of her hair like a pencil, and a candy bracelet on her left arm.

"Nabs, do you have a wholesale card or something? Where the hell do you get all the sweets?"

Nabi nibbled on the bracelet. "My uncle has a membership at one of the stores in Leeds. Brings me loads of goodies."

"You're going to have no teeth by the time you're fifty!"

Nabi scoffed. "I'll have you know I have perfect teeth. Ask my hottie dentist. And I have the metabolism of a child. And...is this really what you want to discuss?"

"No, but I do think you need regular diabetes tests."

Waving a dismissive hand in the air, Nabi arched both eyebrows. "C'mon, spill. What's happened? Cass isn't being an arse, is she? I'll hex her if you want."

Tutting, Harriet curled her feet up, getting comfy. "No, she isn't being an arse, and you couldn't hex someone. You'd feel too guilty."

Nabi shrugged and smiled. "I could hide all her coffee, though."

Laughing, Harriet shook her head. "I don't want you to do that either. Cass has been great. She's really coming out of herself."

"And you still won't tell me what this whole swapping thing is about?"

"It's not for me to say, Nabs."

"Alright, alright. So..."

"I kissed her!" Harriet covered her rapidly heating face with her hands.

A bark of laughter ricocheted around Harriet's living room. "Go, Harriet! Was it good? Tongue or just a peck?"

Still covering her face, Harriet mumbled her answer, "Slip of tongue, and it was fantastic."

Reaching over, Nabi pulled Harriet's hands away. "Start from the beginning. I knew you fancied her, but I didn't expect this."

Sighing, Harriet recounted the whole situation from the first time she and Cass had met. The story didn't seem complete without filling in the background leading up to the kiss. There were layers and intricacies Harriet needed Nabi to understand. Kissing Cass hadn't been a spur of the moment, lust getting the better of her, thing. It had been a buildup of many, many things, sort of thing.

"But she kissed you back?" Nabi's reaction to the whole thing was predictably neutral.

"Sort of. I think she was in shock, but I definitely felt some reciprocation."

"But she hasn't said anything since?"

"Not a dickie-bird!"

Swiping the lolly from her pocket, Nabi popped it in her mouth. Several minutes passed by with only the soft sucking sound of the lolly breaking the silence.

"Okay," Nabi finally announced, causing Harriet to jump slightly. "The choice is simple: Either continue as you have today by ignoring it, or confront her."

"Geez, thanks for such wisdom," Harriet deadpanned. "It's all so clear now."

Nabi rolled her eyes. "It *is* that clear. Overthinking won't get you anywhere. Decide what you want and do it. She'll either run away, which gives you your answer, or she'll talk, which will also give you an answer."

"But what if it's awkward? We still have the rest of the week working together."

Leaning forward, Nabi smacked Harriet square on the forehead. "It's already awkward, dumbass. I should have given you a lecture about shitting where you eat, but that boat's sunk. Now you need to grow a pair and communicate. Cass doesn't come across as the world's most forthright person, so you'll have to handle that part. But you have to talk."

"Cass is *very* forthright!" Why was *that* the point she was arguing?

"No, Cass likes to complain. When it comes to intimate communications, she sucks. We both know it."

"You don't know her!"

Navi laughed. "She's not exactly difficult to read, Harriet. Plus, Kendal told me, so..."

"You've been talking to Kendal about Cass?" A sliver of anger rose in Harriet's chest. "That's not cool, Nabs."

"Whoa, dial it down, Lancelot. No need to plan a rescue mission just yet. Cass was mentioned in the grand scheme of getting to know Kendal, is all. Relax, we weren't gossiping."

Calming slightly, Harriet chugged half her glass of beer. "She confuses me. One minute I think we're thinking the same thing. The next, her walls go back up."

"Well, can you deal with that? If it's part of her character, you need to think long and hard if you can be with someone with those kinds of traits."

She shouldn't ask, but it was too tempting. "Did Kendal say anything? About Cass's predilection for moodiness?"

"No. She just said Cass was a complicated and special person. She said it would take an equally special person to be her partner."

Harriet knew about Cass's upbringing. They'd touched on Cass differing from the other kids growing up and about her introverted ways. She *was* a complicated and special woman. And yes, Harriet wanted to be the person who stood by her. She needed Cass to know she'd be there for the hard times as well as the good, if they were given the chance to become more than friends.

Finishing off the rest of her beer, Harriet turned to Nabi. "I'll talk to her tomorrow after the shop's closed."

"Cool. So, what's your choice? Sticking with her? Or bailing?"

"Sticking."

Nabi playfully punched her on the shoulder. "Knew you'd choose the right one. Keep me updated."

"Will you not tell Kendal? I'd prefer Cass to be the one to spill any beans—good or bad."

"Lips are sealed."

Ero-Tea-Ca was ready to open an hour earlier than usual. Harriet's attempt at sleep ended around half-three. Tossing and turning just wound her up further, so she'd got up and come to the shop. Nothing like paperwork to dull the mind.

Already through three pots of camomile, and half a pot of lavender tea, Harriet almost stalked the clock, anxiously counting down Cass's arrival. She had it all planned out. If Cass hadn't mentioned anything by the end of the day, Harriet would invite her somewhere public for a drink. That way, she wouldn't be tempted to kiss her again.

The back door clinking shut drew Harriet's attention. Cass was here! "Okay, nice and chill, Harriet. Nice and chill."

"Morning," Cass greeted from the open office doorway. Instead of a calm reply, Harriet squeaked—actually squeaked. What the fuck? Sheer mortification was what, especially when she noticed Cass stifling a laugh.

Clearing her throat, Harriet randomly shuffled the paperwork on her desk, which had taken her ages to organise in the first place. "Morning."

"Can I come in?"

"Sure." Gesturing to the empty seat, Harriet continued to fuck up her paperwork in the name of needing something to do with her hands. It was either that or sit on them, because as soon as she'd clapped eyes on Cass, with her hair flowing over her shoulders, Harriet wanted nothing more than to bolt out of her seat and attack Cass's face with her own. She was out of control!

"So..." Cass left the sentence hanging and Harriet on the edge of her seat. "Thank you for giving me some time."

"You're welcome." She'd done the right thing by keeping her mouth shut yesterday. She internally high-fived herself.

"Would you come over tonight for dinner? I'd like to talk properly. But not here. Or we could go to your place. Whatever. I just think we need privacy."

Harriet was already nodding. "Sure. I'm happy to come to you. My place is further away, and it doesn't have a Mr Whiskers."

The smile Cass gave her bolstered her already improving mood. They were going to talk. About the kiss. The knicker-dropping kiss. Now, the content of their impending talk could go either way, but at least Cass wasn't ignoring it or pretending it never happened. That was good.

"Okay. So, tonight?"

"Tonight."

Cass stood. "Would you like another tea?"

Shaking her head, Harriet clamped her legs shut. The mention of more liquid had her bladder shouting in protest. "No, thanks. I've already had too much."

Cass cocked her head and grinned. "Are you doing the pee dance sitting down?"

"Maybe." Harriet grimaced. "Okay, yes. I need to..." Rushing out, Harriet slammed the loo door shut, cutting off Cass's laughter. Great, she could add that to her rapidly growing list of ways she'd embarrassed herself in front of Cass. Whatever. They were going to talk. Tonight. Harriet beamed the entire time she peed.

The queue was already four people deep when Harriet made it to the front of the shop. Cass was happily taking orders and chatting. Not wanting to curb her flow, Harriet slipped in next to her and began making pots of tea.

It really was a wonderful thing to witness. Cass was flourishing in front of Harriet's eyes with every passing second. Where was the skittish sourpuss Harriet knew?

Sure, Cass still frowned when she dealt with a difficult customer, and her bluntness edged on the side of rudeness at times, but she looked lighter.

It was halfway through the afternoon and Harriet had just stepped behind the counter after eating lunch when the true magnitude of Cass's progress really hit home. A young woman waltzed in. She was extremely good looking and confident. There was an air of dominance about her that made Harriet a little weak at the knees.

Cass had finished greeting the new customer in her usual manner when the conversation clearly changed. Just out of hearing distance, Harriet saw Cass stand a little taller. Her back was stiff, but she stayed rooted in place. On the brink of stepping in, she hesitated as Cass walked the customer over to the glass dildos. She stood there talking for several minutes before picking up one of the toys. Harriet saw the slight tremor in her hands, but nothing more.

After a few more minutes, Cass placed the toy in an empty carry box, took it to the till and rang up the order. With her new purchase and a pot of peppermint tea with a side of fruitcake in hand, the woman sat herself in a window seat.

Harriet's attention immediately went to Cass, who was scribbling something in a notepad. As soon as the pen stopped writing, Cass looked over at Harriet. "I'm going to go to lunch now, if that's okay?"

"Sure." Should Harriet say something? Cass didn't give her a chance. She scooted past and headed for the staff breakroom. Taken aback, Harriet dived into work. There were shelves to fill, and cakes to replace. But no matter what she did, Harriet's mind was solely on Cass and what she'd just witnessed.

The rest of the day passed with relative ease. Ronnie came in to pay the bill for Tori's coming out party. They discussed the plans and guest list. Everything was finalised, meaning Harriet could begin baking. Cass served and waited tables. It was easy. Everything in Ero-Tea-Ca was easy, just the way Harriet had planned it.

But then closing time came around, and Harriet found herself suddenly on a cliff's edge. It felt like the outcome of tonight's discussion would lay the foundations of the rest of her life. Dramatic, but true. Cass was different. She held a sway over Harriet, which Harriet had never felt before.

Their budding relationship was delicate, but also built to last. Call it intuition, or too much herbal tea. Harriet just knew Cass was an important part of her future. The problem was communicating that to Cass without her thinking Harriet was just young and idealistic. Maybe part of her was romanticising their situation, but that was normal when you met someone who made your heart flutter, right?

Ugh, she was overthinking again.

Cass flicked the last of the lights off and opened the door, waiting for Harriet to leave the building. "Do you want to come straight over, or go home and change?"

If Harriet was sure tonight would end positively, she'd have chosen to go home, shower, and get spruced up. But she wasn't sure. And if it went badly, she'd just crawl home, eat a tub of ice cream, and fall asleep on the couch. No point doing that with a face full of makeup. "I'll just head home with you."

"Great. Let's go."

20

Cassandra

Everything was prepped and ready. It was the only reason Cass was able to remain so calm and collected all day. After leaving Harriet yesterday evening with a polite goodbye, Cass had spent the night shopping for supplies. She already knew she wanted to have a serious talk with Harriet, who had given her the time she needed to process their kiss. And process she had. After a night of discussing the situation with Kendal, Cass was ready to talk it through.

But the conversation was important, so stocking up on tea, coffee, beer, wine, and gin was a must. Plus, frozen pizza, Indian take-away from Marks & Spencer, and nibbles. Just in case Harriet wasn't super hungry. It had to be perfect.

"Come in." Cass ushered Harriet inside. Mr Whiskers ran at full speed down the hall until he was happily winding his way through their legs. Knowing Harriet would spend a little time fussing over him, Cass headed for the kitchen. "What would you like to drink?" She listed off the options and then proceeded to reel off their food options, too.

"I'll take a beer and Indian, if you're okay with that," Harriet called.

With the food in the oven and two cold beers cracked open, Cass settled on the sofa. Harriet wandered in with Mr Whiskers cradled in her arms. "He's got you twisted 'round his little paw. You know that, right?"

"Of course. But look at him. He's just so gorgeous."

They sat in comfortable silence until Mr Whiskers had his fill of human contact, leaving them alone. Well, it was now or never, Cass assumed. They were here for a reason. Might as well get on with it. The food still had twenty minutes, no point sitting in an atmosphere, waiting.

"So, shall we talk?" Cass put her beer on the coffee table and turned her entire body until she faced Harriet, who mirrored her.

"I'd like that." Harriet looked nervous.

"First of all, I should tell you that Kendal knows about the kiss. I called her after you left, because I needed someone to talk to."

Harriet nodded. "Okay. You should know I told Nabi, then."

"I figured as much. She winked at me when I saw her earlier. It was odd."

Biting her cheeks, Harriet winced. "Sorry about that. She...gets enthusiastic about things."

"It's fine." Cass shuffled in her seat so she could sit a little taller. "Okay, can I just get out what I need to say? I've been rehearsing." She wasn't supposed to admit that part, was she?

Harriet gave her a heart-stopping smile and a little flourish of her hand. "By all means. I'm all ears."

"I'm going to stand." She didn't need to announce that either, but her nerves were a little fried now they were here and getting to the nitty-gritty. "Okay. We kissed. It was a very good kiss—just fyi."

"Noted."

"As I've mentioned before, my interest wasn't in dating. The operative word being *wasn't*. Past tense. We've established I'm attracted to you, and for whatever reason, you get me to open up. I still don't understand it, but it is what it is! Now, moving forward." Cass was pacing now. It helped organise her thoughts. "I shared my worries with Kendal. She's my best friend. It's one facet of my life you'll need to be okay with if we move our friendship to the next level." She sounded like a tech support worker, but stating facts was easier to get out. "Kendal will always be in my life. We'll always love each other."

Cass paused as Harriet raised her hand. "Just wanted to say, I'm completely okay with Kendal and your relationship."

"Right. Okay." Good start. "Next thing—you already know I'm grumpy. It's something I'll try and work on, but mostly, it's just who I am."

"Noted, and happy to continue."

"Are you going to keep interrupting me?" The hands on hips were a bit much, but she supposed it proved the point she was naturally prickly.

Harriet silently zipped her lip, which was cute. "Putting aside the...issue with sex, there are other things you need to be made aware of: My quirks, mainly. I spoke to Kendal, and she told me I should just put it all out there. Let you see the real me and then you can decide if you still want to date me. That way I won't be waiting for you to figure them all out and worrying you'll have had enough and break up with me."

Harriet looked like she was bursting to speak, but instead of saying a word, she took a healthy swig of her beer.

"I don't like cuddling when I sleep. I can deal with it for the first five or ten minutes, but after, I feel restricted. And I can't sleep face to face, because inhaling another person's carbon dioxide makes me feel like I can't breathe properly. I rotate in bed, like a rotisserie chicken. So, if you're a cuddler, that's going to get irritating, because I need space. Shared showers are a big no. When I'm in the shower, it's to get clean and warm. I don't want to share. Never liked it, never will. On that note, shower sex is not what it's cracked up to be. I don't enjoy it. Speaking of...sex...I...I don't like spontaneous sex." Cass could feel her face heating.

Just say it.

"I have hypersensitivity. Which includes smell. I...I need to shower before, you know. And I need my partner to do the same. But I'm okay with doing it around the house. I don't need a bed, so there's one tick in the 'Do I want to date Cass' pro column." It was supposed to lighten the mood, but Cass wasn't sure it did the job. Harriet was sitting with a blank look on her face.

"I can't be around people eating bananas. The sound makes me want to claw my ears off. There are several sounds that make me feel the same way. Mr Whiskers licking his paws is another example. It makes me irrationally angry. I'm defensive. It's my go-to emotion, and it can take a while for me to think things through rationally. That's why I take longer than most to process things." Cass was breathing harder. Jesus, she had a lot of weird shit going on.

"Um...there are other things, but judging by your face, you're probably ready to run out the door by now. I can bag you some food if you like. And I'm okay with just staying friends. No hard feelings." Her confidence had officially left the building. What had she been *thinking*, blurting all that out? No wonder she did better on her own.

Harriet raised her hand again. "Can I speak now?"

Cass ceased pacing and stood still. Her legs wouldn't budge. "Of course." Her voice was one crack away from breaking entirely.

"Right. Let's see if I can cover everything," Harriet began. "I can deal with five to ten minutes worth of cuddling before sleep. I like to curl up on the side of the bed, so it doesn't matter if you rotate all night, and I completely agree with the whole breathing in other people's carbon dioxide. Makes me feel the same way."

Cass was still frozen but a small part of her thawed as Harriet continued to tick off her issues one by one.

"Showering is my quiet time. No desire to share or have sex in one. Been there, done that, got the injury from slipping. As for no spontaneous love making, I think there is a workaround. Anticipation can be just as passion-filled as spontaneity. There's a lot we have to learn about each other before we fall into bed. And communicating is the key. So as long as we can talk about things, I'm not worried. All your 'quirks' are what make you, you, Cass. And I like who you are. I'm excited to learn all your oddities. But don't think you're the only one. I have my fair share of things that might drive *you* nuts. We won't know unless we give it a try."

"What about eating bananas?" It was the stupidest thing she could have responded with, but Cass's brain was still in go-slow mode. She honestly never thought Harriet would still be sitting here, let alone working through everything Cass foresaw as an obstacle in their possible future relationship.

The little snort didn't go unnoticed. Harriet's eyes were full of mirth. "You'll be happy to know I dislike bananas with a passion. Their texture makes me gag. And if there are other things that make your misophonia worse, all you have to do is tell me."

Was it really that simple? Kendal had thought so. She'd practically bent Cass's ear off until Cass agreed to talk to Harriet about the list of things she worried would put Harriet off dating her. Kendal had been certain none of Cass's "quirks" would scare Harriet off. Huh, it looked like she'd been right. Crap, now she was going to have a smug ex-wife to deal with, too.

"What...what about the age gap? I know it's only eleven years."

Harriet held up her hand. "That's what the getting-to-know-you period is all about, Cass. How about we start with one date? If it's a success, we shoot for a second. None of this has to be rushed. We can go at a pace that suits us both."

Cass found herself nodding. It sounded like a reasonable plan. There was still one thing, though, she absolutely had to be clear about. "Okay. One last thing. My experience in the bedroom...is limited. Extremely...vanilla. I think that's what the kids say nowadays. I'm guessing, with your profession, you've had a lot more experience than me."

Harriet's raised eyebrows made Cass re-evaluate that last statement. Shit, had she just inadvertently suggested Harriet was a prostitute? "Not that owning a tea shop that sells sex toys makes you a slapper or anything. Not that sleeping with lots of people is wrong, if that's your thing. Oh, Jesus Fucking Christ, I'm just going to stop talking now."

In a moment of mercy, the universe deigned to offer Cass a break by setting the oven alarm off. Practically running out of the room, Cass cursed herself the entire time she served up their food.

By the time she returned to the living room, Harriet looked fit to burst. Upon seeing Cass's red face and saucer-like eyes, Harriet broke. Loud belly laughs filled Cass's room. It took a second, but suddenly, Cass felt her own laughter build. The whole situation seemed so silly.

Several gut-achingly funny moments passed before they got themselves together. Taking a swig of her beer, Cass took a deep breath. "I know I sound nuts, saying all this to you. But I can't take another rejection, Harriet."

Harriet sobered immediately. "For one, I don't think anything you've said is nuts. It's refreshing to talk like this. Getting it all out there is nice. But please don't worry too much. There is nothing I think we can't tackle, in time. And I know sex is a barrier for you. But look how far you've already come. And...well, I wouldn't find it horrible to be your teacher." It was Harriet's turn to look embarrassed now. Cass chewed the inside of her cheek. She was going to make herself bleed if she kept it up.

"You...um, you'd like to teach me? Sex things?"

The nonchalant shrug did little to clarify exactly what Harriet meant. "Only what you'd feel comfortable with. I'm just saying that your...sexual repertoire isn't fixed, Cass. If you were interested in trying new things, I'd be happy to help. When the time's right."

Well, okay then. "We could, um, talk about that later."

"Of course. Now, shall we eat? I'm starving."

Cass was hungry, but not for curry. What she wanted was to feast on the delectable woman sitting next to her. Once again, Harriet made her feel things she wasn't accustomed to feeling.

Instead of voicing any of that, Cass ate her food. She'd need another couple of days to process tonight, which she instinctively knew Harriet would understand. But this time, Cass wouldn't leave her in limbo. "So, would you like to go out with me? On a date?"

The fork which was about to enter Harriet's mouth paused. Their eyes met, and Cass fought the urge to gasp. Those eyes. They slayed her every time.

"I'd love to go on a date with you."

Cass bobbed her head. "Great. Um, I'll figure something out and let you know."

"I look forward to it."

A tinge of awkwardness settled over them. "I sold a toy today," she declared after several silent minutes.

"I saw. How did you feel? Talking to the customer?"

Cass smiled. "Nervous. But it wasn't hard after a few seconds. After all, it was just another product to sell. No different to tea or coffee, really. I mean, obviously there's a difference. You know what I mean."

Harriet snaked a hand over Cass's thigh and squeezed. "You're very cute when you get flustered." Cass scowled. "And when you scowl." Harriet laughed.

"I'm not someone who usually gets called cute."

"Well, I think you are, so be prepared to hear it more often."

Cass's scowl disappeared instantaneously, replaced by a small blush and a smile. "Thank you."

The small wink Harriet afforded her was just another chunk carved from her walls. Harriet seemed to be the antithesis to Cass's naturally crotchety disposition.

"So, do you think you'd feel confident enough to step up to a sales role? I mean, we all have to serve tea and whatnot, but if you wanted to take the lead on any gift sales, I'd be happy to step aside."

Cass mulled it over. "I think I will. Now I've read up on the toys, and I know the background of the artist who paints the teapots, I think I could do it. There's still a bit to catch up on where all the tea is concerned."

"Don't worry too much. The price tags have short descriptions on them. Enough for you to know if the tea is for relaxation, or stress, etcetera. Don't forget I've been studying and learning about tea for years. Plus, you'll only be in the shop a few more days."

Cass's heart sunk a little at the thought of leaving. But she did miss being surrounded by coffee. "I'd like to be up to snuff for the coming out party, though. That could be a real money maker."

Harriet nodded through a mouthful of korma. "Absolutely. Be aware that it could get a little...rowdy? I don't know if that's the right word. I just mean, there may be more open discussions than you've experienced so far."

Cass figured. She likened it to a Hen Do, or something. There would be crass language and dirty jokes. She couldn't say it would be easy, but she'd do her best to stick it out. "I'm looking forward to it. And...well, with you there, it will be easier."

Harriet reached for Cass's hand. "I'll be there every step of the way."

"I believe you." And she did, which was terrifying but wonderful.

21

Harriet

The new three-tiered cake and sandwich stands were superb. Harriet placed the last one on the only unfinished table. The rest of Ero-Tea-Ca was decked out, ready for Tori's coming out party, which was due to start in ten minutes, meaning the first guests were imminent. Nabi buzzed around, adjusting teacups, cutlery, and napkins.

"I think we're ready," she announced.

Harriet looked around. Yeah, they were ready. "Okay. I'll make sure Cass is okay in the kitchen."

There'd been no more kisses, but things had changed. Cass found every opportunity to touch Harriet. Just little touches. A brush of hands, or a graze of fingertips as she passed by. It was like the slowest, sweetest foreplay Harriet had ever experienced, and she was convinced Cass had no idea what she was doing to her.

"How's my kitchen wench?"

Cass whirled 'round with her signature scowl. "I am *not* a wench! And everything's fine. We have extra sandwiches in the fridge. An emergency flask of coffee for those who have a better sense of taste, and several boxes of the new cake stands."

"I'll bypass the whole coffee thing and stick to the new cake stands. Do you like them?"

Cass blushed slightly but nodded. "They're beautifully painted. The...the scenes are interesting."

Raine, the artist who painted Ero-Tea-Ca's teapots and cups, came up with the idea a few days ago. Harriet and Nabi pounced on the idea, especially when Raine wanted to paint food play scenes on each tier.

"Any particular part of them grab your attention?" Challenging Cass's comfort level was a delicate game. She didn't want to go too far, but Cass definitely seemed open to more and Harriet wanted to encourage that.

Leaning against the kitchen worktop, she waited as Cass fiddled with a plate of sandwiches. It was all about patience. Cass would talk when she was ready. It's not like waiting was a hardship. Harriet got to gawk at Cass's fabulous backside while she did.

"I...uh, quite like the, um...whipped cream depiction."

Interesting. "I see. I'm rather partial to strawberries, so..."

Cass's eyes sparkled ever so slightly. Harriet's breath came a little faster as she watched Cass's subtle reactions to their conversation: The small flush that wasn't embarrassment, the widening of her pupils, and the glint in her eye. Harriet was witnessing a rather turned-on Cass, and she had to admit it was a powerful sight.

Clearing her throat, Cass began gathering up the leftover plated sandwiches. "They go together well."

If Harriet hadn't been listening so intensely, she would've missed Cass's reply. But she didn't and filed that little titbit away for later.

"Tori and Ronnie are here," Nabi shouted through the kitchen door. "And Ronnie has gone all out!" Snapping back into work mode, Harriet left Cass with a small smile and a brush of fingertips against her lower back. She loved the frisson of electricity their proximity conjured.

Ronnie had, indeed, gone all out. She looked like an extra off a Pride float. But she was beaming with happiness, and Tori clearly found her grandmother's outfit entertaining.

"The place looks great!" Ronnie pulled Harriet, and then Nabi, into a tight hug.

"It really does," Tori added. "Thank you so much." Watching her grandmother shuffle off to inspect the nearest table, Tori leaned in and dropped her voice, "I know it's a bit silly to have a coming out party at my age...but it's really lovely."

Nabi shook her head. "Nothing silly about it. You *should* celebrate."

"She's right. Embrace it. And I love that Ero-Tea-Ca gets to play a part."

"Well, I couldn't think of a better place. Having a place like this is a godsend."

Harriet's face warmed with pride. "So, has Ronnie set you up yet?"

Tori laughed. "She's relentless. I've told her I'm not in a rush to date. It's been a journey getting to this point, you know?" Harriet and Nabi understood. No matter what the age, coming to terms with that part of yourself *was* a journey, some more turbulent than others.

"Who has Ronnie deemed good enough for her favourite grandkid then?" Nabi asked, unwrapping a lolly.

Tori sighed. "Seems the old bird isn't picky. I think she's shifted her goals now. Instead of being content with me coming out before she 'kicks the bucket' as she so eloquently puts it, now I think she wants me married and settled. I mean, those are some lofty goals."

The three of them stood laughing. Ronnie absolutely would move the goalposts. Poor Tori. "She's ambitious, all right." Harriet laughed.

"Oh, who's that?" Tori's eyes strayed over Harriet's shoulder. There was only one person it could be. Turning to look, Harriet subconsciously licked her lips as she watched Cass pour hot water in the pre-prepared teapots.

"That's Cass. She owns the café next door," Nabi supplied. "She's helping for a few days."

"Wow, she's gorgeous," Tori replied quietly. The look of lust was plain to see, and Harriet didn't like it one bit. "Is she...on our team?"

Harriet chuckled, masking her discomfort. "She is."

"And is she single?"

Hmm, how to answer that? Maybe she shouldn't. It wasn't Harriet's place to make that statement and she guessed Cass wouldn't appreciate someone answering personal questions like that on her behalf. "You'd have to ask her." Nabi's side-eye didn't go amiss.

Tori smoothed down her strappy top. Harriet could admit she was a lovely-looking woman, and closer to Cass's age. That gave her pause.

"Well, wish me luck," Tori said with a wink. Hang on, was she going over to hit on Cass? Harriet suddenly felt panicked. Didn't Tori *just* say she wasn't ready to date?

Nabi and Harriet pivoted, following Tori's advance. They watched her lean casually over the counter. Harriet watched Cass look up. She waited as they exchanged a few words. Cass's gaze met her own with furrowed eyebrows.

Tori continued to talk until Cass shook her head, and with a confused look, pointed at Harriet. What was she saying? Harriet didn't have to wait long. Cass rounded the serving area and, with Tori, walked over to her.

"Why didn't you tell me?" Tori laughed. Harriet didn't know what she was supposed to say.

"We are dating, aren't we?" Cass asked simultaneously, stealing Harriet's remaining breath. She looked between the two women. Tori chuckled and winked.

"I should get back to my party and my grandmother who has invited as many single lesbians as possible. It was lovely to meet you, Cass. I'll stop in The Beanery sometime."

"Okay." Cass hadn't taken her eyes off Harriet.

"I'll just..." Nabi didn't finish her sentence.

"I thought you wanted to go on a date?" Cass asked as soon as they were alone. Harriet steered them to the corner.

"I do. We are."

"Well, I'm confused then. Tori said she'd asked you if I was single."

"Um...aren't you?"

"Not to date. Not if we're going out?"

"Oh."

"Wait," Cass shot, holding up a hand. "Are you dating other people?"

"No!" Harriet rushed to answer. "Only you. When we finally go out."

Cass studied her face. "Okay. Do you *want* to date other people at the same time as me? It's fine if that's what you want. Um...I just don't think I can do that."

Harriet's body answered before her mouth. Stepping forward, she placed a delicate kiss on Cass's lips. "No, I don't want that."

Cass's shoulders dropped from around her ears. "O-okay, then."

"I just didn't know if you were okay with people knowing about us?"

That earned another set of crinkled eyebrows. "Why wouldn't I be? We're not children, Harriet." Wow, Harriet sure felt like one in that moment—a scolded child, at that. "Sorry, that came out harsher than I meant it to."

"That's okay. I'm just trying to go at your speed, Cass. I don't know what your boundaries are yet."

"How about you find out? Tonight."

"Tonight? As in our first date?"

Cass nodded. "Yes. Why not?"

"Why not, indeed." Harriet couldn't stop the smile from forming, or the excitement from building. All she had to do was get through the party and then she'd be on a date with Cass.

A date!

Tori's party was a smashing success. Not only did everyone have a wonderful time, but Harriet sold ten glass dildos and five gift sets, not to mention the three bespoke cake stand requests. Cass seemed to have enjoyed herself too. She'd effortlessly slipped into hostess mode, looking like she was a permanent fixture of Ero-Tea-Ca's workforce. It was nice.

But now the party was over and the clean-up was done. Harriet had finished putting away the last cake stand in the back when she heard Cass calling her name. Wandering through to the tearoom, Harriet froze. Standing by the most central table was Cass. There was a candle softly dancing on the table, two glasses of wine, and a plate of leftover party sandwiches.

"I didn't have time to plan our first date properly. And I wanted us to be alone, if that's okay. So...um, this is what I came up with. Do you mind, or would you prefer to go to a restaurant or pub? Whatever you want."

Harriet was getting tired of losing her ability to talk. But Cass just had this way of robbing her of cognitive thought when she did things that were sweet and surprisingly vulnerable. "It's perfect."

Looking away, Cass tried to hide her relief, but Harriet saw it. Had she been *that* worried Harriet wouldn't love what she'd done? Was that because other women had scoffed at her efforts? There was still so much to learn.

Rounding the table, Cass pulled out a chair. "Sit, please."

Taking a seat, Harriet took a closer look at the table and wanted to laugh. As well as the sandwiches, there was a small bowl of strawberries and cream. "Huh, I don't remember having those in the fridge."

With a casual shrug, Cass placed a sandwich on her plate. "They came from my fridge next door. I wanted you to have something you liked."

Harriet let out a chuckle that sounded more like a whimper. "You make it quite hard to go slow, Cassandra Beaufort."

"Do I?" she answered with false innocence.

"Mmm. You do. I think I've underestimated you."

"People tend to do that when they pigeonhole me." There was a hint of frustration in Cass's voice.

"Well, I've certainly learned my lesson."

They each took a sip of their drink. "Are you sure this is okay?"

"Cass." Harriet waited until they were looking into each other's eyes. "It's perfect."

"I...um, I was thinking."

"About what?"

"About what you said...or more like offered." The air seemed to grow heady, and Harriet wasn't sure why. What had she offered? "When you offered to be my...teacher."

With uncertainty on the tip of her tongue, clarity suddenly slammed into Harriet's chest. Cass wanted Harriet to teach her. In the bedroom. Oh, wow.

"So I fully understand...you mean—"

"Sex," Cass barked rather aggressively. "Shit, sorry. I didn't mean to..." Cass's eyes closed as she took a fortifying breath. "Yes. I meant sex. I'd like for us to explore...a little."

Twirling the wineglass between her fingers, Harriet let Cass's words sink in. She'd love nothing more than to be a sexual sherpa to Cass, but a seed of insecurity sprouted low in her belly. "Cass..." Shit, how did she ask this without sounding offensive?

"Please just ask," Cass said softly.

"I need to know I'm more than just a means to an end."

Cass cocked her head. "What do you mean?"

Sighing, Harriet placed both hands on the table to steady her. "I mean, I need to know I'm not being used to help you advance your sexual experience and that's it. I mean, I want to help you. But is that all I am?"

Fuck. Cass's hurt and clear offence rippled across every inch of her body. "You think I'd do that?" Her voice was tight, as if it would crack any second.

Well, wasn't this going fantastically? "I...no, I don't, but I had to verbalise it, okay?"

Throwing back the entire glass of wine, Cass looked at the tablecloth for an uncomfortably long time. When Harriet saw her eyes swimming with unshed tears, she cracked. "Shit, I'm sorry, Cass."

Holding up a hand, Cass swiped at her eyes. "No, it's fine. Maybe this wasn't such a good idea."

No, no, no. This couldn't be the end. Harriet had to fix it. Pushing back her chair, she rounded the table and dropped to her knees in front of Cass. "No, please don't say that. I'm sorry."

"I'd never use someone like that," Cass whispered through a tight throat.

Grabbing her hand, Harriet moved until Cass had to look at her. "There. That's one of my quirks," she began. "I voice my unfounded worries, even when they hurt other people. I don't mean to. I didn't mean to upset you. I'm sorry."

"Okay. It's okay. I guess I can understand where you're coming from. I mean, all we seem to do is worry about my stupid insecurities and anxieties."

"They're not stupid." Harriet tried to argue, but Cass carried on.

"But I promise you, Harriet, I'd never do that to you. I couldn't. I simply couldn't let myself be with someone like that if I didn't feel a connection. I certainly couldn't explore things that make me want to curl up in a ball and hide."

Cupping Cass's face, Harriet drew her down into a deep kiss. She needed to transmit her regret at her careless words, and also the need for Cass's closeness. Above all, she wanted Cass to know that she, too, felt their connection.

Being with Cass was nothing like any relationship Harriet had ever known. It required her to be thoughtful of so many things. Cass was barbs and razor blades on the outside, but stuffed full of vulnerability and emotion on the inside. That was how she knew Cass was worth it, though. Harriet wanted to tackle the hard parts. She wanted to be the special person Cass deserved.

The kiss transformed from a statement to a declaration. Harriet wanted Cass, badly. She'd happily strip her in the middle of the shop and show her all the ways Harriet could make her scream. As she went to pull back—because the realistic part of her brain had kicked in—she was surprised that Cass kept her in place by wrapping a strong hand around her neck.

Their tongues glided against each other, exploring. A pressure built in Harriet's centre. She was already pulsing.

Just from a kiss, Cass rendered her a quivering wreck. Happy to follow Cass's lead, she groaned as Cass pulled her up, guiding her to straddle the chair.

Harriet was lost in Cass's heat, a heat that projected Cass's need with startling clarity. Had she really come so far in her journey already, she was about to take Harriet in the middle of Ero-Tea-Ca? It would be the sweetest irony if this is where they made love for the first time.

Instead of following *that* train of thought, Harriet surrendered to Cass's kisses and wandering hands.

22

Cassandra

She felt Harriet everywhere. Not in the physical sense—although Harriet's body was pressed delightfully close. No, Cass felt Harriet's energy wash through her as their kiss heated. An urgency took over as Cass curled her hands around Harriet's back, feeling taut muscles. A shared moan echoed through the empty tearoom as Cass sucked on Harriet's tongue.

"Come home with me." The words left her mouth with as much passion as their kiss. Cass couldn't explain the reason Harriet made her feel like this, so...unlike herself. And right now, she didn't care. There'd be time to analyse and overthink, but now wasn't it. Now, Cass needed to get Harriet home and in bed.

Harriet disentangled herself from Cass's arms and stood up. With tousled hair and swollen lips, she looked down at Cass with unbridled lust. "Let's go." Two words that sent Cass's head spinning. They were doing this—stepping over the line they'd been straddling for days.

Grabbing her purse and coat, Cass followed silently behind Harriet as she switched off the lights and locked the door. Now the spell had been temporarily interrupted by their relocation, Cass's brain was catching up. She didn't want to think about things. For once, all she wanted to do was go with the flow. But as they walked towards Cass's house, the little voice that so often derailed things piped up.

How sexy would it be when Cass asked Harriet to shower first? It wouldn't. Surely this...thing they were feeling would shatter into awkwardness. It happened every time. And even if Harriet managed to get over *that* blundering mess, how would she feel when Cass inevitably lacked the diversity and knowledge Harriet was no doubt accustomed to? Cass was going to humiliate herself.

"Stay with me, Cass." Cass felt a hand slip into hers and tug her forward. They'd made it to Cass's house in record time. Harriet led the way, almost running the last few metres. She whirled around, pinning Cass with those deliciously salacious eyes. "Keys."

Cass handed over her keys with a shaking hand. Harriet took them without comment. This was it. Where Cass would ruin things by asking—

"Bathroom," Harriet stated, pulling Cass along. When they arrived outside Cass's en suite, Harriet pulled her back in for a toe-curling kiss. Cass was not in charge of this *at all*. She was barely functioning, too caught up in shock. "Shower. When you're done, I want you on the bed. Preferably naked, but I'll leave that up to you."

She felt Harriet turn her body by the shoulders. It was only when she stumbled through the bathroom door that she finally became cognisant of what had just happened. Harriet had taken away any possibility of Cass's need to clean-up from turning into anything resembling awkward. If anything, she'd made the situation more fraught with delectable tension.

Discarding her clothes at an accelerated rate, Cass jumped in the shower, washing off the day's grime. Her mind was reeling, and her body was aching. Was this really about to happen? The nagging thoughts surrounding Cass's upcoming performance skated on the edge of her mind as she rinsed off the soapsuds and stepped out of the cubicle.

"Don't ruin this before it's even begun," she whispered to herself. Wrapping the towel around her body, Cass entered her bedroom and immediately forgot her own name. Standing at the foot of the bed in all her naked glory was Harriet.

Stepping forward, Harriet brought her lips to Cass's ear. "On the bed." Stepping aside, Harriet waited for Cass to move. It took a second for her legs to cooperate, but eventually Cass moved. Turning, she watched Harriet eye her from head to foot. The slow lick of her lip nearly had Cass moaning out loud.

"I'll be five minutes. Feel free to start without me."

Did she mean she wanted Cass to...touch herself? Mutual masturbation was one thing. Having a person watch her go solo without participating was new. Biting her lip, Cass listened as the water started. Harriet was in her shower. Naked and wet. That was all the imagery she needed to throw caution to the wind and drop her towel.

Climbing on the bed, she settled against the headboard. Her heart was through the roof, but not entirely due to nerves. A large percentage was the fear of the unknown. Regardless of her general insecurities, the first time sleeping with a new partner was always a little nerve-wracking. All the unknowns to contend with.

Shaking her head in a bid to clear her mind, Cass closed her eyes and concentrated on the sound of the water. Her mind swam with visions of Harriet soaping up. She witnessed Harriet's hands gliding over her soft skin, dipping between her legs.

Oh, wow.

Cass was so lost in her imaginary world and the feelings she stoked with her own hands securely between her legs, she didn't hear the bathroom door open. It was only when a low moan emanated from its general direction, her eyes snapped open. Harriet was still naked and still looking at her as if she were a meal. Only now, Harriet's hand was rubbing slow circles around her left nipple. "You are gorgeous. Please don't stop."

Swallowing hard, Cass re-engaged her fingers. Soft touches around her clit before dipping into her wetness had her gritting her teeth, willing her body to slow down. Cass's eyes never left Harriet. Not when the first signs of an orgasm approaching built in her abdomen, or when Harriet dropped her other hand between her own legs. It was only when the breath-stealing climax finally rocketed through her clit that Cass had to succumb and close her eyes.

She heard her own loud groan carry through the room. Then Harriet's gasping cry of delight. Blood pumped through her ears as her chest rose and fell rapidly. Her lungs needed more air than she could inhale. "Oh, God," she panted.

"That...was so bloody hot, Cass!"

Peeling her eyes open, Cass cast her gaze back to Harriet, who was bent at the waist, hands on knees. "Are you okay?"

Holding up her index finger, Harriet nodded. "That sucker ripped right through me. Wow."

A smile formed. Had the sight of Cass masturbating really done that? Made Harriet fold over in wonder? There was something wholly satisfying about it, even though Cass would've preferred her fingers had been the ones to do the touching. Maybe next time.

Realising she was still exposed to the room, Cass closed her legs. What now? Usually, Cass was a one and done, but the sight and sound of Harriet coming kept the fire burning. Her clit was already responding to the pressure of her closed thighs.

"Can I get on the bed with you?" Harriet was vertical again and standing at the foot of the bed. Nodding, Cass bit her lip as she watched Harriet crawl towards her. Jesus Christ, she was gorgeous, sexy, and way out of Cass's league.

When Harriet arrived at Cass's side, she languidly trailed a finger up Cass's stomach, causing her muscles to clench. "Can I straddle you again? I really liked it earlier."

"Y-yes. Please."

God, could she be more pathetic? Shouldn't Cass be the one taking the lead? After all, she was the older one. The books she'd read usually portrayed the older MC as the debonair, confident, take-charge sort of person. Shouldn't that be Cass in this particular situation?

"Come back to me, Cass."

Zoning out in the middle of sex was also pathetic, so Cass was doing really swell so far. She rolled her eyes. Harriet giggled. "Did you just roll your eyes at me or yourself?"

"Myself."

"Do you want to talk about it?"

"Not one bit."

Studying her for a beat longer, Harriet shrugged. "Okay. Then I'll do what I wanted to do in the tearoom."

What Harriet had wanted to do in the tearoom was grind her wet centre into Cass's, apparently. Grasping her hips, Cass helped deepen the roll. Her mouth was in reaching distance of two very pink and erect nipples.

Forging past her usual indecision, Cass leaned forward and sucked in one of those teasingly perfect breasts. Harriet gasped before burying both hands in Cass's hair and holding her to her chest, encouraging Cass to suck harder.

They settled into a rhythm that left both women clawing at each other. Cass had never gotten worked up a second time around so quickly. But the feel of Harriet's pleasure coating her lower torso was exquisite. She still couldn't wrap her head around the fact that *she* was the one getting Harriet so excited.

As they continued to build up to what was bound to be another soul-shattering orgasm, Cass took a chance—one that left her red-faced, even at the idea. But call it intuition, or blind faith, Cass just knew if she ran her finger just over—

"Oh, fuck, yes," Harriet shouted the second Cass's middle finger ran over her puckered entrance.

Feeling more confident, Cass let go of Harriet's nipple with a pop. Her finger continued its soft assault on the rear as she captured Harriet's lips in a devastating kiss.

The smell of sex permeated her senses, but she was too lost in the moment to care. Her hypersensitivity had latched on to Harriet's butter-soft skin, and for once, Cass was happy for it.

With Harriet practically squirming, Cass had to wrap her free hand around the base of her neck to keep the rhythm from slipping. Sensing Harriet needed more, Cass relied on her instincts, planted both hands on Harriet's hips and flipped her over, pinning Harriet's back to the mattress. Without pausing, she settled between her legs and slipped two fingers inside. She began pumping, hard and deep, relishing in Harriet's cries of pleasure. Adding a third finger, Cass curled the tips, brushing Harriet's G-spot. The curse words which flew out of Harriet's mouth were obscene, but all they did was drive Cass to work harder. She felt the walls clamp and the rush of liquid seep through her fingers. She braced herself as Harriet's body vibrated and shook. All she could do was watch in wonder as Harriet arched her back and screamed into the night.

Slowing her movements, Cass laid gentle kisses on Harriet's chest as she panted and gasped for breath. Eventually, she pulled out and sat back on her haunches. Looking down on a wrecked Harriet Kirkwell was possibly the best view in the world and Cass needed to savour every second, because, quite frankly, she couldn't quite believe what she'd achieved.

Never in all her sexual history had she felt so...powerful. Like she was finally the person she'd always hoped to be: A normal person who wasn't hung up on sex, and just a regular woman who knew how to satisfy a partner without all the worrying. Cass moved so she was lying at Harriet's side.

"I think I'm dead." Rolling over to her stomach, Harriet turned her head and eyed Cass. "You killed me."

"Was...was it okay? Um, did you enjoy it?"

She could have done without Harriet laughing. It didn't instil confidence, even though she was pretty sure she'd done a good job.

"Was it okay?" Harriet chuckled. "Cass, you just liquified my lady garden!"

Of course, Cass blushed fire engine red. "Well, that's...good."

Harriet buried her head in the duvet and continued to laugh. Cass sat with a shy smile on her face, her eyes poring over every contour of Harriet's body. When she no longer heard laughter, Cass leaned over to see if Harriet had fallen asleep.

The contented sigh didn't really help. Was that a sleeping sigh, or a just-taking-a-minute-to-bask sigh? Unsure what to do, Cass laid down so her body was flush with Harriet's. If she was asleep, Cass had no problems snuggling up. Sure, her vagina still ached, and she might have to sort that out before she could sleep, but as long as she was there, next to Harriet, it didn't matter.

"I've not forgotten about you." Harriet's voice was muffled, as she still had her face planted in the bedcovers. Cass was starting to grow concerned about her air intake. Slowly, Harriet turned her head. With flushed cheeks and glassy eyes, she looked adorably...fucked.

"You can sleep if you want."

"Oh, no. I'm just getting my second wind. There are still a lot of things I want to do to you. If you're comfortable."

Cass let her hand stroke long gentle paths up and down Harriet's exposed back. "I'm comfortable with you."

Rolling to her side, Harriet placed a hand on Cass's hip. "Is there anything you don't like?"

"I...uh, wouldn't like you doing what I did to you, if you know what I mean."

Harriet's eye flashed with mirth. "Got it. The back door is permanently closed."

Cass wrinkled her nose at the analogy, which only caused Harriet to titter. "Something like that."

"Do you like penetration?"

"Yes."

"And oral?"

Bloody hell, Cass had never had so many questions fired her way when naked. "Very much so."

The smile Harriet conjured was blinding. "Oh, good, because all I want to do right now is taste you."

"Oh."

"Is that okay?"

Wetting her lips, Cass nodded. She couldn't remember the last time she'd had a woman taste her. "I like circles. Is that okay to say?"

Pushing gently on Cass's shoulder, Harriet slipped on top. "It is more than okay to say. I want to know what gets you off, Cass. I find it very sexy when a woman knows what she wants and isn't afraid to ask for it. Never be worried about that, okay?"

"Okay. Should...should I have asked about doing what I did?" It occurred to Cass that maybe they should have had this discussion before getting naked.

"No, don't worry. There isn't much I don't like, but thank you for checking in. Boundaries are important, and continued consent is a must. If there is anything you want to happen, or more importantly, not happen, just talk to me, and I'll promise to do the same."

Clasping Harriet's bum cheeks, Cass leaned up and kissed those plump lips. "Deal. Right now, I'd really like to feel your mouth on me."

"Jesus, you're so hot," Harriet groaned, already sliding down her body.

Cass wanted to return the compliment, but she was a little too distracted by the sight of Harriet going down on her to form words. Her fingers fisted the in sheets the second Harriet's tongue made contact. She felt every millimetre as it slid slowly through her folds. The noise that fell from Cass's mouth was less a groan and more a whimper of unintelligible gibberish.

No longer able to keep her eyes open, Cass let her head fall back. Every part of her body was attuned to Harriet's movements. Her nerves were firing on all cylinders as she fell into sexual bliss. Harriet was taking her apart with each lick and suck.

"Inside," she pleaded.

Harriet grunted something, sending vibrations through her clit. Before Cass could ask if everything was okay, two fingers entered her and immediately curled.

"Don't come yet," Harriet commanded. She must have felt the strong clench of Cass's muscles as soon as she entered her. It was pure bliss.

Cass's hips bucked off the bed, but Harriet held her down, never letting up the pace in which she pounded into Cass. It was hard, but not painful. Just the right amount of roughness to make Cass plead to whatever deity was looking down on her, because if Harriet didn't let her come soon, she was going to get really upset. "Harriet," she growled.

"I'll tell you when to let go, Cass. Just a little longer."

Only seconds passed, but it felt so much longer as Cass's orgasm rounded on her. "Harriet, I can't..."

"Now." Harriet clamped onto Cass's clit and added a third finger, sending Cass into the rafters. The scream that tore itself from Cass's throat was animalistic, but it was all she could do to stop herself from shattering altogether.

23

Harriet

L apping up the last of Cass's pleasure, Harriet almost purred in happiness. She'd waited so long to get her mouth on the woman, and it was as spectacular as she'd hoped. Cass was soft as silk, with a small patch of neatly groomed dark hair nestled between her legs. Harriet rubbed her nose through it for the millionth time. God, she could live down here and die a happy woman.

Cass was still crooning with every delicate touch of her tongue, and it was perfect. She was so responsive...and wet! They'd definitely need to change the sheets. But Harriet planned to have her wicked way with Cass a few more times, so no point interrupting their fun with laundry just yet.

Their entire time together this evening had been divine and a little surprising, if Harriet were honest. She'd thought Cass would be shy...timid even. Harriet had every intention of leading their first time together, but Cass had taken control in the most delightful way. Actually, she shouldn't have been that surprised. Cass liked to keep her guessing. And, boy, was she happy about *that*!

Cass may still have a way to go until she felt truly confident in herself, but tonight had certainly gone a long way towards helping. Harriet hoped it had, in any case, because there was no reason for Cass to be anything but smug. She'd unravelled Harriet masterfully. Twice. And hopefully she'd do some more unravelling as the night wore on.

"Mmm." Cass's hips dropped to the bed and inched away from Harriet's tongue. "Sensitive."

Squeezing Cass's bum and licking her clit one last time, Harriet made her way up Cass's phenomenal body, one open-mouthed kiss at a time. She tasted of sex and sweat. Delicious.

She couldn't help but linger for a moment on Cass's breasts. They were just a little more than a handful and heavy. Utter perfection. Cass's nipples were a shade darker than Harriet's and a little larger. She studied the hard peaks before giving each one a gentle kiss and suck. Cass drew in a ragged breath. Happy with the response, Harriet settled between damp thighs and stroked Cass's hair from her face.

"You taste delicious." There was so much more to say, but all in good time. Harriet needed to digest this sudden change in their relationship before admitting how she truly felt, which, by all appearances, was ga-ga over Cass. Her heart gave a sudden thump as she looked down into Cass's eyes. She was falling fast and hard. There was no doubt about it: Cassandra Beaufort wielded a power over Harriet she wasn't entirely sure she could, or wanted to, fight.

Bringing both hands to Harriet's face, Cass smiled. "Kiss me."

The kiss was slow and indulgent. Harriet savoured every second as their tongues slid together, filling each other's mouths. When the kiss came to a natural end, Harriet laid her head on Cass's chest and listened to her heartbeat.

"I'm not too heavy, am I?" Her voice was laden with exhaustion. The rhythmic thud in her ear was like a lullaby.

Cass responded by curling both arms around Harriet's back, holding her tighter. "It's getting late."

Ah. Harriet stiffened. Their moment came to a stuttering halt. Was that Cass's way of asking her to leave? They hadn't discussed sleeping over. Hell, they hadn't discussed sleeping *together*, but here they were, post-sex, and in Harriet's case, unsure of what to do next.

Deciding to act like an adult and not a sulking teen, Harriet shuffled off Cass. With a smile that didn't quite reach her eyes—even though she tried—she began searching the floor for her clothes. "I'll just..." Pointing to the bathroom, Harriet made to leave until Cass grabbed her arm, looking confused.

"Are you leaving?"

Oh, okay. Maybe she'd got it wrong. "Well, I didn't want to assume, and you said it was getting late."

"Because it is getting late, I need to feed Mr Whiskers."

Her shoulders dropped in relief. "So, that wasn't a subtle way of getting me to leave?"

Cass sat up, wrapping the bedsheet around her. "Since when am I subtle?" Fair. "If I wanted you to leave, Harriet, I would ask you to."

Running a hand through her hair, Harriet laughed. "Okay. So, I take it you don't want me to leave?"

"No! Unless you do. You're free to do as you please."

Oh, here was Cass's snarky side. Harriet recognised it as a defence mechanism. Cass was feeling vulnerable and getting pissy to cover it up. Dropping her clothes, she sauntered back to the bed and promptly straddled Cass again. "Then I won't go. I'd love nothing more than to wake up with you...assuming breakfast is included." She added a little wink, hoping to lighten the somewhat tense mood.

The lines between Cass's eyes smoothed as she relaxed, pulling Harriet closer. "I can do breakfast."

"Good. Now, before we go for the next round, maybe we should feed your other pussy first."

"Oh, for God's sake," Cass grumbled. Harriet's shoulders shook. It was a little pleasurable getting Cass riled up. "But yes, Mr Whiskers *does* need feeding. Considering we didn't finish our sandwiches, would you also like something to eat?"

"Whatever you're having," Harriet murmured. She was too busy slowly rocking her hips to fully engage. Cass was like an industrial magnet, pulling her back for more. The second their bodies touched, her clit begged for friction. And who was she to deny herself such pleasure?

"I'm not going anywhere if you do that," Cass groaned, sinking her fingers into Harriet's thighs.

On the verge of answering, a loud cry from a rather disgruntled cat echoed through the door. Dropping her forehead to Cass's, Harriet laughed. "Go. Feed Mr Whiskers and then hurry back."

Watching Cass scramble out of bed naked, Harriet licked her lips. God, she wanted to do naughty things to that woman. Smiling, she laid back and closed her eyes, reliving their time together so far. It had been a great first date.

Sunlight danced across Harriet's closed eyes, rousing her from sleep. Sitting up, she arched her back, throwing her arms in the air to deepen the stretch. Everything felt wonderful until she realised she'd clearly fallen asleep before Cass returned from feeding Mr Whiskers last night.

Crap!

Turning her head, she noted the empty space. Running a hand over the mattress, she surmised Cass had been awake for a while, considering there was no residual heat left. How could she have fallen asleep? Well, several explosive orgasms would be the answer. Her body ached and she felt sticky between her legs. Yeah, it had been one hell of a night.

Listening intently, Harriet worried her lip. There was a strong chance Cass's barriers would be back up this morning. They'd shared something intense but unforeseen last night, and Harriet wouldn't be surprised if Cass retreated to process it all.

Mid thought, Harriet's attention was snagged by the bedroom door creaking open.

"Oh, you're awake. Damn." Cass looked adorably put out.

"I can pretend to be asleep if you want to go out and come back in." Seeing Cass, hair messy and wearing yoga pants and a light T-shirt, made Harriet happier than it should have.

Cass rolled her eyes. "No need. I just wanted to bring you breakfast in bed and wake you with a kiss. Never mind. Next time."

Cass said it so matter-of-factly, Harriet couldn't help but chuckle. But along with amusement, Harriet felt relief. Cass wanted there to be a next time, and by all accounts, she wasn't freaking out or pulling away.

Setting the tray on the bedside table, Cass sat next to Harriet. Her hand travelled the length of her leg, sending ripples of electricity through her extremities. "I hope you like muesli because it's all I have. I made you some tea as well, but it's nothing fancy. Just Tetley. Did you know they've put the bloody prices up again?"

Completely swept away by Cass's rambling, Harriet pulled her in and kissed her thoroughly. They melted together until they both became breathless.

"I love muesli."

Cass's eyes remained firmly on her lips as she answered, "Good. Well, eat up."

Halfway through her breakfast, Harriet had to ask the question which plagued her since waking up. "Are you okay? I mean, after last night. Are you feeling good?" Ugh, she wasn't asking it right, but her tongue felt tied.

Placing her spoon in her bowl, Cass turned. "You're wondering if I'm freaking out, right?"

Shrugging, Harriet braced for the answer. Cass took both their bowls and set them on her bedside table before reaching over and lacing her fingers with Harriet's.

"Normally, I would be," Cass began, "but like I said, you do something to me, Harriet. I'm not myself when you're close to me. Maybe I should be panicking or feel embarrassed, but all I feel is bliss. Is that okay to say?"

"It's perfect. I feel the same. Last night was everything. The best first date I've ever had."

Cass pulled away and covered her head with her hands. "Oh, God, I ravished you like a horny teenager on our first date. How improper."

Curling her lips, Harriet stopped herself from laughing. Cass was too much sometimes. "I know. I mean, shouldn't we have waited until we're married? For propriety's sake? We're ladies after all."

She expected the playful bat and Cass's best scowl. What she didn't expect was to be tackled to the bed and tickled.

"You enjoy mocking me, don't you?" Cass growled into her neck, which ceased all amusement immediately and set Harriet on fire.

"I don't know what you mean." Harriet's voice dropped an octave and grew breathier as Cass skittered her lips across Harriet's neck.

"Mmm, likely story." Cass sounded just as worked up as she did. Pushing Cass to a sitting position, Harriet stood from the bed. "I'm going to shower."

Cass's eyes widened. Harriet wanted to ask why she looked so surprised, but felt it was more prudent to get washed so they could get dirty again as quickly as possible.

"Cass. Hey, Cass, there's someone at your door."

Harriet huffed out a laugh as Cass mumbled something before turning her head away. Peeling herself out of bed, Harriet hunted for something to wear. Cass's silk robe would do. All she had to do was get rid of whoever was pounding on the door and then she could slip back into a peaceful sleep. Maybe she'd get a cuddle in first. It wasn't as if Cass would wake up. The woman would sleep through the Apocalypse.

Tying the belt securely, Harriet ripped open the door, ready to tell whoever it was to bugger off. Her mouth snapped shut as her eyes connected with Kendal.

"Hey, hi. Hello."

Smooth.

Kendal's eyes sparkled and creased in amusement. "Harriet. Hello, what a pleasant surprise."

"Indeed. A lovely surprise."

It was not.

"Is my wayward business partner around?"

Harriet cast her eyes to the stairs. Kendal's light laugh made her chuckle too.

"She's asleep, and for the life of me I can't get her to wake up." She opened the door further and waited for Kendal to come inside. It was okay. She could get through this with minimal embarrassment. Not that there was anything to be embarrassed about. It was just a tad awkward standing in nothing but a silk robe with your lover's ex-wife. They entered the living room and sat down.

Nodding through her amusement, Kendal held up her index finger, cleared her throat, and bellowed, "Lolita, oh my God, what are you doing here?"

There was a crash, then several curses, before a half-dressed Cass came bounding down the stairs before skidding to a halt.

"My hip didn't hurt," she babbled, still half asleep.

Kendal smiled widely as Harriet covered her mouth with a hand.

It took Cass several seconds to come around, and she was not amused. "There's a place in hell for people like you."

Kendal scoffed. "So dramatic."

"What do you want, Kendal?"

"Oh, got our grouchy knickers on today. Okay." Harriet was losing the battle not to titter. "I wanted to go over next week's schedule. You're back on tomorrow, right?"

"Yes." Cass stood with her arms crossed, eyebrows furrowed. "Is there a problem?"

"I'm taking a long weekend. Shauna's booked a spa."

Rubbing sleep from her eyes, Cass wandered over to the sofa and sat next to Harriet, who was trying to make herself invisible. She had no idea how Cass wanted to handle their situation with her ex-wife.

"Okay. I'm sure we'll be fine." Cass looked from Kendal to Harriet. "Morning," she whispered. The softest kiss Harriet ever had, landed on her lips, lighting her up from the inside. She couldn't help but cast a glance at Kendal, who smiled brightly.

"It's afternoon," her ex-wife clarified.

Cass placed a second kiss on Harriet before turning back to Kendal. "Huh. Time flies when you're having...fun, I guess."

Was that a wink? Did Cass just make an almost naughty joke?

"I'm happy for you both."

Cass went red. Harriet beamed and placed a hand on Cass's leg. "I'm happy too. Would you like some tea or coffee?"

"No, no," Kendal said, standing. "I'll leave you to it. See you tomorrow, Cass."

Harriet stayed seated until Cass came back from seeing Kendal out. "Are you okay?"

"Yes, why wouldn't I be?"

"Well, because your ex just turned up to your house where your new...um, girlfriend? Answered the door in your robe."

It was Cass who did the straddling this time, causing Harriet's breath to hitch. "I'm perfect. And you don't need to add a question mark to the girlfriend part of your sentence. I want that. And you also need to stop worrying about me. If there is a problem, Harriet, I will come out and say it. I know I can be hard to read sometimes, but I promise, I won't play games. I'm thrilled this is happening. Unless you want to keep it quiet, I'd like everyone to know."

Leaning forward, Harriet placed a kiss on the end of Cass's nose. "Would you come to Ero-Tea-Ca with me tomorrow night? I'm having a few friends over for a book club meeting. We decided to start one ourselves after offering out the teashop to others."

Cass was silent. Her eyes scanning Harriet's features. "Do they know I was horrible to you when we met?"

"Yes. But they also know you apologised. They're good people and they mean the world to me. I'd very much like you to meet them."

"O-okay. But...well, what if they don't like me? What if the age thing is a problem, or they think I'm too miserable for you? I'd completely understand, but—"

"Hey. Stop. Cass, they'll love you. And...well, I think it would help you feel more comfortable if you met them. They're an eclectic bunch. Some are outgoing and loud. But others are introverted and quiet. I want you to see it's okay to be who you are. There will be no judgement. Ero-Tea-Ca is a safe place, full of safe people."

Cass huffed and sat back. "I don't want our relationship to be all about me and my issues, Harriet."

"And it won't be. But right now, you need this. Look how far you've come already. I just want you to feel at ease, but if I'm pushing, I'll back off."

"Can I think about it?"

Harriet nodded immediately. "Of course. Now, can we get back to the kissing and fondling?"

Cocking her eyebrow, Cass smiled. "There was fondling?"

"Well, there will be."

24

Cassandra

"Cassandra. It's good to see you again. How are things?"

Cass got herself comfortable in the chair. "Better. I wanted to ask your advice on something."

Dr Herman smiled. "That's not how this works."

Waving a dismissive hand, Cass forged on. "No, I understand. I've come to a decision, and I'd just like you to tell me if it's a healthy choice."

"Okay, I'll bite. What's the decision?"

"I plan to talk to my mum. As in, *really* talk."

Dr Herman placed her pen down. "Before I give you my opinion, I'd like you to unpack your reason for wanting to talk to her. In the past you've said your relationship with your mum makes it difficult to communicate effectively. Has that changed?"

Shaking her head, Cass replied, "Not at all, and that's why I think we need to sit down and talk. Nothing will change if we keep going the way we are."

"I agree. But you still haven't told me where this is coming from."

Taking a deep breath, Cass tried her best to answer fully. The truth was, since Harriet had asked Cass two months ago to meet her friends for her book club, Cass had been in her head. She'd thought about it, but eventually declined to meet them. Harriet had been understanding, but it left Cass feeling hollow. As far as she'd come with regard to sex and her comfort level with the subject, the truth of the matter was Cass triggered easily.

And, as sure as Harriet was that her friends wouldn't judge, Cass couldn't promise she wouldn't react to the smallest of innuendos or coarse language. The last thing she wanted to do was put Harriet in an awkward position.

Within those two months, they'd had several more dates and slept with each other multiple times. In fact, they spent nearly every free minute they had wrapped up in each other. Cass visited Ero-Tea-Ca daily and felt comfortable, especially with the customers she'd befriended when working there for the week. With Harriet, things were easy. But Cass couldn't expect Harriet to wait around forever before taking the next step of meeting each other's loved ones. So, Cass had to get a grip on the thing stopping her from moving forward.

"Remember the teashop which opened next door?"

"The erotic teashop, yes. As I recall you were staunchly against it."

Cass's face heated. "Yes, well...I'm dating the owner."

"That's certainly unexpected."

Cass smiled. "Harriet was unexpected."

"I can see that."

"She's like no one I've ever met. I tried to resist the attraction at first. Also, I'd acted badly towards her, so that didn't help." Dr Herman gave her a knowing smile. "But we got to know each other, and I found myself opening up to her. About...things."

"You felt comfortable talking to Harriet about sex, and your mother?"

"Yes. And so, I ended up working in the teashop for a week. A sort of immersion therapy."

"And how did that go?"

"Well, it wasn't as bad as I thought, and Harriet was amazingly patient. She's just amazing altogether, really."

"She's certainly made an impression if that smile is anything to go by."

Cass couldn't argue with that. "She made me want to...help myself. I know on some level I'll always be a little awkward and reserved, but I know I can grow where certain things are concerned. I have grown. I've shown myself to her completely. I mean, my quirks," Cass quickly clarified.

"That was a big thing to do."

"Kendal helped. I've met her new partner, by the way."

Dr Herman's eyebrows raised. "You have been busy. But let's table that for a moment. You've opened up to Harriet, and things are going well?"

"Better than I could have hoped for. She's so thoughtful, but I don't want our relationship to always come back to my problems."

"Alright. Has something specific happened to make you feel this way?"

"Harriet asked me to meet her friends. They were having a book club meetup in the tearoom."

"And you didn't want to?"

"I did. I'll admit I was nervous because they all know I'd been a bit of a bitch in the beginning. But that wasn't what stopped me."

"So, what did?"

"My mother." Cass scrubbed her face. "It all comes back to her. Memories of embarrassing moments. How loud and over the top she was about sex, and how all I wanted to do was hide away. As soon as Harriet asked me to go to Ero-Tea-Ca, I instantly panicked. What if her friends started making jokes that triggered me? Because that's what happens. I know now, my reaction to things is a trauma response. That's right, isn't it?"

This was where Cass needed Dr Herman to help her out. "It is. You respond with either aggression, in the form of caustic words, or you run away."

"So, to that end, I figured an honest conversation with my mother might help pave the way to moving on."

"And how do you see it going? What are your expectations?"

Sighing, Cass crossed one leg over the other. "Nothing erases our past. I don't want to, because as much as this has been an issue for me, my mum did a great job. She loved me unconditionally. We just don't understand certain parts of each other. I'd like to explain some of my parts to her without reacting first. I think that's why we're not very good at communication. I've always been *reactive* to her. I'd like to try something different."

"I think that's a healthy view."

"So, I should talk to her?"

"You've already made the decision, Cassandra. You know what's right for you. I think it would be wise to pick up our sessions again, on a regular basis. You still have triggers I believe we can work through. Pairing that with the conversation you plan to have with Lolita, and with Harriet's support, I think we can make a real difference. You're working hard and I'd like to help."

"O-okay. I'd like that. Thank you, Dr Herman."

"No thanks needed. As I said, you're doing the hard work. Now, shall we address Kendal and her new partner?"

Cass wrinkled her nose. "I sort of did the opposite of what you suggested."

A knowing smirk formed on the good doctor's face. "You ran right over and asked Kendal if she was seeing someone new?"

"Something like that," Cass mumbled. "But we were able to talk it through."

"And you met her?"

"Shauna. Yes. Kendal invited me over for dinner. I asked Harriet to go along."

"When was this?"

Squinting her eyes, Cass tried to pinpoint the exact date. So much had happened lately, it was hard to keep track. "A few months ago. Before Harriet and I started dating."

"So even then you trusted Harriet to support you?"

"Yes. Like I said, she just gets me."

"And how did the meeting go?"

With a forced laugh, Cass admitted she'd been a bit of an arse. "But Harriet called me out on it, and I ended up having an enjoyable time. Shauna thinks the world of Kendal. They seem happy."

"I sense a little melancholy, Cassandra."

"Only because it's truly the end of an era. Obviously, Kendal will remain in my heart forever. Apart from Harriet, she's the only lover I've had that took the time to know me. To accept me. But now I know we weren't meant for more than deep friendship. How could we be when she's so happy with Shauna?"

"And you're happy with Harriet?" Dr Herman finished.

With a shrug, Cass nodded. "It's still early for us. And, as shown today, I have plenty to work on still. But for once I think I might have landed on my feet. Sure, there's still the odd time I expect Harriet to walk away, grow tired of my silly habits, but she hasn't so far."

Dr Herman sat forward. "It's important you recognise that, Cassandra. If you're always waiting for her to bolt, *you* are the one with one foot out the door to begin with. You'll never fully trust the partnership."

"I agree. I'm doing my best to talk to her. It's difficult at times. My first instinct is to retreat, but with Harriet, a bigger part of me wants to stay and work it out."

"That's wonderful to hear. Really. I can only see you progressing if you maintain this attitude. But remember, trauma takes time. There is no set deadline. There will be days when you feel on top of the world and then suddenly, you'll be triggered. It's important to understand that. You'll feel like you've taken a step back, but that simply won't be true."

"I just wish I'd done this sooner."

"Everything in its own time, Cassandra. The important thing is you're addressing it now."

"Should I meet Harriet's friends? Am I being too cautious?"

"Not necessarily. Only you know if you're ready. But as you've said, you trust Harriet. Lay out your fears and worse-case scenarios. She'll help you through it. Maybe even offer a perspective you can't see."

Cass could do that. Like with her mum, a deeper conversation needed to happen. "Okay. I'll do that."

"Let's set up another session for next week. I'd like once a week for the next couple of months. You're on a roll, Cassandra, and I want to strike while the iron's hot."

With the next three appointments secured, Cass strolled through the park. She was expected at The Beanery in fifteen minutes, giving her enough time to call her mum. Usually she was sent to voicemail due to Lolita's lack of service as she travelled, but not today. "Cass, my love! It's so wonderful to hear from you."

"Hi, Mum. Um...I was wondering when you planned to visit next?" It could be tomorrow or six months from now, and Cass didn't want to wait in limbo.

"Well. I'm still in the area, actually. Remember Henry?"

"The guy you met when you visited."

"That's him. Well...we're engaged."

Cass had to physically stop herself from barking down the phone by biting her knuckles. "Engaged?" she managed to grit out.

"I know, I know. It's really quick." That was a bloody understatement. "But he's the one, Cass."

Now, Lolita Beaufort might have had a man at every port over the years, but she'd never once declared being in love. This was new. "Right. Okay."

"Would you meet him?"

It wasn't the way the conversation was supposed to be going, but Cass rolled with it. "Of course. But I'd like to talk first. Just me and you. Is that okay?"

"Sure, honey. Is tomorrow too soon?"

Not soon enough! "Tomorrow's perfect. Bye, Mum."

Letting out a long, slow stream of air, Cass slumped against the nearest tree. What a morning. Shaking away her emotional fatigue, she started towards the café. Before entering, though, she detoured to Ero-Tea-Ca. There was only one person she wanted to share her morning with, and that was the blonde beauty serving behind the counter.

Harriet lit up as soon as she saw Cass. "Hey, I didn't think I'd get to see you until later."

"I just wanted to see you."

"Well, that's sweet. Hang on." Harriet whispered in Nabi's ear and then ushered Cass into the back, where she promptly pushed her up against the wall and devoured her mouth.

Cass couldn't get enough of Harriet like this. So open and wanting. But they were in a place of business and Cass's responsible side kicked in before she plunged a hand down her girlfriend's pants.

"We can't do that here," she panted.

Harriet pulled back, her lips swollen. "I know. Sorry." The grin and mischievous flash in her eyes said she wasn't sorry in the least.

"Will you come over tonight?"

"If you want. I can bring dinner."

Cass licked Harriet's bottom lip because...she could, and it was *right* there. "Can we talk?" Timing wasn't Cass's strong suit. Harriet reared back with panic in her eyes. "It's about my mum," Cass blurted.

"Is she okay?" At least Harriet didn't look on the verge of an anxiety attack anymore.

"She's getting married!"

"Oh. Um...what?"

Cass laughed. After hours of talking, Harriet knew all about Lolita and her man-eating ways. "Yeah, that was pretty much my reaction. Anyway, can we talk about it tonight? I need to get to the café now. Kendal will tan my arse if I'm late again, especially if she sees me coming out from your shop. She tends to start making kissy faces." Cass screwed up her face. Kendal was really annoying sometimes.

With a bark of laughter, Harriet gripped Cass's cheeks. "She knows what we get up to on your visits, methinks. And of course we can talk tonight."

With one last kiss—okay, three more kisses—Cass left for work. As predicted, Kendal spotted her exiting Ero-Tea-Ca and instantly began mocking her. "You've got lipstick on your mouth."

Cass stupidly wiped her lips, even though Harriet didn't have lipstick on today. "You're a child," she grumbled, walking past Kendal to deposit her bag in the back.

Wiping the counter, Kendal shrugged. "Maybe, but I find it highly entertaining."

They worked side by side for a solid half an hour as an unexpected rush descended on the café. After Gordon, the last one in line, was served, Cass had time for an espresso. She and Gordon chatted about the price of tea bags, which validated Cass's ire at the supermarket, because he, too, was suitably miffed. Kendal just rolled her eyes and changed the subject.

The afternoon passed with no fanfare. It had been just a steady day. It was only when they were upturning chairs and wiping down for the night that Cass approached Kendal regarding her session with Dr Herman. She felt she owed her ex-wife an apology. "Hey, Ken. Can we talk?"

"Sure thing." Patting the barstool next to her, Cass waited for Kendal to get comfy. "Everything alright?"

Cass took Kendal's hand and held it between hers. "I wanted to say I'm sorry."

"What on earth for?"

"For not sorting myself out sooner. I'm back with Herman."

Kendal shuffled in her seat until they were facing each other. "Is this a good or bad development?"

"It's good. Really good. But I'm now realising I should have done it years ago. Maybe then you wouldn't have had to put up with so much."

"Cass, you make it sound like you were a monster, which you weren't. We had a good marriage. A great friendship."

"We did," Cass agreed. "But you deserved more."

Kendal furrowed her brows. "Cass, I didn't lack for anything."

"Maybe not. And I know there's no point wishing for do-overs. I wouldn't even if I could, because I think we're both where we're supposed to be. *With* the people we're supposed to be with."

"That's true. You're my best friend, Cass. Always. But Shauna...she's my person. Is that awful to hear?"

Maybe a few months ago it would have been, but all Cass could think about was how that statement rang true for her and Harriet. "No. I...shit. I think Harriet's my person. It's far too early to be thinking like that. But I feel it here." Cass laid a hand over her heart.

"She's turned you into a big softy." Kendal laughed, causing Cass to scowl playfully.

"Poppycock."

"Hey. It's a good thing, Cass. If Harriet's the one who has inspired this growth, I would wholeheartedly agree she's your person. As for us, I need you to stop putting blame on yourself. Let it go, sweetie."

Bringing Kendal's hand up to her lips, Cass laid a delicate kiss on her knuckles. "I will. I'll let it go. And, for what it's worth, I think Shauna's great. I'm thrilled for you."

"Thank you. It means a lot. Now, stop being a coward and tell Harriet how you really feel. That woman is bonkers about you. Whether it's weeks or years, if you love her, tell her."

The L word made Cass's mouth dry up. Not because she didn't feel it. But because it was such a big thing to declare. And until Cass could walk into Ero-Tea-Ca and meet Harriet's friends and family without a shred of self-doubt, she just couldn't voice that word. Harriet deserved her to be the best she could be. And that wasn't Cass right now. No, she just had to work a little longer and harder and then she'd tell Harriet exactly how she felt.

25

Harriet

Harriet couldn't understand what she was witnessing. Why was Cass holding Kendal's hand? Scrap that. Why the hell was Cass *kissing* her hand?

Shaking her head, Harriet refused to jump to conclusions, any more than she already had. There was no reason to feel insecure about Cass and Kendal. Cass had always been upfront about her and Kendal's friendship. No need to make a mountain out of a molehill. As she finished banishing thoughts that would only lead to hurt, she caught Cass's eye.

Cass gave her a heart-stopping smile before giving Kendal a quick peck on the cheek and hopping off the barstool.

Opening the door, Cass pulled Harriet inside. "Hey, I just need to grab my coat and I'll be ready to leave." If Cass caught any of Harriet's minor concern, she didn't let on. Instead, she leaned in and kissed her lips, immediately settling Harriet's nerves.

Hurrying off to the back room, Cass left Harriet standing with Kendal. For the first time since meeting the woman, Harriet felt uncomfortable, and she didn't like it. Being jealous wasn't in her nature, and she certainly didn't want to start now.

"Thank you," Kendal said suddenly, breaking the silence.

Meeting Kendal's eye, Harriet gave a questioning smile. "What for?"

"For being who she deserves." Harriet opened her mouth, but nothing came out. "She adores you."

"I adore her too."

"I know." Kendal winked before giving Harriet's hand a gentle squeeze.

"Okay, I'm ready. Will you be okay locking up, Ken?" Cass was fighting to get her coat on as she spoke. Harriet laughed, trying to help her untangle an arm.

"Shauna will be here in a moment, so no worries. Have a good night."

Grabbing Harriet's hand, Cass dragged them outside. The air was frigid, but it meant Cass held Harriet close, so she wasn't going to complain.

"Did you have a good afternoon?" Cass asked. Harriet was in two minds whether to bring up the scene she witnessed between Cass and Kendal.

"Not bad. We had a couple of rowdy guys come in." It wasn't the first and wouldn't be the last time she had people visit Ero-Tea-Ca with the sole purpose of making a menace of themselves. Young men particularly enjoyed it, showing their immaturity to the world.

"Pepper spray. Shove that in their faces and they'll not come back." Cass's concern and penchant for violent solutions warmed her more than the arm around her shoulders.

"I can't go 'round assaulting people, Cass." Harriet laughed.

"Shame. It would make working with the public a lot nicer."

Shaking her head, Harriet leaned into Cass. "How you run a successful business that *relies* on public opinion and patronage is beyond me."

"The coffee's good. Simple as that. I suppose Kendal being nice helps, too. If it were left to me, I'd have Gordon and that's about it." Cass's eyes sparkled with mirth.

"At least you can recognise that about yourself."

Cass grinned. "It's less about recognising that about myself and more about regularly being told I'm a miserable sod." They laughed as they walked. The knot in Harriet's stomach unfurled a little.

"Hey, so you and Kendal looked serious when I turned up. Everything okay?"

Cass let out a deep breath. "Yeah. I went to my therapist today and worked through some stuff. I felt I owed Kendal an apology."

"Right. Um...do you want to talk about it?"

"I do. But can we get home first? My feet are killing me, and I want to be curled up on the sofa with you for that conversation."

"Of course. Although we need to make a pit stop because I didn't order any food."

"Fish and chips?"

"Deal."

Content with their evening plans, Harriet marvelled at how different Cass was from when they'd first met. There was the casual mention of going *home* together, and her willingness to talk about things Harriet knew she found difficult. Is that why Kendal thanked her? Because Cass was coming out of her shell?

Whatever the reason, Harriet was happy—genuinely happy. The only thing still causing a slight pang of worry was Cass's refusal to meet her friends. Two months after the initial invite to their friends-only book club, and Cass hadn't yet mentioned being ready to attend.

A surge of guilt swarmed Harriet's mind. Cass was working so hard on herself, and here Harriet was getting upset because Cass needed a bit more time before meeting her people. Jesus, could she be more selfish? Cass was constantly stepping out of her comfort zone. Surely, the least Harriet could do was be a supportive girlfriend.

"That's a serious face. Everything okay?"

"Just eager to get in the warm," Harriet lied. If anyone was failing to do their bit in this relationship, it was Harriet. She'd asked Cass to communicate with her, and yet she was the one finding it hard to say what was on her mind. Maybe a little self-reflection was in order.

They wandered to Cass's house in companionable silence. As per usual, Mr Whiskers stole the limelight as soon as they stepped through the door. Cass set about her nightly routine, leaving Harriet to snuggle the cat.

After a plate of greasy fish and chips and a glass of wine, Harriet was in heaven. She was so relaxed it took a second to register Cass's shift in mood.

"Can we talk now?"

Peering from under half-closed eyelids, Harriet saw Cass's nervous demeanour. Sitting up and tucking her legs under, she prepared herself. "Sure."

"First thing—my mother is getting married."

"It's sudden," Harriet commented.

"It is. I plan to talk to her about it tomorrow. I suppose if she's happy, I should support her, right?"

Harriet weighed her answer. "I'd wait and see what's said tomorrow. If you get the feeling something isn't right, I wouldn't blindly support it without raising your concerns. But you know your mum. Maybe go on gut feeling?"

Cass looked to be mulling over Harriet's opinion. "Mmm, you're right. But actually, the reason I ended up talking to Mum in the first place was because of what I spoke to Dr Herman about. Um...can I tell you?"

Scooting forward, Harriet hooked two fingers under Cass's chin. "You can tell me anything."

Cass proceeded to tell Harriet about her session. There was a lot to take in, and Harriet had to stop herself from interrupting several times, but eventually Cass sagged back into the couch, finished talking, looking at Harriet for a reaction.

"I think it's great you're going to talk to Lolita. If I haven't said it recently, I'm very proud of you, Cass."

Her blush was adorable, so Harriet had to kiss her soundly. It was like a girlfriend law or something. If not, it should be. Adorable Cass should always get kisses.

"As for meeting my friends. I'm glad you brought that up. I have a small confession." Cass furrowed her brows. Harriet ploughed on. "I was starting to worry. Selfishly, I might add. I was getting impatient that you didn't want to meet them, and I'm sorry. It's a big deal, and I shouldn't have just sprung it on you like that."

Cass shook her head. "You didn't. You asked, and I answered. And for the record, I *do* want to meet them. But like I just explained, I'm so worried I'll make an arse of myself or embarrass you."

"You couldn't embarrass me, Cass."

A humourless laugh burst from Cass's mouth. "Oh, yes, I could. I wouldn't do it on purpose, I can promise that. But like Herman said, my reflex when triggered is to either lash out or run. If I did that in front of your friends, it would absolutely embarrass you and I'd be mortified."

"Okay. So, we wait. We're in a good place, right?"

"Very." Cass leaned in and kissed her. "We're only a few months in, and yet I feel so settled with you, Harriet. Is that okay to admit? Tell me if it's too forward, or too soon."

"It's more than okay to admit. So, let's not rock the boat until you feel more confident."

Harriet's eyes fluttered as Cass traced her jawline with a light finger. "The thing is, honey, it could take years to work through my triggers. I can't put our relationship on hold like that. So...maybe you could, um, talk to your friends. The ones you want me to meet? Tell them a little about my...issues?"

Searching Cass's face, Harriet saw vulnerability, but also a resolve she hadn't seen before. Cass was taking massive steps, and Harriet knew they were partly for her, and for their relationship. Sourpuss Cass was the most loving and warm person she'd ever met, and Harriet was completely in love with her.

Wow!

The words were on the tip of her tongue, but instead of saying those three words, Harriet chickened out. Instead, she asked, "Are you sure?"

"Yes. At least then, if I have a setback, they won't think I'm a raving lunatic."

Harriet laughed. "You might think *they're* all raving lunatics!"

"Maybe." Cass smiled. "As long as I get their blessing, that's all I care about."

"Oh, sweetie. You don't need their blessing. I love my friends and family, but they don't get a say in my relationships. Ever."

"But it would be nice if we all got along, right?"

"Well, yes—"

"So, I want to make a good impression. I've already got some ground to make up after ratting you out to the council for smoking pot."

"We weren't actually smoking pot, so really you just made yourself look a bit of a tit doing that." Harriet smirked. She jerked her body away from Cass's tickling fingers.

"No need to rub it in," Cass replied playfully.

A buzz from Harriet's bag interrupted their banter. Pecking Cass on the nose, she grabbed her phone and read the incoming message. "Crap!"

"What's wrong?"

With a dramatic flair Kevin would be proud of, Harriet flung her head back and stared at the ceiling, letting out a loud huff. "It's Diane's birthday next week and she wants a family meal to celebrate."

"Okay. And you don't want to go?"

"I had a bit of a falling out with my parents," she admitted.

"When? Why didn't you tell me?"

Good question. "I didn't want to burden you with it, I suppose."

Cass sighed. "But that's not how partnerships work. I'm here for you. Well, I want to be if you let me."

Settling further into Cass's side, Harriet breathed her in. "You're completely right. I'll do better. This thing with my parents is tiring. It was nice to concentrate on something good in my life, especially when I finally won you over and got you to admit how great Ero-Tea-Ca is."

Cass scoffed. "I've said no such thing."

"Mmm hmm. I promise I'll do better."

"It's not about doing better. It's about you trusting me with that part of yourself. That's all I want."

"I do, Cass. It's scary how much I trust you—trust us. Maybe that's partly the reason for being secretive with this whole parental blowup. Once you're involved in all my family drama, there's no going back. It's a big step. Although, I've already started planning our future together in my head!"

Oh, she didn't mean to say that out loud. Or maybe she did. Cass was right. She'd put her faith in Harriet. A lot of faith. It was time Harriet returned it. Her parents weren't easy, but they were a part of her life. She wanted Cass to know her, entirely, messy relationships and all.

Cass's arms held her tighter. "What have you been planning?" There was an edge of wonder laced in her words. Harriet looked up into inquisitive eyes.

Shifting nervously, Harriet drew in a breath. "I've thought about us living together. Getting another cat to keep Mr Whiskers company. Going on holiday. If you'd ever consider getting married again...and kids. There, happy?" She wasn't sure why she felt raw, but she did, and it made her agitated.

Leaning forward, Cass grinned. "Hey, I'm the only one in this relationship who gets to be snarky. You're the sunshine to my clouds."

"I wasn't being snarky," Harriet shot back. She'd just left her heart out there for the world, aka, Cass, to see, and she was getting mocked for being a bit on edge. Charming.

"You've really thought about all that?"

Harriet melted into Cass's body the second her arms pulled her in. She felt Cass's breath ghost across her forehead and the warmth of her lips kissing her gently.

"Yes. I have."

"I want to come with you to Diane's birthday meal if that's okay?"

Pulling back, Harriet met Cass's eyes. "You do? But my parents will be there and it's going to be awful."

"Exactly why I want to be there with you. And why I want to meet your friends. Let's say the week after next? You're having another book club, right?"

Pushing back until Cass was at arm's length, Harriet stared until her eyes felt too dry. "Cass, are you sure?"

"I am." Cass pulled her back in. "On the condition that you talk to me, Harriet. Please. No more keeping secrets or worrying how I'll react. If all those fantasies are to come true, we have to be a team."

Swallowing, Harriet breathed in Cass's scent. Did that mean Cass wanted what she did? "So...we can talk about living together in the future? And marriage?"

"We can talk about anything you want. Talking doesn't mean we have to rush into anything. But I like the idea of us planning our future. It makes me feel safe."

"Oh, Cass." Harriet needed the talking to stop and the lovemaking to start. She wanted to show Cass just how safe she was in Harriet's care. "I need you in bed, Cass. Now!"

26

Cassandra

Cass couldn't stop her knee from bobbing up and down. In hindsight, the third espresso was probably a bad idea. Unfortunately, she'd gotten around two hours sleep. Partly because Harriet debauched her for hours, and partly because, after the fun was over, Cass couldn't shut off her mind.

Having an in-depth conversation with her mother might be good for their long-term relationship, but it was doing a number on her short-term nerves. She'd wracked her brains all night, to no avail, trying to come up with an opening statement.

So here she was, waiting for her mum, with nervous energy making itself known in the way of awkward bodily movements. How she wished Harriet were sitting next to her. She'd offered to come along, but there was no way Cass would wrangle her mum in if she met Harriet in an official *you're my daughter's girlfriend* capacity.

"Cass, love," she heard Lolita call from the other side of the pond. With a small wave, she took in her mum race-walking towards her with a smile lighting up her face.

"Hi, Mum, you look good," Cass said as soon as Lolita was within a suitable hearing distance. No need to screech from across the park.

Walking into Lolita's arms, Cass took a second to calm herself. This time around, she wouldn't get irritated or run away. Cass was determined to have a healthy discussion, once and for all.

"You look wonderful yourself, love!"

Smiling shyly, Cass tugged gently on her mum's sleeve to set them off walking. Motion was necessary to ward off a panic attack. If they sat down, Cass's nerves would build to an explosive level.

"So, I know you want to talk about Henry," Cass began. "I do, too. But could we chat about something…that's sort of difficult for me to talk about?"

Lolita was smiling at a small puppy stumbling over its ball. "'Course, love. Chat away."

Reining in a frustrated sigh, Cass navigated them away from the adorable dogs. She needed her mum's undivided attention. "Mum, this is serious."

Thankfully sensing Cass's tone, Lolita turned to her and gave a nod. "I'm listening, sweetheart."

Oh, boy. She had to say it now. There was no backing out. But how the hell does a person say what Cass needed to say without it sounding as if she were blaming her life's issues on the one person who'd always been there for her? As best she could, anyway.

"I've been seeing a therapist." Good place to start, right?

Lolita pulled them to a stop. "Oh?"

Biting her lip, Cass took a steadying breath. "Yeah, um...ah, this is really hard to say!"

"Cass, baby, just say it. I'll listen with an open mind."

"We don't always communicate well, Mum. I think that's a fair assessment, right?"

Lolita tipped her head from side to side. "I guess."

Cass forged on. "I know I'm quick to react. Usually negatively."

"You've always had a short temper." Lolita laughed.

"Because I've felt embarrassed, Mum," Cass shot. Closing her eyes, she chastised herself for snapping. "Growing up, I didn't fit in. I'm reserved. Kids took that as an excuse to bully me."

"I know you had a few problems, but was it that bad?"

"Yes, Mum, it was. And...God, I don't know how to say this without upsetting you..."

"Cassandra, please just say whatever you need to say."

Peering at her feet, Cass summoned the words. "You made it worse, Mum. I know you didn't mean to. I don't even think you realised how your behaviour affected me, but it did. Enduring all the comments from kids and adults about you being...*loose*—not my words, may I add. Everything just ended up being about you and your men. Plus, you weren't shy about telling me about them. Or about sex in general. And I know you didn't cross any boundaries, as such, but it all made me so uncomfortable, Mum. To the point where anything to do with sex had me recoiling. It's been...hard."

Well, she'd officially word vomited, and her mum looked on the verge of tears. Shit!

"I..."

"I'm sorry, Mum. Maybe I could have put it better. Shit, I just wanted to be honest with you. I'm working hard to get over some stuff, and believe me, it's not all because of you and our relationship—"

"But most of it is?" Lolita's voice wobbled with emotion. "I traumatised my kid and sent her into therapy!"

"Oh, Mum." Cass hugged Lolita fiercely. "Please don't cry." This was the first time in many years they'd properly embraced. Cass closed her eyes, feeling the sting of tears. "I pushed you away. Instead of opening up to you, and working it out years ago, I pushed you away."

It took several minutes, but eventually, Lolita dried her tears. "I was so young when I had you, Cass. I thought I could carry on being me, even with a kid. I wanted us to be friends. I thought treating you that way would make us closer, because, Lord knows, I didn't know how to be a single mum."

"You did. You gave me everything. I...I just didn't turn out like you. Outgoing, I mean. I'm introverted, and I struggle with social situations. They drain me."

"And all I did was push you to be like me, without figuring out you couldn't."

"I'm really not here to place blame." Cass gripped Lolita's shoulders. "I want us to be closer. And to do that, we need to know each other better. I also don't want you to change. I love you how you are, I just need..."

"For me to understand you."

"I *want* you to understand me."

Letting her mum guide her to the nearest bench, Cass sat down, never letting go of her mum's hand. "Remember Harriet?"

"The owner of Ero-Tea-Ca?"

Cass nodded. "Well...we're dating. And it's serious." Lolita's face immediately brightened, and Cass saw the moment she went to ask something, but stopped herself. "She's younger than me, and eternally positive, which was irritating to begin with."

"She was lovely when I met her briefly."

"I realised I wanted to change some of my ways when we started seeing each other. Now, she knows I'm never going to be Ms Sunshine, or one hundred percent comfortable with certain things, but that's okay. Because I know she likes me, for me."

Lolita cupped Cass's face. "I couldn't wish for anything more for you, honey." She sighed. "I think I knew, deep down, my dating history had an effect on your romantic views. I worried that was why you and Kendal split up."

"No, we wanted different things."

"You never told me the reason."

"I wanted kids and she didn't. I'm sorry I didn't confide in you more."

"Why would you if you didn't feel comfortable? But I need that to change, Cass. You're my only daughter. Of course I want to know you. The good, bad, and the ugly."

"Same. So, where do we go from here?"

Blowing out a breath, Lolita took a second to gaze over the park. "One day at a time? I think we'll need more than one conversation, and maybe...maybe I could attend therapy? If that would help?"

"You'd come to therapy with me?"

"Cassandra, I'd do anything for you! Maybe I could learn something about myself, too."

"I love you, Mum."

"My sweet Cass. I love you too."

Feeling lighter than she could ever imagine, Cass hugged Lolita again. They were on the road to recovery, and Cass hadn't known how badly she needed that to happen.

Pulling away, Cass swiped a rogue tear. "Do you want to tell me about Henry?"

"He's wonderful, Cass. Kind, gentle, and a fantastic lo— He's perfect for me."

"And you're sure you want to marry him? He's not after your money or anything?"

Lolita snorted. "Cass, he's loaded! If anything, *his* kids should be asking that, not you."

"So, he has kids?"

Cass settled in and listened to Lolita gush over her new love. It was a side Cass had never seen before, and she decided love suited her mother well.

"You'll meet him, then?"

"Of course I will. Is he here?" Cass cast a look around the park.

"He's waiting in the car."

"Okay, shall we go to him, or do you want to wait here?" Cass was suddenly nervous again.

Lolita whipped out her phone and sent a message. "He'll be five minutes."

Sitting in silence, Cass began processing the morning. She'd need more time to fully digest their conversation, but at first glance, she thought it went as well as could be expected.

Noticing Lolita sitting a little taller, she followed her mum's gaze. A handsome man beamed back at them. He was tall, probably around six feet with salt-and-pepper hair and a groomed beard—nice suit, too.

Stepping up to Lolita, he dropped a sweet kiss on her cheek before turning to Cass and offering his hand. "It's lovely to meet you, Cassandra. Lol has told me a lot about you."

Lol? Cass grinned at her mother, who blushed. "It's lovely to meet you too," she replied, shaking his hand. "Fancy grabbing a coffee? I know a place."

Henry chuckled. "Sounds great! Lol." Offering his arm, Lolita stood and wrapped her hand around his bicep.

"Why thank you, kind sir. Lead on, Cass."

They walked slowly through the park, chatting. Cass learned of Henry's two children, both actors trying to make their fortunes, but both struggling. Henry spoke a little about his company. Cass was reassured he wasn't work obsessed. She didn't think that would work well for her mum. But Henry allayed those fears when he explained he was semi-retired, looking to make it permanent by the end of the year.

By the time they got to The Beanery, Cass was a little in love with the man herself. He was genuinely kind and treated Lolita like a queen.

"Lolita!" Kendal called, jogging over to give her a hug.

"Kendal, my love. This is Henry. My fiancé."

"It's a pleasure," Henry said, shaking Kendal's hand. "Lovely to meet you. I'm Cass's business partner."

"Oh, I've told him all about you."

"All good things, I hope. Sit down, I'll bring you all some coffee."

"Actually," Cass interrupted. "Would...would you like to go next door?" She needed to see Harriet, and she wanted her to meet Lolita...officially in a *this-is-my-girlfriend* kind of way.

Kendal scoffed playfully. "Pilfering your own customers? Not a savvy business move, Beaufort!"

Rolling her eyes, Cass looked at her mum. "What do you think?"

Pulling Cass to the side, Lolita leaned in. "Are you comfortable with that?"

"I am. I go in there daily, and...I'm much better with things now. Plus, I really want you to meet Harriet."

"Then I'd love to. Sorry, Kendal, we'll catch up next time. I have a girlfriend to assess."

Whirling around, Lolita was out the door before Cass could blink. Scrambling to catch up, she laughed silently at her mum's antics.

"Hang on. Don't go barrelling in there. You'll scare her. She doesn't know she's about to formally meet you."

"I'll be on my best behaviour. I've told Henry how much I've wanted to visit the new tea shop."

Cass smiled, appreciating the fact her mum hadn't added a descriptor, which she most certainly would have before their talk this morning, probably adding something like *saucy* or *kinky*.

Stepping over the threshold, Cass tried to see Ero-Tea-Ca from the perspective of a new customer. It was gorgeous. Her mum clearly agreed, as she gushed over everything from the table settings to the vintage-style counter.

Nabi and Kevin were working the floor and service area. "Hey, Cass, she's in the back," Nabi called over her shoulder as she stacked tea boxes on the shelf.

"Thanks." Ushering her mum and Henry to the only open table, Cass told them to order whatever they wanted. "I'll be back in a second."

Slipping through the door and into the stockroom, Cass cleared her throat, not wanting to startle her girlfriend, who was balancing precariously on a small ladder.

"Oh, hey, babe. One sec," Harriet said, straining to reach the top shelf.

"Oh, for God's sake, get down," Cass bit out. Harriet was going to break her bloody neck. Marching over, she took Harriet by the hips and lifted her clear off the ladder.

Ignoring Harriet's protests, Cass hopped up, plucked the box from the shelf and handed it over.

"You need to learn health and safety."

Harriet smiled. "Why, when it means my gorgeous lover comes to my rescue? I got a fabulous view of your arse just then."

Trying to remain serious, Cass stepped closer. "Try and keep that feeling when you walk into the tearoom?"

"Why?" Harriet cocked her head. "Is there a disaster waiting for me? Did Nabi break something?"

"No disaster. Just one Lolita Beaufort."

Harriet's eyes went wide. "Your mum's here?"

"Yes. We talked. It went...less catastrophically than I thought. We're going to work on our relationship. But she's here to meet you. Officially."

Harriet let out an honest-to-God squeak. "Cassandra," she hissed, "I'm a mess. I can't meet her looking like this."

Playing with the hem of Harriet's apron, Cass smiled. "Harriet, you look beautiful. She'll love the smiling teapots."

Harriet huffed, planting hands on hips. "I can't believe this."

"Hey, you don't have to meet her if you're not ready." Cass couldn't exactly get upset if Harriet didn't want to go out there and talk to Lolita. She'd refused to meet Harriet's friends, after all.

Scrunching her nose, Harriet eyeballed Cass. "I want to meet her. Just know you've got some making up to do tonight." Oh, no, however would Cass cope? Making love to Harriet as a punishment? How terrible! "Stop smirking."

Cass laughed. "Sorry. No smirking or smiling of any kind. I'll do whatever you like this evening to make up for my oversight."

As much as Harriet tried, she couldn't hide her own smirk. "Ugh, you're impossible. Okay, let's do this."

Straightening her shirt and fluffing her hair, Harriet held her head high and strolled over to Lolita and Henry. In true Lolita style, she scooped Harriet into a tight hug and whispered something in her ear that left her blushing. Cass decided she didn't want to know.

Cass sat back and let Lolita do her thing. She didn't exactly interrogate Harriet, but she did ask what her intentions were, before bursting out into laughter. After that, the tension drained from Harriet's body, leaving Cass feeling better.

Henry and Cass chatted as Lolita asked Harriet every question under the sun about Ero-Tea-Ca. There were several moments where her mum paused before speaking, looking over at Cass.

Not wanting to draw attention to it, Cass continued happily talking with Henry, and then Nabi when she sauntered over with a lollipop and a cup of tea for an impromptu meeting. Cass couldn't have asked for more. Harriet seemed to get along with her mum like a house on fire, and Henry definitely fit in with Cass, being a little more reserved than Lolita.

Cass's heart swelled. Things really were looking up.

27

Harriet

Pacing was good. Pacing helped stave off the nerves and resentment. Pacing was going to wear a hole through Harriet's shoes if she didn't stop sometime soon. She did stop now and then to stare at Cass, who leaned casually against Harriet's parents' front garden wall, waiting patiently. Cass, who exuded confidence in the face of meeting Harriet's family.

Diane owed her big time for this. She didn't care if it was her sister's birthday. Forcing her to interact with Patsy and Ronald after she'd set clear boundaries was out of order, but Harriet couldn't deny Diane this. Not when her sister had supported her without question over the years. Harriet would just have to suck it up and hope the Kirkwells were polite enough to her and Cass until they could make an escape.

"Okay, I'm ready!"

"Okay." Cass didn't move from her spot. Probably because Harriet was still pacing. Maybe one more minute.

"Will you get in here?" Kevin called from her parents' door. "You look deranged."

Shooting him her best Cass-inspired scowl, Harriet stepped up to her girlfriend and buried her head in Cass's long hair. "Let's go," she moaned.

Cass squeezed her bum playfully before standing and taking Harriet's hand. "It will be fine."

"Why aren't you nervous?" After Cass reacted so strongly about meeting Harriet's friends, she was sure meeting the parents would send her running for the hills. Instead, Cass stood by her side as a pillar of strength, bolstering Harriet's confidence in getting through the dinner.

"Because I know how to handle these kinds of people," Cass replied easily.

It made sense, Harriet decided. She'd once joked Cass and the older Kirkwells would get on really well because they all shared a rather negative and ornery outlook on life. But that was before Harriet got to know Cass. Yes, she might be prickly regarding certain things, but she wasn't a snob. Deep down, Cass only cared what others thought of her on a surface level. And even then, it was a trigger response.

With every passing day, she came a little further out of her shell. The more relaxed her rules became, the less she gave a shit about society's views on her. It was kind of lovely to witness. Patsy and Ronald Kirkwell, on the other hand, were cemented in their snobbishness and disapproval of all things *different*. They never bent, or even swayed, from their rigid outlook on life, even if that meant falling out with their kids.

Bolstered by Cass, Harriet walked them up the garden path. "Before we go in, I just wanted you to know you look really hot." She should've commented sooner. Cass looked delicious in fitted black jeans and a ruby red T-shirt hidden away underneath a sport coat. The high heels were a surprise, though, and one Harriet intended to explore later. She liked casual Cass. No doubt she'd have dressed to the nines if Harriet hadn't firmly told her the dinner was a relaxed affair. Well, as relaxed as a dinner could be with her parents sitting at the table.

Smiling with a small blush, Cass leaned in and kissed Harriet just below her ear. It was a particularly sensitive spot, and one Cass knew would get her revved up.

"That's mean." Harriet mewled her response. Cass was also coming out of her shell where these little touches and caresses were concerned, especially in public.

"Just wanted to give you something to focus on," Cass whispered in her ear before gently biting the lobe.

Kevin's hand grabbing Harriet's collar and yanking her through the door broke the spell. "The quicker you get in here, the quicker we can go home," he hissed. Since her dramatic exit the last time Harriet had dinner with the family, Kevin had become especially salty, his carefree attitude waning with every acerbic comment their parents threw his way. He'd clearly not realised how much shit Harriet had had thrown at her until she was out of the picture and all of Patsy and Ronald's ire got directed his way.

Stripping off her jacket and taking Cass's, Harriet hung them closest to the door. If they had to make a dash for it, she wanted their belongings in easy reach. Resolute to her fate, Harriet followed Kevin.

Diane stood up and greeted them with hugs. Mitchel, her husband, gave them a wave and looked equally pissed off to be there, too. The only bright side was getting hugs from her niblings.

As soon as the pleasant members of the family had been kissed and hugged, Harriet turned to her parents, who were sitting in their usual chairs with the TV on mute.

"Mum, Dad, I'd like you to meet Cassandra Beaufort, my girlfriend."

Cass stepped forward and extended her hand. "Nice to meet you both."

Ronald stood and shook her hand. Patsy took a little longer, her eyes assessing. If her intention was to intimidate, it failed, because Cass didn't waver one bit and Harriet loved her for it.

"Cassandra, you own The Oxford Beanery, correct?" Ronald asked.

"Co-owner. I run it with my ex-wife."

"You're a divorcée?" Patsy shot.

"I am."

"How old are you?"

"Mum!" Harriet wanted to scream. It'd taken her mother less than five minutes to start causing trouble. Harriet knew all too well how shitty her mother could be when she felt like it.

"I'm forty-one."

"And you think it's appropriate to be with someone a decade younger than you?" Patsy was a dog with a bone.

"If that person wants to be with me, then yes. I believe there's a seven-year difference between yourself and Ronald."

Harriet did a double take. How had Cass found that out? Not that she was upset about it—far from it—it was just a surprise, a happy one, because her mum looked like she was sucking a lemon. "Seven years isn't so small either. But I'm sure you'll agree, it's about the couple rather than the number."

"Drinks," Diane announced, effectively ending the conversation. "Is wine okay, Cassandra?"

"Perfect. And please, call me Cass."

"What's it like running a café?" Robbie asked.

"It's hard work but fulfilling."

"Do you travel to find new coffee?" Robbie was seemingly enamoured. Harriet could understand. It seemed her favourite niece took after her aunt in more ways than one.

"I've travelled. My last venture was to South America." Harriet saw a flash of discomfort. She knew Cass was still a tad miffed she'd missed out on purchasing the shop Harriet now owned because of that trip.

"Wow. I'd love to travel like that."

"No reason you can't."

The rest of the family chatted away happily. Harriet gave Diane a gift certificate for Ero-Tea-Ca because it's the only thing she could think of. Diane had everything and the money to buy whatever else she wanted.

It was only her parents who remained silent, even when they sat down to eat. Thank Christ, Diane had ordered food instead of making them all suffer through a bleak roast dinner.

They were half an hour into the meal when Harriet got a creeping sensation up her spine. Patsy was eying Cass closely, a hint of something glistening in her eye. Before Harriet figured it out, her mother gently cleared her throat.

"Cassandra, aren't you the same person who sent in a complaint against Harriet's...shop?" God, the woman could barely say the word. Harriet wanted to roll her eyes. So, this was her parents' plan: to humiliate her.

"I did," Cass replied with no trace of awkwardness.

"We can't blame you," Ronald interjected. "It's unbecoming having a place like that on the high street. Did you ever get a response? Are they taking action?"

Harriet's mouth dropped open. She was sitting *right* there, and her parents were...Jesus, she couldn't even articulate it. They were unbelievable. Kevin and Diane must have agreed because they sat wide-eyed and slack-jawed. Diane, the eldest who usually jumped in and smoothed things over, was gobsmacked, as were the rest of the table's inhabitants.

"They are not, thank God." Cass continued to eat.

"Oh, you're not pursuing it?" Patsy enquired.

Chuckling, Cass placed her knife and fork down before wiping the corner of her mouth with a napkin. "I most certainly am not. What sort of person would I be to actively hurt someone I care about? As her parents, you must understand that. I'd be a terrible woman for wanting to cause that kind of pain, and I'd be unsuitable to be Harriet's partner. I was misguided when we first met. I can also admit I was upset my plan to buy the shop hadn't panned out as I wanted. Unfortunately, Harriet took the brunt of it, and I'll regret my behaviour for a long time to come. Thankfully, Harriet is entirely wonderful and accepted my apology. As for Ero-Tea-Ca being unbecoming of the high street, I'm happy to inform you, you're wrong. Ero-Tea-Ca has injected new life into the street. We are getting more footfall. Other businesses are seeing an increase in sales because of the new clientele Harriet is attracting."

Harriet stared at Cass, dumbfounded.

"But that isn't all. Harriet has created a safe space for a myriad of people. The community is benefitting in more than one way because of her and the teashop. You must be very proud. I know I am."

Giving Patsy and Ronald a smile, Cass picked up her utensils and began eating again. The room was silent for several moments. Harriet couldn't find the words for what Cass had just done.

It seemed Cass wasn't finished, though. "Oh, I also forgot to mention she's a finalist for the Best Shop Owners Award."

Harriet's eyes snapped to Cass. "I'm what?"

"Yes. It's between you and The Bookworm. The winner will be announced..." Cass spied her watch. "Oh, in an hour. That's exciting."

"Harriet, that's amazing!" Robbie screeched, jumping up from her seat and hugging her tightly.

"Wow, sis! I knew you could do it." Kevin gave her a beaming smile and two thumbs up.

Diane had tears welling in her eyes. "Congratulations, Harriet. We are so, so proud of you."

"I...but...what?"

Cass laughed. "Please don't be mad I kept it from you. I wanted it to be a surprise."

"But I've only been open a few months!" Harriet couldn't get her head around it.

"It doesn't matter how long you've been open. The fact is, Ero-Tea-Ca is booming. You're elevating the high street, and people recognise that."

"We have to celebrate," Diane announced, standing. "Everyone grab your coats, we're going to the pub. Mum, Dad, you're welcome to join us if you want."

Harriet completely forgot her parents were there for a moment. But the reality of what they'd tried to do minutes before came rushing back. "I doubt you'll want to come and celebrate such a thing. Not for a shop that's bound to fail. Isn't that what you said?" Harriet was angry, but she wouldn't let them take this moment from her. "Let's go." She didn't give Patsy or Ronald the chance to speak.

Putting on her coat, Harriet noticed Cass hadn't followed her into the hall. The rest of the family was already making their way outside. Concerned, Harriet headed back to the dining room. She'd lose her shit if her parents were giving Cass any more grief.

"You'll lose her," she heard Cass say, "if you continue like this. She'll leave and never come back. No matter what you think of me or her shop, she is your daughter. Do better." And then Cass whirled around. Not wanting to be caught eavesdropping, Harriet scuttled to the front door. She redid her zip to look as if she was simply preparing to leave. Cass stepped up next to her, grabbed her chin, and kissed her soundly.

"Let's go celebrate."

"Oh my God, that was so much fun! I'm so pleased the shop is closed tomorrow. I need a morning in bed after that." Harriet was on top of the world. The celebration turned out to be a full-on party by the end of the night. Harriet had immediately called Nabi to come to the pub when Ero-Tea-Ca was announced as the winner. They'd spent five minutes squealing in delight. Nabi even cried, which was out of character.

"It was. Diane is nice."

Harriet pulled them to a stop, only yards away from Cass's front door. "Thank you!"

Cass nipped her nose. "Nothing to thank me for."

Harriet scoffed. "There is and you know it. I couldn't have gotten through that dinner without you, Cass. You were perfect."

"I doubt I've earned myself a return invitation, but as long as you're okay, that's all that matters. I'm sorry they behaved like that."

Harriet shook her head. "I wasn't surprised. A little shocked at one point, I suppose."

"Understandably. As long as you know they're wrong. You have worked your lovely derriere off, and you're succeeding. Ero-Tea-Ca is a universal triumph."

"Wow, could I get that in writing? You know, for when you're being all moody and pissy, that my shop is better than yours!"

Harriet stifled a laugh as Cass growled. "I'll never admit that! The Oxford Beanery is a beacon in these parts. And a three-time award winner."

Dragging her index finger across Cass's pouting lips, she grinned. "I do love it when you get all het up like this. It's sexy."

"You're incorrigible. Get in that house!"

"Yes, ma'am."

Laughing, they stumbled through the door. Harriet reached for Cass as soon as their coats were off. Running her hands through Cass's hair, Harriet tugged slightly, knowing Cass liked a bit of hair pulling, even if she wasn't aware of it herself.

Over the course of their budding relationship, Cass had inadvertently shown Harriet she was far from the "vanilla sex" person she regarded herself as. Cass liked hair pulling. Spanking and dirty talk, too; none of which they'd discussed, but were things Harriet observed.

"Shower," she breathed into Cass's open mouth. She swallowed a moan as Cass sucked on her tongue and grabbed her ass, giving it a delightful squeeze and knead.

They fumbled each other's clothes off without breaking contact. This was Harriet's favourite part: their utter urgency to get naked with each other. Breaking away to shower added to their foreplay. Harriet loved seeing Cass's eyes blown wide open with lust, but unable to satiate her thirst straight away. Sometimes Harriet liked to tease further by taking an extra-long soak. Cass became almost feral when she did that, especially when she masturbated in the shower, knowing Cass could hear her. It was their game, and Harriet was a master at it.

Tonight, Cass seemed extra wound up. She was waiting for Harriet in the bathroom when she stepped out of the cubicle. "Wait there," Cass demanded, pointing to her sink. "And no towel."

Harriet's heart rate tripled. She watched Cass wash her body, all the time picturing what she wanted to do to her and where she wanted her mouth and fingers. Her sexy daydream was broken as Cass stepped out of the cubicle and into her personal space.

"Turn around."

Harriet bit her lip. This was new. They'd had sex in the bedroom many times, once in the kitchen during a food break, which followed a particularly long session of lovemaking, but never anywhere else.

"I said, 'turn around,'" Cass repeated in a low tone.

Cassandra Beaufort was far from vanilla. How had Harriet got so lucky?

28

Cassandra

Cass smoothed her hand down the plane of Harriet's naked back. She was sublime. Perfection in human form, and she was all hers.

"Bend," Cass murmured, still entranced by Harriet's body.

She watched Harriet buckle at the hip until her upper torso laid flat over the bathroom sink, her hands gripping the edge of the worktop until white. She was enjoying it. But nowhere near as much as Cass.

Snaking one hand up and into Harriet's hair, she gently massaged her scalp before grabbing a handful of her silky locks. Pulling slightly, Cass tilted Harriet's head back. Their gazes locked in the mirror.

Unable to look away, Cass trailed her fingers down the base of Harriet's back until she felt pliable flesh under her hand. God, Harriet had a great arse.

Stroking gently, she took her time dipping between Harriet's legs from behind. A quiver ran the length of her girlfriend's spine. She was divine. Truly magnificent.

Cass had wanted to touch Harriet for hours, ever since picking her up to go to her parents' for dinner—an experience Cass wasn't in a rush to replicate any time soon. Harriet tried to warn her how bad they were, but even Cass was shocked at their brazen criticism against, and contempt of, Ero-Tea-Ca.

Shame had spiralled in her gut when she realised she'd been no better than them when she first met Harriet. Having her back and fighting her corner was the least she could do to show Harriet she didn't feel or think like them. It was Cass who nominated Ero-Tea-Ca for the award in the first place, though she wouldn't tell Harriet that.

"Cass," Harriet panted. Shaking away any thoughts of the past, Cass concentrated on giving Harriet what she needed, what they both needed.

"Patience." A word she was struggling with herself. A bead of her own need dripped down her thigh. Gritting her teeth, Cass stepped forward until her sex rested teasingly against Harriet's backside. The pressure of her own hand nestled between Harriet's legs added just the right amount of friction.

Swiping two fingers through the length of Harriet's slit, Cass hummed in appreciation at the sheer volume of wetness slicking her hand. "Oh, Cass."

No longer in control of her urges, Cass parted Harriet's lips and slid in. Tight and warm, Cass couldn't hold in the moan she felt rising in her throat as Harriet adjusted to let her in further. Gripping her hair a little harder, Cass withdrew her fingers, slowly.

The protest died on Harriet's lips as soon as Cass rocked back into her with three fingers, timing her thrust with another pull of her hair. "Oh…" The gasp was music to Cass's ears. It told her that her ministrations had stolen Harriet's breath clean away.

Feeling her own clit pulse violently, Cass waited until she was on a forward thrust before rocking her hips in time. The movement sent a shockwave through her entire lower body. Harriet began pushing her arse back into Cass's hand, which put even more pressure on her clit. Together, they were driving each other crazy.

"H-harder," Harriet mewled, her head dropping. Picking up the pace and force, Cass gave Harriet what she needed. A flood of liquid ran down her hand and wrist as Harriet lost the battle to hold on any longer.

As her groans turned to screams, Cass careened off the edge. She fell forward, rolling her hips, riding out the orgasm as it pulsed through every nerve. She heard her own moan but muffled it by biting down on Harriet's shoulder. The action sent Harriet off the deep end for a second time. Their movements were messy, but it didn't matter. Cass rode Harriet's ass as she orgasmed again. Only when Harriet lunged forward, dislodging Cass's fingers, did she stop rocking.

No words were spoken as they both tried to catch their breaths. Cass released Harriet's hair and held on to her hips. She couldn't lift her head. Their bodies stayed locked together, hot and sweaty.

"Jesus!" Harriet spluttered finally. "That...that was fantastic."

Cass nodded against Harriet's back. "Yeah." Sucking in a fortifying breath, she straightened up, placing a kiss on Harriet's shoulder. "Bed?"

"Give me like ten seconds. I'm not sure I can walk."

Grinning, Cass guided Harriet up and away from the vanity area. "I can help with that." Now, Cass might be in her forties, but she was no slouch. Years of working in the service industry had given her a core of steel and some pretty decent biceps. Scooping Harriet up, Cass laughed, as Harriet squeaked in surprise and then giggled as Cass carried her to the bed.

"Oh my God, I can't believe you just did that!" Harriet laughed. Cass grinned, quite happy with herself. She wasn't too shabby at this romance malarky.

"Are you tired?" She hoped Harriet would say no, because she certainly didn't feel it. Her body was alive and needed more. More of Harriet.

"No. I'm not tired in the least. What did you have in mind?"

"Can I taste you?"

Cass's eyes dropped to Harriet's mouth as she ran the tip of her tongue across the lower lip. It was a signature Harriet move, and it drove her nuts. "Yes, please," Harriet finally said.

Climbing on top, Cass took that teasing tongue and sucked on it. They devolved into a deep, passionate kiss

Cass was in no hurry to get out of, even if she *did* want her mouth a little farther south.

Harriet's hands began to wander. She gripped Cass's hips in a bid to move Cass down. Happy to oblige, Cass broke the kiss and made her way down Harriet's body, showering her skin with soft kisses and nipping teeth.

"Cass."

With one last nip on Harriet's lower torso, Cass dipped her head to where they both wanted it. Harriet smelled of sex: rich and musky. She tasted equally good and completely addictive. Cass could lose herself in Harriet's heat for days, she was sure of it.

Losing patience, Harriet moved a hand to Cass's head, guiding her closer. It only took a second for Cass's face to be covered in the vestiges of Harriet's last orgasm. Lapping freely, Cass worked to clean her up before attempting to get her dirty all over again.

Harriet groaned and shifted as Cass's tongue moved around her lips. She played with her entrance, dipping in and out but never fully committing. Harriet was a gibbering wreck by the time Cass inhaled her clit. She sucked rhythmically until Harriet spouted nonsense. Her head thrashed from side to side as Cass took her with no reprieve. After Harriet almost levitated, Cass retreated to catch her breath.

Holy crap, that was fantastic.

Moving slowly to Harriet's side, Cass laid down, burying her head in those gorgeous golden strands. Harriet was yet to speak, her chest rising and falling with speed. Her cheeks were painted red and sweat beaded on her forehead.

It was perfect. Cass didn't need anything. She was happy to spend the rest of the evening in blissed out silence. Her eyes flitted closed as she listened to Harriet's breath even out.

The incessant buzz of Harriet's mobile woke Cass. Her body felt heavy and not just because her girlfriend lay sprawled over her chest. The heaviness originated in her muscles, sore from their antics the night before.

"Harriet, your phone."

Nothing. Harriet didn't stir. Her soft breaths continued evenly to skate across Cass's bare chest.

Hating to break their cocoon of comfort, Cass sighed and rolled gently, dislodging Harriet, who grumbled. It worked, though, because she fluttered open her eyes and winced at the intruding light.

"Why's it so sunny in here?"

"Because the blinds are open. Your phone is buzzing."

Cass smiled lovingly as Harriet sat up like a zombie rising from the grave. She was totally disoriented and her hair puffed out magnificently. Eighties, eat your heart out.

"Where is it?" She looked around without seeing, causing Cass to chuckle.

"It's here. I'll go and make coffee."

"Noooo. Let me just see what's going on and then we can go back to sleep. I was having a wonderful dream."

Kissing the side of her head, Cass climbed out of bed and pulled on her robe. "You can go back to sleep if you want, but I'm awake now."

She ignored the irritated grumble and left Harriet to reply to whoever needed to get hold of her so badly. They should talk about putting their phones on *Do Not Disturb*. That way, they might get a lay-in now and then.

Mr Whiskers made his contempt known to the entire street. Cass rolled her eyes. She was less than two hours later than usual. Surely he wasn't dying of starvation quite so quickly.

She spent a little time giving him chin rubs while the coffee percolated. Apart from the interruption of their lay-in, the morning was turning out perfectly. Maybe they could stay in bed all day making love. Wouldn't that be nice?

Cass's reverie was shattered by Harriet letting out a string of expletives. Grabbing their coffees and a box of croissants, she made her way back to the bedroom. Harriet sat against the headboard, tapping away on her phone.

"Everything okay?"

"It's Kev," she began. "He's told everyone about the award and they've decided to throw a celebratory book club session. In thirty minutes."

"That's nice, isn't it?" Cass asked, climbing back into bed.

"I wanted to spend the day with you." Grumpy Harriet was adorable. She didn't quite have it in her to be convincing, though. Her sunny disposition took away any true disquiet.

"Am I not allowed to come with you?"

Harriet laid the phone down and looked straight at Cass. "You want to come? To meet everyone?"

Shrugging, Cass broke off a piece of croissant and shoved it in her mouth. *Mmm, buttery.* "I've met your parents. They can't be much worse than that."

"They're not worse, just different. I've not had a chance to talk to them...about you. I mean, they know we're together. I just haven't mentioned your..."

"Issues? It's fine. I'm sure I can handle it."

Crawling from her spot, Harriet climbed in Cass's lap. "I'd love for you to meet them."

Brushing a hand through Harriet's hair, Cass kissed her gently. "Then it's settled."

After a rather hasty breakfast, Cass walked hand in hand with Harriet to Ero-Tea-Ca. The lights were on and voices could be heard laughing and joking behind the door. Cass felt the familiar feeling of anxiety start to creep its way into her mind. She'd tried to play off meeting Harriet's friends as something she wasn't too concerned about. It was a tiny lie. Yes, she'd met Harriet's parents, which under normal circumstances should be a lot more nerve-wracking than meeting a group of friends. But it wasn't quite so straightforward.

Cass had known how to handle Patsy and Ronald. Dealing with snobbery, rudeness, and just general negativity was well in her wheelhouse. But the friendship group? She didn't know how to handle them. Harriet had warned her they were an eclectic lot. How was Cass supposed to prepare for that?

Harriet paused as she entered the shop. Cass saw her body stiffen, which couldn't be good, right? Whirling around, Harriet looked worried. "I'm sorry. I didn't know."

Forming her hands into fists inside her coat pocket, Cass gave a tight smile. "Let's go." She'd face whatever was inside, even though it was still morning and already felt far too early for any kind of celebration. It definitely felt too early to have a Dominatrix staring you down. It wasn't even time for elevenses.

What in the world?

Ero-Tea-Ca was packed full of people. They all cheered when Harriet entered. Cass recognised Nabi and Kevin, but that was it. She certainly didn't know the woman clad in black leather, holding a riding crop.

"Here she is," Kevin bellowed. "Shop Owner of the Year, in the flesh!"

Cass held herself back as Harriet was swept up into cuddles and kisses.

"Oh my God, you guys. What is happening?" Harriet laughed.

A tall person stepped forward with flair. This had to be Gogo. Harriet and Kevin spoke of them often. They were known to be rather dramatic, apparently. "Well. As this was an unscheduled book club, we had to do it early. Some of us have plans, darling. But there's no way we wouldn't celebrate with you. So, it's a morning tea party. But a little naughtier."

The sharp smack of leather turned everyone's attention. Gogo laughed and clapped. "Harriet, you know Mistress Black?" Harriet went red and nodded. Cass bit the inside of her cheek. Mistress Black was the leader of the Domme book club. Were she and Harriet friends? "Well, to commemorate this wonderful achievement, we thought—"

"*You* thought." Kevin interrupted, casting a glance towards Cass.

"*I* thought," Gogo laughed, "it would be nice to live up to the tea shop's name. So, Mistress Black is going to give you a little taste of what it's like to be rewarded in the naughtiest of ways."

Cass felt like she'd been punched in the chest. Was she expected to stand there and watch Harriet get pleasured by another woman? What the hell? Everything in her body wanted her to turn and leave. Storm out of there in a cloud of offence. But she didn't. Instead of fleeing, she took a deep breath and waited for Harriet to reply.

"Um...I don't think that's really appropriate, Gogo." Harriet looked as awkward as Cass felt.

Waving their hand in dismissal, Gogo stepped forward. "Nonsense. It's a bit of fun." Looking directly at Cass, Gogo grinned. "You've always been a bit daring, my dear Harriet. Nothing like a quick spank to wake you up in the morning. Your girlfriend can join in too if she wants."

All eyes turned to Cass, and she knew her face was on fire. "No thank you," she managed to grit out. Cass stood her ground, refusing to embarrass Harriet by leaving. She wanted to, but she wouldn't.

Gogo pouted. "Such a stick in the mud. Don't tell me you don't like your ass smacked, Cassandra."

"Gogo," Kevin warned.

"What I do and don't like done to my body is none of your concern." Cass heard the vitriol in her own words.

If Gogo picked up on her anger and discomfort, they didn't let on. Instead, they chuckled and cocked a hip, planting their hand on it. "Darling, if you want to be with Ms Harriet, you need to be a little less uptight than this. It's only fun. Don't be so vanilla, sweetie."

Cass knew then, Gogo had some inkling of her difficulties regarding sex. It was the only explanation, which meant either Kevin or Nabi had discussed it with them. She knew Harriet had spoken to her brother and best friend weeks ago. It helped pave the way for them becoming friends.

Well, Cass thought they were friends.

29

Harriet

This was a disaster. She had no idea what Gogo was playing at, but Harriet was both mortified and incensed. She'd known Gogo for a long time, and experienced their bitchy side many times, but it had never been directed towards someone she loved. And she did love Cass. Head over heels kind of love. Which was why she couldn't stand by and watch her be humiliated like this, in a room full of people she didn't know.

"Gogo, enough."

Cackling, Gogo turned to Harriet. "Wow, she's got you as uptight as her now. Don't tell me you've gone all frigid too, Harriet."

The smack of Cass's palm on the table next to her rang around the room. Harriet held her breath. She could see Cass desperately trying to hold back tears. "Enough," she croaked. The room was silent. Harriet didn't know what to do. Her heart told her to take Cass into her arms, but her brain said the opposite. Cass usually needed space when feeling overwhelmed, but what if she interpreted it as Harriet not standing by her?

"G, you're out of line," Nabi said, shaking her head.

"I'm out of line?" Gogo snorted. "I was just having a bit of fun. But I think you're all forgetting she was the one who caused Harriet sleepless nights when the shop opened. Let's not forget Harriet had a life before she met Cass. Now we never see her because she's shacked up with Ms Beaufort over there, playing house. And from what I gather, she's got more baggage than Heathrow Lost and Found. That's who you want to see Harriet with?"

Before Harriet uttered a word, Cass stepped forward. "You're correct. I was awful to Harriet when we first met, and I have apologised for that. Harriet chose to forgive me and we moved forward. As for Harriet and I playing house, you do your friend a disservice by treating her choices with such disdain. I believe Harriet is with me so much because she wants to be. Because we are a couple. In *love*."

Harriet's breath hitched as Cass looked into her eyes. She smiled and nodded her head. Yes, they were in love, and she needed Cass to know she felt it too.

"If you wish to see Harriet more often, maybe you could call her instead of acting like a petulant child." Gogo looked stunned. Few people had the gall to stand up to them. They were menacing in height and had the attitude to match sometimes. "As for my baggage, I would have thought someone who has had their fair share of unwarranted harassment and discrimination would know better. You don't know me well enough to have an opinion, no matter what you've heard, or from who. But I am a part of this community," Cass said, gesturing to the room full of queer people. "I thought it was supposed to be a safe space, void of the petty bullshit we have to put up with out there. Clearly not, if you so easily try to use my perceived weaknesses as a way to hurt me, and, by default, Harriet."

Kevin stepped to Cass's side. "I think you should leave." For a second, Harriet panicked he was talking to Cass. But when he took Cass's hand in his own, she relaxed. "This was supposed to be a celebration and all you've done is attack Cass, for no good reason. I've always defended you, G. Every time you said too much, or got out of line, because I love you. But not this time. Cass is a part of Ero-Tea-Ca. She's family, and you don't treat family this way."

"Kevin," Gogo said, looking rattled.

"No. I asked you to be sensitive to Cass's needs. You've made it look like I gossiped, and I can't have that." Kevin turned his attention to Harriet. "I swear, Harriet. I asked G to tone it down a bit. I wanted Cass to feel comfortable."

"It's okay," Cass said, her face still red but missing the murderous tinge.

"It's not okay." Harriet moved until she was nose to nose with Cass. "It's not okay to be treated this way." Turning, she pinned Gogo with her eyes. "Ero-Tea-Ca is a safe space for everyone. You know that. You were a person who needed that, so how dare you use it as a way to make someone uncomfortable within their own skin? All you had to do was talk to me, and I would have allayed any worries you had regarding our relationship, although I don't owe you, or anyone, an explanation."

"Harr—"

"No." She held up her hand in warning. "Stop talking. Go home. I will talk to you when I'm ready, G. Until then, you need to get out."

The room remained deathly silent as Gogo picked up their jacket and bag. Their head hung low as they made their way through the throng of people.

"Alright, let's get back to celebrating!" Nabi shouted. "Come on, chop chop."

Ignoring everyone, Harriet took Cass's hand and led her to the stockroom. "I'm so sorry, Cass." She pulled Cass into a bone-crushing hug the second they were alone. "I don't know what the hell got into them."

"Should I leave?"

The vulnerability in Cass's voice shattered Harriet's heart. "Please don't go."

Nodding, Cass buried her head in Harriet's hair. They stayed holding each other for a long while.

"Did you mean it?"

Cass pulled her head back slowly. "That we're a couple in love?"

"Yes. Did you mean it?"

She watched Cass swallow thickly. "I know I can't speak for you. But yes. I love you. I'm in love with you."

Taking Cass's face, Harriet hiccupped a sob. "I love you too. So much."

"Even though I'm old and grumpy?"

"Not old and occasionally grumpy. Even then."

"And you're not rethinking us? After what Gogo said?"

Shaking her head, Harriet kissed her fiercely. "Not one bit. I'll have it out with them. Find out what the bloody hell that was about. But right now, my only concern is you."

"I'm okay. A little shaken...I really wanted to leave."

"But you didn't."

Cass leaned her forehead against Harriet's. "No. Not this time. But...well, are you friends with Mistress Black?"

"I only know her through organising her book club."

"Okay. I just wondered why Gogo thought you'd like to celebrate...with her."

Harriet rolled her eyes. "Because they're an ass. Sure, we've all joked about liking a good spanking. I've never actually taken part in a scene or anything."

"A scene?"

"Dom/sub play scene. It doesn't matter."

Harriet could *feel* Cass thinking. "If...if there's anything you want...in the bedroom I mean, I need you to tell me. Not hide it because you're worried it might upset me."

"Hey," Harriet began, her fingers caressing Cass's face. "Our sex life is fantastic. I love discovering new things with you. I promise I'll talk to you if I want something new."

"Okay. Because I'll try it. If you want."

Grinning, Harriet grabbed Cass's arse. "Maybe. But right now, I love what you do to me, without accessories."

"You mean the riding crop, right?"

"Yes, Cass." Harriet laughed. "Please don't get in your head about it. We're good. You're great. And we love each other. That's everything."

The party spread out over the rest of the day. Wanting to share the joy, Harriet opened up to the public, welcoming Ronnie and Tori, plus Tori's new girlfriend. It was amazing how many loyal customers Ero-Tea-Ca had in such a short amount of time.

Throughout the celebrations, though, Harriet kept a watchful eye on Cass. Unease settled in her gut as she replayed Gogo's outburst. Cass was putting on a brave face, and for the most part looked as if she were enjoying herself, but Harriet couldn't help but worry. Would the confrontation set her back? Trigger her? God, she could throttle Gogo.

"Hey, sis. You okay?"

"Mm hmm." Harriet still wasn't sure if she were pissed at Kevin.

"Hey, now. I didn't do anything, Harriet. I promise."

Setting down her teacup, Harriet turned in her chair to face him. "What, exactly, did you say? Because that was way over the top, even for G."

Kevin shook his head and sighed. "I literally just said that Cass had a few things she was working through, and you'd appreciate it if they could rein in the banter a little."

"That's it?" She eyed him suspiciously.

"Harriet, I may be smitten with them, but I would never defend them when they were out of line like that. I really don't know why they took it as a personal affront."

Harriet sighed. "You know how sensitive they get about being told to be 'less than', even though I know that's not what you meant. I'm guessing Gogo took it that way."

"Fuck, you're right." Kevin looked completely dejected. It was well known Gogo had a bad time growing up and coming out. Throughout their entire life, they'd had people telling them to stop being so loud, open, and generally themselves. When they broke free of that life, they made it their personal mission to be as flamboyant and outspoken as they wanted. If at any time a partner, or friend for that matter, tried to tell them to reel it in, Gogo took it badly. Most of their relationships had ended because of that.

"But it still doesn't excuse them from behaving like that towards Cass."

Kevin placed his arm around her shoulders. "So, you're in love, huh?" His teasing tone helped diffuse the tension.

"Yes. That was the first time she said it. I doubt she wanted us to have that conversation in front of a bunch of people while being attacked."

"Ah, shit. I'm sorry, Harriet. Jesus, I really screwed the pooch, didn't I?"

Letting her head drop to his shoulder, Harriet puffed out a breath of air. "No. You were trying to look out for her, and I appreciate it. I just hope this won't set her back."

"Talk it out. I'm sure she's fine. Look, she's even chatting to Mistress Black."

Harriet scanned the room. And yes, Cass was indeed talking to Mistress Black. Harriet's heart raced. Surely Cass knew who she was talking to, right? She'd be fine. It was just that after the earlier events, Harriet was on edge.

Kevin leaned in, his voice dropping to a whisper. "You need to trust her, Harriet. She'll let you know if she needs saving. But after how she handled G, I wouldn't worry too much."

He was absolutely right. Cass had a vulnerable side, but she wasn't weak. She didn't need Harriet rushing in every five minutes, trying to save her. She just needed to stand by Cass's side being supportive—as she herself would want to be supported.

Catching Cass's eye, Harriet winked. It'd been too long since they'd been near each other and Harriet was getting antsy. Smiling internally, she watched Cass politely excuse herself and make her way over.

"Are you enjoying yourself?" Cass asked, bending to drop a kiss on Harriet's lips.

"More now you're next to me."

"Sweet talker." They grinned like idiots. Dropping into Kevin's now-vacated seat, Cass leaned back and took a deep breath. "You have some lovely friends."

Harriet's hand made its way to the back of Cass's neck. There was something relaxing about playing with the fine hairs. She watched her friends laughing and joking, feeling utterly content. "I'm glad you like them."

Falling into comfortable silence, Harriet cast her gaze around the tearoom. "What did you want to do with the place, if I hadn't bought it?" They were past it being a sore subject, but Cass had never revealed her intended plans for the shop.

"I wanted to turn it into a sort of library/bookstore."

"I can see that." Harriet pondered, "What about the upstairs space? Never thought of using that?"

Cass shrugged. "I thought about it."

"And?"

"I think it'd be too small. Especially if I wanted comfy tables and chairs." Another shrug. "It just wasn't meant to be. But," she turned and nuzzled her nose just below Harriet's ear, "I think I got a better deal in the end. Don't you?"

Feeling a rush of heat make its way south, Harriet shuddered under Cass's lingering breath. "Y-yeah. I think we both got a pretty sweet deal."

"How much longer do we need to stay?"

Flexing her hands, Harriet smiled at a few people passing by. She couldn't let them see how turned on she was. Not because she felt uncomfortable, but because she didn't want them lingering to rib her for it.

"I'll start the goodbyes. Be ready to go in ten minutes." Not wanting to waste a second, Harriet bolted from the table and began thanking everyone for coming. She noticed Cass smirking, but didn't care. The only thing she cared about was getting everyone out of the shop and Cass back to bed.

Nabi was the last to leave after helping her and Cass tidy up. By the time she dragged Cass back to the house, she was overwhelmed with need. "Take your clothes off."

Cass shut the front door and chuckled. "Okay."

"Shower and then wait for me on the bed."

Cass bit her lip. "Okay."

Harriet waited until the bathroom door was closed before hurrying around the room, lighting candles. She put on some soft instrumental music, stripped naked, and waited. Cass stepped into the room a mere five minutes later. Her eyes were wide as she scanned the dim room.

"On the bed, Cass. I won't be a minute."

Hurrying through her cleaning ritual, Harriet had to remind herself to breathe. Suitably clean and smelling of Cass's favourite shower gel, Harriet opened the bathroom door and leaned against the frame. Cass lay with one hand behind her head, legs crossed. The other hand trailed light strokes up and down her own torso, causing both nipples to stand erect.

Licking her lips, Harriet calmed her raging libido. "You're beautiful."

Giving her own left nipple a pinch, Cass flared her nostrils but remained silent. No longer able to wait, Harriet stalked across the room until she reached the bed.

"There's something we need to talk about," she began. Her knees hit the duvet. Cass looked momentarily concerned. Continuing her path, Harriet crawled up Cass's body, stopping now and then to place kisses on her overheated skin. As she slipped between Cass's legs, Harriet basked in the feel of their bodies uniting. Was there anything better than a lover's naked skin making first contact? Harriet didn't think so. Her clit twitched impatiently.

"Harriet," Cass breathed. Her hands no longer fondled her nipples, but settled on Harriet's hips.

Ignoring Cass's attempt to get her to roll her hips, Harriet bent her head, nuzzling her nose against Cass's. "Something important happened today. Something monumental and we've not discussed it properly."

"W-what?"

"We said the L word, Cass. We're in love. That needs celebrating, don't you think?"

Cass nodded frantically. "Yes, it does."

30

Cassandra

Something was going on with Harriet. Cass was sure of it. Since the impromptu party last week, Harriet had been acting weird—secretive, almost. Twice now, Cass had popped by the shop, only to find Harriet gone. Nabi was no help. She either didn't know where Harriet was or she was keeping quiet.

Even more frustrating was the fact Kendal was also AWOL a lot at the moment. Cass thought maybe she was nipping off for a bit of nookie with Shauna, but then Shauna rang the café asking for Kendal, so Cass was stumped.

Although she couldn't get too indignant about being kept in the dark because she wasn't so innocent herself. Cass had a secret—a dirty, whip-wielding secret.

"Come in," Mistress Black said in her usual honeyed tone. Cass looked left and right down the street, looking for signs she'd been followed. It was ridiculous, but her mind wouldn't stop worrying. "How have you been, Cassandra?"

No matter how many times she'd asked Mistress Black to call her Cass, the woman purred her full name every time.

"G-good. Thank you. Um, yourself?" She followed Mistress Black to the living room.

"Perfectly splendid. Now, are you ready?"

Cass slipped off her coat and sat on the sofa. "Yes. I'm ready."

Mistress Black took a seat in the high wingback chair in the corner of the living room. Crossing one long leg over the other, she rested both hands on her lap, regarding Cass. "Are you sure? We've been here before, and you were not able to complete the task."

Swallowing away her anxiety, Cass sat up straight. "No, I'm ready this time."

"Good. Then I'll ask you the question you failed to answer on your first and second visit. Why are you here, Cassandra?"

This was Cass's third time in front of Mistress Black. She'd not been able to answer the question the first two times. As soon as she had opened her mouth, she froze, anxiety crippling her at every turn. Mistress Black had sat patiently each time. But Cass couldn't answer.

She'd decided to seek out Mistress Black after their brief conversation at the party. The woman exuded a confidence Cass had never seen before. It'd taken a lot of gumption to approach Mistress Black in the first place. She'd half convinced herself the woman would instantly whip out a paddle or ask Cass to drop to her knees. But of course, that hadn't happened. They had chatted like regular people. About the weather, no less.

During their conversation, Cass noticed how commanding Mistress Black was without actually asking anything of anyone. She just radiated dominance and confidence. And that's when the idea struck.

What if Cass could emulate Mistress Black? She didn't want to become a Domme, or enter that life, but she did want some guidance. She wanted someone to show her how to be confident in her sex life, confident with all things sexual, without baulking.

The good doctor was working with Cass on her triggers and history. But Cass needed more than that. She needed to stop being the woman who ran away from sex and anything associated with it.

Her last session with Dr Herman was a revelation of sorts. Not that it was a surprise, but to hear the doctor name what Cass was doing helped. Cass rejected sex or anything perceived as salacious, in a way to make sure she didn't turn out like her mum.

Now, that sounded harsh at first and Cass felt awful, because deep down she knew it was true. But she also knew her mum hadn't done anything wrong. She'd only ever been herself.

Thankfully, Dr Herman put it into perspective. According to her, Cass was still working with a child's perspective of her mother. Instead of looking at things through a forty-one-year-old's mind, Cass reverted to the painful teen years anytime something scandalous came up. The embarrassment, gossiping, and judgement she heard whispered about her mother, triggered her to withdraw and distance herself.

So, with that in mind, Cass hoped working with Mistress Black could help nudge her into an adult's mindset. She'd already come a long way on her own. Things bothered her less and less, but the lingering self-doubt and panic still reared its ugly head now and then, meaning

Cass still snapped and withdrew. She was tired of it. Sure, she would get pissed off at the price of living, or the local council would still bring out her ornery side, but she didn't want her love life to do that. Harriet didn't deserve it, and neither did Cass.

"Because I want to own my power. I want to feel confident in my own skin. I'm doing this for me and for Harriet."

"How do you think this will help you feel comfortable?"

"I'm hoping to learn control. Within myself. I want to control my anxiety and fear. Turn it on its head and make it work *for* me, instead of against. You're one of the most confident women I think I've ever met. I want you to teach me how to be like you."

"And your limits?"

"No touching. I'm with Harriet. I'm not looking to be taught how to be a Domme or a sub. I'm not looking to enter the scene." Cass silently patted herself on the back for remembering the terminology. "Or the lifestyle. Harriet and I...we..." Oh, God, she was struggling again.

"Take your time, Cassandra."

"We have a fulfilling sex life. I know there are things Harriet would like to try, but she's reticent—scared I'll freak out."

"Things like what?" Mistress Black remained stoic. She never gave away a thing she was thinking.

"Like...like toys. I know she has them. I've got a vibrator myself, but we never use them."

"Have you initiated that particular conversation?"

Cass shook her head. "No, and that's the problem. Conversations like that should come easy, but they don't. I want to take the lead. It shouldn't be up to Harriet all the time."

"But so far, you don't feel confident to talk to her about it?"

Cass sighed in frustration. "I second-guess myself."

Mistress Black drummed her perfectly manicured nails on her knee. Cass waited. "Okay, Cassandra. I'm going to help you. We'll work on your self-awareness, self-confidence, and above all, acceptance."

Cass was confused. "I know who I am. I accept myself just fine."

"No, you do not. But you will. Give me a few weeks and you'll be exactly where you should be. Dominating your life, entirely."

Not entirely sure what that meant, Cass cast her worries aside. She needed to do this. For her. For Harriet. "When can we start?"

"Right now, Cassandra. After tonight, I expect to see you here at least once a week, until I say otherwise. Clear?"

"Clear."

This was it. Cass could feel it. With Mistress Black's help, she was going to become the best version of herself.

Cass had visited Mistress Black three times a week for the last month. And boy, was she feeling good! She was still a little nervous, but that was to be expected. Mistress Black, or Selina, as she now referred to her, had coached Cass for this very moment, nerves included. No longer under her tutelage, Cass and Selina were more than happy to be friends. Selina was fun to be around. She was a lot more laid back than Cass first thought.

Harriet continued to be preoccupied, which for a while had Cass concerned, but she trusted her girlfriend.

Harriet would fill Cass in when she was ready. That was what she repeated to herself daily, anyway.

To be fair, Ero-Tea-Ca was always slammed, so Harriet definitely had her hands full. It was the evenings she begged off from seeing Cass that puzzled her. Harriet had said she had some work to finish up but never elaborated.

Knowing there were some negative feelings brewing, Cass spoke to Dr Herman, asking for advice. "Talk to her," was the width and breadth of that convo. Cass absolutely should have talked to Harriet, but some old insecurities took root and stopped her from communicating. The voices which told Cass that Harriet was already growing bored with her and was distancing herself, whispered in her mind.

Selina, being stupidly observant, made Cass confess all her spiralling thoughts and feelings, which then led to some very intense sessions. By the end, though, Cass came out the other side feeling stronger. She had a choice: Trust Harriet or don't. Simple.

Cass chose to trust her, so she continued with her plan, a plan to show Harriet that Cass was all in. She chose Harriet and the teashop. She chose a life of sexual innuendos and naughty teapots, of awkward questions and eclectic friends. Because from the moment Cass allowed herself to be with Harriet, she knew this was it. This was her forever.

Checking her watch, Cass scanned the tearoom one last time. Sunday afternoons were usually reserved for book clubs, specifically Selina's book club today; however, Mistress Black had graciously allowed Cass to hijack her time as long as the Domme club could use The Oxford Beanery as a replacement. With Kendal's enthusiastic blessing, Cass agreed.

Instead of paralysing nerves, Cass felt excited bubbles in her belly. Smoothing down her slacks one last time, she positioned herself in front of the counter facing the door. Harriet was due any second, lured to the shop under a false "emergency" pretence. Thank you, Nabi!

A shadow fell across the door. Harriet's long hair billowed in the wind. Even as a silhouette, she was breathtaking. Standing tall, Cass smiled. She was ready.

The door burst open. Harriet looked around frantically. "I'm here. Is everything okay? Nabi said something about a fire!"

Cass rolled her eyes. She'd asked Nabi to get Harriet to the shop, not induce a stroke. Cass planted her feet slightly wider than her hips and raised a hand to stop Harriet, then took a deep breath. Showtime. "The shop is fine. No fire. Please shut the door."

Harriet hesitated for a second, but complied. Cass watched her take in the room with arched brows. "Cass, what's going on?"

Pointing to the single chair sitting in a clearing in the middle of the teashop, Cass schooled her face and waited. Eventually, Harriet moved and sat down. Cass smirked when Harriet's gaze raked up the length of Cass's body, her eyes wide and appreciative.

Wearing fitted black slacks, black high heels, and an Ero-Tea-Ca shirt open at the front to reveal the tops of her breasts and a sneak peek at the lace bra, Cass felt smug. Harriet was practically drooling. She had weighed up whether to keep her hair loose, but in the end opted for a high, tight ponytail and dark eye makeup.

"Cass?" Harriet's voice was lower than usual.

Turning to the counter, Cass picked up a box and placed it on the table closest to Harriet. Happy she had her girlfriend's undivided attention, she flicked off the lid. Harriet strained to see inside but couldn't, leaving her to frown, and Cass to smile devilishly.

"I'm going to lay some things out on the table, and you are to choose your favourites."

"What things? Cass, what's going on?"

"I won't repeat myself, Harriet."

Harriet's eyes shot to Cass. Her nostrils flared and pupils dilated. She was turned on by Cass's commanding presence. Perfect.

Slowly and methodically, Cass emptied the box, ignoring Harriet's sharp intake of breath. "Choose your favourite."

Harriet looked from the items, to Cass, and back again, several times. "I-I like that one."

Cass picked up the double-ended dildo and placed it to one side. "Anything else?"

Harriet bit her lip. Cass could see she wanted to choose the handcuffs and blindfold. Picking them up without a word, Cass put them next to the dildo. "Is that it?"

Harriet nodded. Happily, Cass placed the unselected items back in the box and returned it to the counter. "Next, I want you to choose anything from that tray." Cass pointed to a silver platter filled with different food. She'd researched popular food play items and laid them out for Harriet to choose from.

Clearing her throat, Harriet briefly scanned the plates and bowls. "The strawberries and squirt-y cream."

Nodding, Cass took them and placed them with the toys. "Stay there." Taking the platter full of food back to the kitchen gave Cass a chance to breathe. So far, things were going well.

Harriet hadn't moved a muscle. She was looking thoroughly confused, but Cass saw the excitement in her eyes. "Please take your coat off. Make yourself comfortable."

Hanging her purse on the back of her chair, Harriet shucked off her coat, laying it on the closest chair. Cass watched her for any signs of discomfort, but she didn't detect any at all. Happy she could continue, Cass slipped behind the counter and picked up the tray with Harriet's favourite naughty teapot design, a cup and saucer, and a selection of erotic-themed mini cakes.

"The tea is steeped. May I pour you a cup?" Harriet remained silent but nodded. "I know you're wondering what's going on. But I'd like to take care of you first. Is that okay?"

"Y-yes."

"Good," Cass purred. "Now, while you sit there with your tea, I want you to tell me all the things you want me to do to you with regards to the items you've chosen."

It was a good thing Cass hadn't handed over the tea yet, because she was sure it would've ended up on the floor. Harriet gasped, her hands gripping the edge of the chair until they were white. "What do you mean?" she spluttered.

Cass circled her slowly, allowing her fingertips to gently run over Harriet's shoulders, causing the skin to react. "I want you to tell me how you'd like me to fuck you with the dildo. Would you prefer to be tied up and blindfolded first, or would that come later?"

"Cass!"

Bending slightly until her lips were next to Harriet's ear, Cass traced the tip of her tongue around the lobe. "Would you like me to lick cream off your nipples while handcuffed to my bed, Harriet? Or maybe you'd like me to leave a trail of it down your back, allowing me to snack on you as I take you from behind?"

"Jesus Christ." Harriet's voice was almost a whisper.

"Drink up." Cass handed over the teacup. She watched as Harriet handled it with visibly shaking hands. Wandering over to the door, Cass flicked the lock. The last thing they needed was to be disturbed.

31

Harriet

It was like someone had plucked one of Harriet's most sexy dreams right from her head and made it a reality. Cass looked phenomenal. Even though she had zero clue what the hell was going on, Harriet was all for it.

There was an air about her girlfriend that'd started showing itself a few weeks ago, but this display was beyond that. Cass radiated confidence and sex. Harriet almost choked on her tongue when she got a proper look at Cass in her outfit. Sure, it was slacks and a shirt, but Cass carried it in a way that left Harriet in no doubt Cass knew she looked fucking hot as hell. That black lace bra Cass wore would be the death of her.

Upon first arrival, Harriet had been so distracted by the possibility of an emergency, she'd completely missed Cass looking like she did and the way the tearoom had been rearranged. She was most definitely paying attention now.

With the sound of the door lock being flicked, Harriet willed herself to remain still and not spill her tea everywhere. She desperately wanted to know what was going on, but Cass had been quite clear Harriet would have to wait for answers.

A not-so-small part of her worried Cass felt she needed to put on a show because they'd been spending some time apart recently. The separation had been all Harriet's doing, but it was for a good reason. She just couldn't explain that to Cass until now. But maybe she'd already caused damage to their relationship if Cass felt she had to do this.

Harriet couldn't imagine how awkward and hard this must be for her to do. Should she put a stop to it?

"Head back in the room, sweetheart." Cass's voice was like honey.

"C-Cass. You don't have to do this."

"Shh. No more talking unless it's explicitly about how you want me to service you."

"S-service me?" Harriet was a stuttering mess.

"Yes, love." Cass slinked around the chair, dropping to her knees in front of Harriet. "Mmm, you smell good. My favourite shower gel again? I want to service you. Would you like that?"

Of course, she'd bloody like that. But this was so...out there for Cass. "I would. But—"

"Oh, no. Remember what I just said."

Harriet nodded dumbly. Heat pooled between her legs. Looking into Cass's eyes, she was surprised to see her looking...well, not how Harriet thought she would. There was no panic. Not a hint of anxiety. In fact, she actually looked like she was enjoying herself.

"I'll tell you what. While you mull it over, I'll start things off." What did *that* mean? Cass stood gracefully and took a step back, then another. Harriet couldn't look away. Slowly, Cass brought her fingers to the buttons on her shirt. One by one, she flicked them open, revealing more of that delicious bra.

"Oh my God," Harriet mumbled.

Smiling wolfishly, Cass continued until all buttons were undone. Dropping her eyes to Cass's magnificent cleavage, Harriet fought the urge to stand up and bury her face between her fantastic breasts.

Seemingly reading Harriet's mind, Cass tutted, "Now, now, Harriet. You're supposed to be thinking of all the ways I can pleasure you. Are you ready to say them out loud yet?"

If it meant Cass stopped doing what she was doing, then Harriet was keeping her mouth shut! With a bite of her lower lip, Cass shrugged, seemingly happy to continue. The shirt fell from her shoulders and hit the floor.

Trailing her fingers south, Cass hovered over the clasp of her slacks. "Hmm, I'm missing something."

Harriet was in Wonderland. Wherever this rabbit hole went, she was happy to go along. Watching with rapt attention, a lump formed in her throat. Cass opened the box again and pulled out a small silver bullet vibrator.

"Now, you don't know this about me, sweetheart, but this little gizmo is one of my favourite things to play with. Shall I show you?" She couldn't mean? Harriet whimpered as Cass sauntered over to the table in front of her, placing the vibe down before unhooking her trousers.

"Slacks on or off, Harriet. Your choice."

Miraculously, Harriet still held her cup of tea. Gingerly, she took a small sip, hoping it would clear up the desert feeling currently making itself at home in her mouth and throat. Suitably lubricated, Harriet swallowed. "Off." Placing the teacup on the floor next to her chair, Harriet waited.

Well, she might as well commit. Cass didn't look to be stopping anytime soon, and Harriet really wanted to see what was underneath those trousers.

"Off it is."

With the grace of a feline, Cass slipped off her high heels, unzipped her trousers, and turned around. Looking at Harriet over her shoulder, she bent at the waist, slowly peeling the slacks from her legs.

Gaping at Cass's thong and therefore, almost bare arse, Harriet had to wonder if she really *was* dreaming. Her hands balled into fists on her lap as she continued to watch. Cass took her time picking up her clothes and neatly folding them. She knew Harriet would wait for as long as necessary, which turned Harriet on even more.

Hitching herself onto the edge of the table, Cass lifted her legs, placing her feet on two separate chairs. Without breaking eye contact, Cass used those deliciously toned legs to push the chairs to the side, revealing her lace centre to Harriet.

Positively salivating, Harriet watched in earnest as Cass snatched up the vibe. "Ready to tell me what you want yet?"

"Nope."

Chuckling, Cass brought the vibe to her mouth, letting her tongue coat it in saliva before trailing it down her torso. "Okay, Harriet. You've got until I scream to make up your mind." Panting, Harriet nodded. Nothing mattered but this. Cass twisted the toy, making it vibrate. Harriet traced every movement as Cass ran it gently over the top of her thong. Even though the underwear was black, Harriet could see Cass's excitement soak through the material.

The air was thick with tension and heady moans. Both Cass and Harriet were losing themselves. Harriet watched Cass's chest rise and fall in quick succession.

"Press harder," she urged, needing Cass to take it further. To her utter dismay, Cass pulled the vibe away.

"No," she gasped. "Remember, the only thing I want to hear from you is how you want me to fuck you, Harriet."

"Sorry. Sorry." Harriet snapped her mouth shut. Cass arched her brow, daring her to speak. She didn't. Lesson learned. Satisfied, Cass resumed her play. This time however, she slipped her hand underneath the thong.

Cass dropped her head back, eyes rolling skyward. "Oh, yes."

Gritting her teeth, Harriet shifted in her seat, trying desperately to relieve some of the ache she was experiencing in her crotch. She watched in wonder as Cass took herself higher and higher, moaning into the room with no regard to her volume. She was utterly free and euphoric. With one final jerk of her hand, Cass tumbled over the edge with one long, deep shout to the universe.

"Cassandra...that..."

"Mmm, was very satisfactory. But time's up. Are you ready?"

Right, she was supposed to be coming up with the best way for Cass to debauch her. In her own teashop. With toys. "That was pretty fantastic, Cass. I'm not sure how to beat it."

Dropping both feet to the floor, Cass gracefully folded one knee over the other, her hands slightly behind to prop herself up. "If you're uncomfortable, you can say no. It's a full sentence, sweetheart."

"I'm far from uncomfortable."

"Would you like to stop?"

"No." Harriet didn't want this to ever stop.

"Then what do you want? What are your fantasies?"

"I want you to take me on a table with the dildo." The words fell from her mouth. "And then I want to tie *you* up as I eat cream from your body."

Smiling like the cat that got the...well, cream, Cass slinked off the table. She whipped her thong off with such speed and precision, Harriet wasn't sure it had actually happened until she spied Cass's neat patch of curls glistening.

"Are you happy to undress or would you like to keep your clothes on? Either way is fine with me. Hitching your skirt over your hips is quite a visual."

"May I stand?"

"You can do whatever you want."

If Cass could stand in the middle of Ero-Tea-Ca near naked, Harriet could do the same. And honestly, she was so turned on by the mere thought of what Cass was about to do; her skin was on fire and the clothes weren't helping.

In a move far less seductive than Cass's strip tease, Harriet practically ripped off her clothes until she was down to her underwear. "Which table?" she asked.

"Dealer's choice."

Harriet couldn't give a monkey's backside; she just needed Cass to...what was it? Service her. And service her *now*. Stepping up to the table Cass had just pleasured herself on, Harriet hoisted herself up on the varnished wood, making a mental note to disinfect every square inch of the place once they were finished.

Smoothing her palms on the tabletop, Harriet rested her weight on her arms, letting her legs drop open. No sooner was she situated than Cass stepped forward and pushed apart her legs even further.

"I've been very much looking forward to this," Cass whispered.

Forgoing any protestations when her knickers got ripped in two by Cass's sheer determination to get her naked, Harriet closed her eyes and waited. "Please, Cass."

After a few moments with no touching, Harriet thought Cass may have changed her mind. But her worry was for naught. Soft hands settled on her hips. "Sorry, had to get the thing positioned right."

"T-take your time," she stuttered, as Cass coated the dildo with her excitement.

With a scoff, Cass brought the tip of the dildo to Harriet's entrance. "We've waited long enough."

Sweet pressure radiated from Harriet's inner walls as Cass thrust deep and slow. "Is that good?"

Nodding, Harriet wrapped her legs around Cass's waist and concentrated on regulating her breathing. The whole experience had her careening towards a premature end. Reaching forward, she held on to Cass's hip. "Nice and slow, Cass."

"Mmmm."

The slow and steady rhythm only worked for so long, though. Harriet felt wetness drip between her arse cheeks and her centre tighten with every thrust. "I...I need..."

Unable to finish her request, Harriet moaned, gripping the table with her free hand. In a bout of pure genius, Cass brought Harriet to orgasm with a slide of her fingers. Reaching down, she drew tight, forceful circles on Harriet's clit, setting off a chain reaction that saw her screaming into the ceiling.

Harriet grumbled as Cass pulled out. Seconds later, two warm arms circled her, helping her stand. Inhaling Cass's scent, Harriet let her head drop to her shoulder. Warm lips stroked her temple and then her cheek.

"Are you okay?"

Wetting her dry lips, Harriet summoned the energy to look up. "I have no words, Cass. That...that was...what *was* that? Not that I'm complaining, but I'm still in a state of shock, I think."

"Let's get dressed and we'll talk. We can take the food back to my place later if you want?"

"Oh, I want."

On wobbly legs, Harriet haphazardly dressed. Cass looked suitably pleased, which Harriet couldn't fault her for because, hell, she'd just ruined her in the space of an hour.

Wiping her hair from her rather sweaty face, she watched Cass clean off the table with a wipe and replace the pot of tea, along with Harriet's teacup and erotic cakes.

Settling in the chair opposite, Cass leaned back and smiled. "I suppose you'd like an explanation?"

"Not an explanation. Maybe...I don't know...the story behind it? Is that better? I don't want you to feel like you have to answer to me for *anything* you do."

"I appreciate you saying that. But I do owe you an explanation. I've been seeing Mistress Black." Harriet stilled, her heart plummeting to her stomach. "Not as a client," Cass rushed to say. "She's been mentoring me."

"To be a Domme?" Harriet almost screeched.

Laughing, Cass leaned forward and took Harriet's hands. "No, sweetheart. She's helped me...accept myself. Turn my anxiety into something I can use to boost my self-confidence and worth. Along with Dr Herman, she's taught me how to cope better with things that used to make me want to hide away."

"I...wow." Harriet was stunned and a little upset with herself for not being as involved with Cass's self-treatment as she should have. "Are you still seeing her?"

"No, but we are friends now. Is that okay?"

"Of course. So...what does this mean, exactly?"

Shrugging, Cass popped an erotically decorated French Fancy into her mouth. "Nothing, and everything, I guess. I don't want that life, Harriet. Unless that's something you want to explore."

"Not really. I loved what just happened and would be ecstatic for something like that to happen again."

"Me too. I...I like feeling dominant. But not over you, if that makes sense. If I can dominate my fear, I feel better equipped to face parts of life I usually get upset over. But that doesn't mean I want to be in charge all the time. I like it when you get bossy, too."

Harriet smiled and winked. "Duly noted. So why the teashop?"

Cass winced. "Are you mad?"

Harriet laughed. "Nothing about this makes me mad. Just curious."

"Well," Cass began, "it's where we started. It's where my anxieties hit a high point, but also where I found my calm and strength." Harriet was about to cry. "Plus," Cass shrugged with a grin, "I figured Ero-Tea-Ca should see some action. You know, to live up to its name."

Harriet burst out laughing. "That's fair. We will need to clean, thoroughly."

"Done. Now, shall we go back to mine?"

Worrying her lip, Harriet decided it was time. "Actually, there's something I need to confess, too."

Sipping her tea, Cass waited. There was a hint of worry Harriet needed to erase. "Remember the surprise award party?"

"Yes."

"Remember our conversation?"

Cass frowned. "Um, which one? Is this about Gogo? Are you still not talking?"

Harriet shook her head. "No, that's all sorted. They've been nice to you right?"

"Yes. I think they're thawing."

Harriet rolled her eyes. "They'll do better than that if they want to remain friends."

"So, if it's not about Gogo, I don't know which conversation you're referring to."

"The one where you told me you'd planned to open a bookshop-slash-library."

"Oh, right. Okay."

Harriet sat up straight. She wasn't sure how her plan would be received. Hopefully, as an exciting adventure. But she wasn't sure. "I...well, I wanted to make your dream come true. Obviously, I can't change Ero-Tea-Ca, but I thought...well, I thought we could become partners. If we converted both upstairs areas into one giant space, we could have a bookshop, with tables and chairs."

Cass remained silent, staring, so Harriet chose to carry on. "I...I approached Kendal. Just to see if it would be something she'd ever consider. Of course I was going to talk to you, too, but I became a little lost in the planning. I made a presentation to show you and everything. I also wanted to make sure I was financially viable to be an equal shareholder in it. I am, by the way. So, the missed dates and meetings...that's what I was doing. Are you mad?" Cass stared and then stared a little more. "I swear nothing has been done without your permission; it was just a fact-finding mission."

Harriet rolled her lips as Cass held up her hand. "You want to open a bookstore with me?"

Harriet nodded, not confident in her voice.

"As my partner?"

"In life and work," Harriet whispered. "Cass," she said a little louder, "I'm in this. I want a life with you.

Marriage, kids, the works. I'm not going anywhere, and I want to give you everything you want—including a bookstore. Together we can do it. I even came up with a name." She smiled. "The Oxford Beanery Ero-Tea-Ca Bookstore."

Cass chuckled. "Makes sense, I suppose."

"But we can stock all kinds of genres. Not just smut."

"Well," Cass grinned, "we need some smut. It's in the name after all."

"So, you want this?" Harriet held her breath.

Standing, Cass held out her hand. Taking it, Harriet let herself be pulled into Cass's warmth. "I want all of it, Harriet. All. Of. It. I'm yours."

"Even the sexy teapots and glass dildos?" She was joking, but not entirely. Harriet needed to know Cass was comfortable in this life, surrounded by these things, and not just tolerating them for her sake.

Hearing the unspoken truth in Harriet's joke, Cass hooked two fingers under her chin. "I want all the erotica you can give me, Harriet Kirkwell."

Pulling Cass forward, Harriet claimed her lips, sucking and biting. "Careful what you wish for."

Epilogue

"**U**nacceptable," Cassandra hissed to herself as she peered through the blinds. "I won't stand for it," she growled as she watched the moving van's rear door open. "They'll ruin us all."

"Now you're just being dramatic," Kendal scoffed from behind. "And repetitive. You did this when Ero-Tea-Ca opened and look where that got you."

"But they're just hauling boxes like they don't contain our livelihood! Who hired these clowns?"

"You did." Kendal laughed. "And they're hauling books. I doubt they'll be doing much damage, Cass."

Whirling 'round, Cass hooked a thumb over her shoulder. "Tell that to the beat-up paperbacks. The biggest oaf hasn't found a box he hasn't dropped since starting!"

"Harriet, come out here and talk some sense into your insane girlfriend."

"I'm not insane," Cass grumbled, turning back to the blind and incompetent movers.

"Your window-watching days are over, my love," Harriet cooed in her ear. "The movers are doing their job. No need to watch over them. Why don't we nip next door and have a nice cup of tea?"

"Kendal needs help." Cass wasn't ready to let her sour mood go just yet.

"No, I don't, you know, considering we're closed. Go away and relax. Shauna will be here soon, and you don't want to stick around while we get all mushy."

Cass wrinkled her nose. "You're right, I don't. Come on then," she said to Harriet, grabbing her hand and leading her out the back door. She couldn't guarantee she wouldn't say something to the burly men ruining their new stock if she stood face to face with them.

The inviting scent of cakes and tea wafted up Cass's nose the second they stepped inside. Ero-Tea-Ca felt like home now, just as much as The Beanery. "I'll have a camomile please," she said to Harriet, who was already boiling the kettle. As well as embracing the teashop wholeheartedly, Cass also drank a hell of a lot more tea. It would never beat coffee, but she could see the benefits, especially on days like this.

Banging and loud thumps echoed from upstairs, setting Cass's nerves alight once more. They had one week to get the bookshop stocked and organised before the grand opening. Thank God their friends were coming over this afternoon to help.

"I need to order pizza," she said out loud to herself. "Maybe wine. Hmmm, although that might inhibit progress rather than aid it."

Putting two teapots on the staffroom table, Harriet sat opposite Cass with a warm smile directed her way. "Pizza and pop will do, Cass."

"I'll order five pizzas. Gogo will eat two by themselves."

Harriet chuckled. "They will. Now, will you please just take a minute to relax. Everything is under control."

Cass shook her head. "I don't know how you're so calm."

Harriet shrugged. "We have help, and I know we'll get things done in time. I want to enjoy the experience."

"Selina has booked the space for the first Sunday. That's eight days away."

"And Selina will also be here this afternoon to help. Sweetie, please relax. Do you need…" Harriet left the sentence hanging but raised her eyebrows.

Cass flushed. "Later. If we start that now, we'll miss the rest of the day."

"Because you can't get enough of me?" Harriet wiggled her eyebrows, making Cass laugh.

"Exactly. And you know how I like us to take our time." Her voice dropped seductively, which made Harriet shiver. Cass smiled smugly.

"Fine, no sexy time. Do you want to head upstairs and start unpacking boxes then? That way you can micromanage and not drive me nuts by sulking."

Cass huffed. "I do not sulk."

"Oh, yes, you do. Come on, sourpuss."

They worked together for an hour, shifting heavy boxes. Cass managed to hold her tongue around the movers who dropped the last box—literally—before mumbling a goodbye and leaving them to it.

Kendal and Shauna were the first to arrive. Kendal's hair gave away just how mushy they'd gotten in the café.

Cass leaned against her ex-wife's side and whispered, "I hope you cleaned down whatever surface you did it on."

Kendal blushed. "I don't know what you mean."

"Your fly is undone, Ken."

Whipping around, Kendal fixed her jeans, snorting with laughter. Cass chuckled alongside her as Shauna and Harriet gave them an amused look.

"Hello? Are you up there?" Lolita's voice sang, before the woman herself danced into the room. Lolita and Henry were really into their dance nowadays, meaning they waltzed and foxtrotted their way through life.

"Hey, Mum." Cass swooped in, kissing Lolita on the cheek and squeezing her tight. They had, in fact, gone to therapy together for a few months. Dr Herman had been fantastic, helping both mother and daughter reconcile their past and find a way to move forward. Lolita was still the same wild woman Cass knew and loved, but she now took the time to consider her words before speaking them out loud. Cass worked on herself and accepting her mum, meaning they were closer than ever.

Henry was like a father to Cass and Harriet. He was the calm to Lolita's chaotic personality. Plus, they'd moved closer to Cass, so months didn't go by without her seeing hide nor hair of her mum.

"Where's Henry?" Harriet asked while hugging Lolita.

"He's picking up Mr Whiskers."

Cass was confused. "What? Why?"

Lolita rolled her eyes. "Because a bookshop called Ero-Tea-Ca has to have its own pussy...cat." Biting her lip, Lolita tried to hide her snort with little success. Harriet chuckled, covering her mouth with a hand. Cass looked between them before shaking her head.

"That was terrible. The equivalent of a naughty dad joke. For shame, Mother. For shame."

Lolita finally burst, her laugh contagious. By the time Henry stepped in with a rather put out Mr Whiskers, the five women were in hysterics. Henry beamed and laughed. "Looks like the party's started. Here's your kitty. He wasn't best pleased I moved him, though."

"The fun has arrived," Nabi shouted from the bottom of the stairs. They'd decided to use the stairs in the teashop and add an adjoining door from the café to allow access. It was less construction, meaning neither shop had to close for long.

Thunderous steps echoed around the empty bookshop. Nabi, Kevin, Gogo, Selina, Diane, Mitchel, and Robbie crammed through the door, looking far too excited.

"You're all nearly two hours early," Cass shouted over the din.

"Harriet called and said you were stressing so we decided to get here earlier," Gogo replied, pulling Cass in for a hug. "We got you, honey. By the night's end, this place is going to look as fabulous as me in a sequined dress."

Feeling a sudden rush of tears, Cass buried her head in Gogo's chest. "Thank you."

Peeling herself away, Cass took Harriet by the waist and pulled her close. "I love you."

Nuzzling her neck, Harriet sighed. "I just want you to be happy, baby."

"Let's get to it," Nabi called. She already had a lollipop unwrapped and heading towards her mouth.

The day was finally here. Cass, Harriet, and Kendal would open their doors to the public. The Oxford Beanery Ero-Tea-Ca Bookstore would welcome their first patron in just over three hours.

Snuggling a little closer to Cass's warm, naked body, Harriet smiled in utter contentment. She had so much to be happy about. Both the café and teashop were performing brilliantly. The buzz about their joint venture was the talk of Oxford, so Harriet expected today to be another success.

Cass pulled her closer and sniffed her hair, which meant she was awake. "Mornin'."

Shifting away, Harriet lifted her head and looked into Cass's eyes. "Good morning."

"Have you been awake long?"

"Only ten-or-so minutes. I was surprised to beat you." Cass was usually up and out of bed by seven at the latest. It was now 8 a.m.

"You wore me out last night."

Harriet grinned. They'd definitely worked off some energy last night. She was momentarily lost in the memory when Cass chuckled. Rolling them so she was on top, Cass leaned down and kissed Harriet good morning. "Want a repeat performance?"

Grabbing Cass's bum, Harriet grinned. "Yes, but before that, I have a present for you."

"Why?"

Harriet laughed at Cass's brusque response. "Because I love you and wanted to. Is that okay?"

Cass blushed. "Of course it is. Sorry."

Shaking her head, Harriet wrapped her legs around Cass's hips and reversed their positions. "Wait there."

Digging through her bag, Harriet pulled out the package. She hoped Cass liked it and found the funny side. Over the past several months, Cass had relaxed a lot when it came to sex and sex-related topics. She was more easily able to laugh along with their friends, even cracking her own saucy jokes from time to time.

"Is it a book?" Cass grinned.

Huffing, Harriet placed the box on the bed. "Does it look like a book?"

"Can I open it?"

Nodding, Harriet worried her lip as Cass tore through the paper wrapping. She watched Cass pull out the teapot and examine the artwork. Her eyes bugged and her mouth dropped open. Harriet was on the verge of apologising, when Cass hugged the teapot close to her naked breasts.

"I love it! Oh my God, Harriet, it's beautiful."

Falling back dramatically to the bed, Harriet let out a loud, "Phew."

The bed dipped as Cass leaned over. "Is it Raine's work?"

"Yup."

Cass's face took on a tinge of red. "I can't believe she painted our afternoon sexcapade in the teashop. How will we look her in the face?" Cass laughed.

"Raine has painted so many erotic scenes, they all blur into one."

"But she got our features spot on. And the bit where you're on the table."

"Good, right?" Harriet leaned up, nipping Cass's lip. "I thought it would be nice to have our very own Ero-Tea-Ca collection."

"Are there teacups?"

"Not yet. I wanted to see how the teapot went over first."

"I appreciate that," Cass began, "but I'm fine. It's a beautiful gift."

"Then I'll ask Raine to go ahead with the rest of it. I ordered a cake stand as well. For when we have our own naughty tea party."

Cass grinned. "My my, you have thought this through."

Harriet shrugged. "I'm always thinking about you, Cass."

"You know what would make the tea parties easier?"

"What?"

"If we lived in the same house." Harriet stilled. Did she mean... "Move in with me. I want to live with you and wake up with you every morning."

Letting out an excited squeal, Harriet wrapped herself around Cass. "Yes! Oh my God, yes!"

This time Cass let out a dramatic, "Phew. Good, because if you'd said no, I would have to cancel the movers for next weekend."

Giggling, Harriet booped Cass on the nose. "We wouldn't want that."

"Indeed."

Losing themselves in each other, Harriet and Cass almost missed their own grand opening. Only when the incessant ringing of both phones pulled them out of their sex bubble did they realise they had ten minutes to get to the shop.

Speed walking, they made it to the front of both shops with two minutes to spare, earning a frown and playful punch on their arms from Kendal.

The crowd was significant. Harriet saw old and new faces smiling at her, clearly eager to check out the new add-on. With the café taking the brunt of the disruption during the renovation, the three partners decided to leave it open for trade and close Ero-Tea-Ca for the morning to open the bookstore. With a ribbon across the door, Kendal motioned to Cass.

"Thank you for coming," she began. "It's an absolute dream and honour to open the bookstore with Harriet and Kendal. Although it started as my dream, I know we share a deep love of the place. I think I can safely speak for us all when we say this has been a labour of love. A safe space to relax and read." Cass looked at Kendal and Harriet, who were both beaming. Unable to stop herself, she leaned down and kissed Harriet. With a smile and a light heart, Cass turned back to the crowd. "So, without further ado... Welcome to Ero-Tea-Ca! We're open!"

The ribbon fell to the floor as Kendal, Harriet, and Cass gave it a good tug. The door opened, and the patrons streamed in, all heading for the staircase.

"It's called *The Oxford Beanery* Ero-Tea-Ca Bookstore, babe," Harriet murmured in her ear.

"I know," Cass said. "But it's a mouthful and we're standing outside Ero-Tea-Ca."

Kendal snorted. "I can't believe you said the word *erotica* in front of a crowd full of people."

Cass grinned. "I didn't even blush."

"I'm proud of you," Harriet said, patting her bum playfully.

"Wait until I conduct my first book club. Then you'll be really proud."

Gasping in faux shock, Kendal grabbed Cass by the shoulders. "Are you going to read a naughty book, Cassandra Beaufort?"

Swatting her away, Cass led them into the shop and up the stairs. "Yes. And I'll even provide naughty cakes."

"See, I told you Ero-Tea-Ca would be good for the street," Kendal sang smugly.

They stood in the doorway watching people browse the shelves. Several were already settled in the comfy seats with either a coffee or a pot of tea.

"You did, Ken. And I couldn't be happier to be proved wrong."

Harriet leaned into Cass. "We've done something good."

"You started it," Cass replied.

"Maybe. But together, we've created something truly wonderful."

Nabi bustled over with three cups of tea. "Here, freshly brewed."

Picking up their cups, Cass, Harriet, and Kendal clinked them together. "To a new start," Kendal said.

"To the bookstore," Harriet added.

"To Ero-Tea-Ca," Cass finished.

Afterword

Thank you for reading Welcome to Ero-TEA-Ca: We're open!

Please spare a few more minutes of your time by heading over to Amazon and Goodreads to leave a review.

Other Titles By Alyson Root

A Dance Towards Forever

Diving Into Her

Always Emilie

Broken Parts Included

Love & Other Wild Things

Finding Molly Parsons

Keeping Carmen Ruiz

The Wisdom of Bug

Sleigh Bells Ring

Risking Immortality

Waiting for Eternity

Fighting for Infinity

Mob's Seduction

Playing Her Heart

About the author

Alyson was born and raised in the heart of England. She moved to Paris in 2015 when she met her wife. Together they moved to the west of France, where they now live with their two dogs. Alyson spends her time reading sapphic fiction books, writing and Scuba Diving.

Alyson discovered her love of writing in her mid-thirties. Her debut book, *A Dance Towards Forever,* was inspired by her wife and their very own love story. Alyson wrote *Diving Into Her* and award-winning *Always Emilie,* which added with her first book, created The French Connection series.

www.alysonroot.com

a.rootauthor@alysonroot.com

HUMAN
AUTHORED™

THE
Authors Guild®

3626044